JUST AS YOU ARE

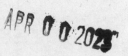

JUST AS YOU ARE

A NOVEL

CAMILLE KELLOGG

THE DIAL PRESS
NEW YORK

Just as You Are is a work of fiction. Names, characters, places, and incidents are the products of the author's imagination or are used fictitiously. Any resemblance to actual events, locales, or persons, living or dead, is entirely coincidental.

A Dial Press Trade Paperback Original

Copyright © 2023 by Camille Kellogg
Dial Delights Extras copyright © 2023 by Penguin Random House LLC

Published in the United States by The Dial Press, an imprint of Random House, a division of Penguin Random House LLC, New York.

THE DIAL PRESS is a registered trademark and the colophon is a trademark of Penguin Random House LLC. DIAL DELIGHTS and colophon are trademarks of Penguin Random House LLC.

LIBRARY OF CONGRESS CATALOGING-IN-PUBLICATION DATA
Names: Kellogg, Camille, author.
Title: Just as you are: a novel / Camille Kellogg.
Description: First edition. | New York: The Dial Press, [2023]
Identifiers: LCCN 2022035925 (print) | LCCN 2022035926 (ebook) |
ISBN 9780593594704 (trade paperback) | ISBN 9780593594711 (ebook)
Subjects: LCGFT: Romantic fiction. | Novels.
Classification: LCC PS3611.E4439 J87 2023 (print) |
LCC PS3611.E4439 (ebook) | DDC 813/.6—dc23/eng/20220816
LC record available at https://lccn.loc.gov/2022035925
LC ebook record available at https://lccn.loc.gov/2022035926

Printed in the United States of America on acid-free paper

randomhousebooks.com

2 4 6 8 9 7 5 3 1

First Edition

Book design by Jo Anne Metsch

*To everyone who's doubted if there's a
happy ending out there for them*

JUST AS YOU ARE

1

——

Everyone knows that when you throw a dinner party for a bunch of lesbians, at least half of them will be vegan. Which, unfortunately, was why Liz was going to be brutally murdered by her roommate.

Liz paused outside her apartment door, still panting from her sprint through Crown Heights to their third-floor walk-up. The weekend train from Manhattan had been agonizingly slow, and then she'd had to push through a million people on Franklin Avenue to get home: a crowd of parents waiting outside the karate studio, a line of couples outside the trendy pop-up restaurant, a large family barbecuing on the sidewalk, and dozens of people walking tiny, slow-moving dogs.

Liz said a quick mental prayer that Jane would be in a forgiving mood. Tonight's party was going to be tense enough without them fighting, too. Then she flung open the front door as dramatically as possible.

"I'm the worst," she said between breaths, bending over and grabbing her knees. "I know it. You don't have to say it. You can have my firstborn child as repayment."

Jane, a dark-skinned Black woman with her hair in long, thin braids, let out a loud *humph* noise from the kitchen, where she was shaking a pan of what seemed to be sizzling onions.

"You were supposed to be here two hours ago." Jane released the pan without looking up and yanked open the oven with a clang.

"No," Liz said, unlacing her Doc Martens and leaving them in the pile of shoes by the door. "I was supposed to be here an hour ago. Not two. You look great, by the way. And wow, it smells amazing in here! Is that risotto?"

"I said four." Jane pulled out a tray of mini-quiches and laid them on the stove. She still hadn't looked at Liz. "It's six."

"But we all know that you said four knowing I'd be an hour late and get home at five. So, really, I'm only an hour late." Liz eased herself onto one of the stools on the other side of the breakfast bar, which was covered in a truly impressive number of onion skins.

"Which would have been helpful if it had worked." Jane's voice was clipped. "Now there's not enough time to steam the beets."

"Luckily I've solved that particular problem for you," Liz said, trying to sound optimistic, "by not bringing beets." She started cleaning up the onion skins so she would look helpful.

Jane finally turned around. "Are you serious?"

Liz did her best puppy dog eyes. "The store was closed by the time I got there."

Jane clanged a lid down on a pot with more force than usual. "I'm going to tell everyone it's your fault that we don't have any vegan food."

"No!" Liz abandoned the onion skins to clasp her hands together and beg. "Please. Charlotte will make me watch those videos on animal cruelty again, and I really can't take that tonight. I'm fragile, okay?"

Jane glared down at the onions, now caramelized, as she transferred them to a platter. Liz studied her, worried that her roommate might actually be mad.

"Look, Jane, I'm really sorry," Liz said, in a serious tone this time. "You're right. I should have been back here, I should have gotten beets, it's just—"

Jane started cackling. She uncovered one of the pots in front of her and tipped it toward Liz so she could see the perfectly steamed beets inside.

"Katie!" Jane yelled. "I owe you ten bucks."

There was a triumphant scream from behind them. One of the doors in the living room opened and their roommate Katie popped her head out of her bedroom.

"I *knew* it," Katie shouted, running into the kitchen wearing nothing but a lime-green towel. "Liz is the queen of five-hour dates. I knew there was no way she'd be back in time to get beets."

"I am *not* the—"

"Wait, wait," Jane interrupted. "Was it a Tinder date, a Her date, or a Lex date?"

Liz froze mid-sentence and narrowed her eyes. "Why?"

"No reason," Jane said innocently. Katie giggled.

Liz crossed her arms and peered suspiciously between her roommates. "Her," she finally admitted.

"Yes!" Jane pumped her fist. Katie booed.

"Okay, okay," Katie said. "That's five bucks off your tab. But you still owe me fifteen from that night at Scissors, when you thought Liz would go home with that drag king and I bet that she'd chicken out."

"Will you stop betting on my life?" Liz went back to gathering the onion skins. "Also, I did not chicken out."

"You really did," Jane said, patting her shoulder. "He was so hot, and you totally blew it."

"How did the date go, by the way?" Katie sat down on one of the stools at the breakfast bar, putting severe strain on her towel's ability to cover her body. Katie was on the curvy side, which made her the only one of the roommates whose pants Liz could borrow on a regular basis. She had warm-brown skin, and her curly hair was usually styled up to show off her undercut, when it wasn't still dripping from the shower.

Liz groaned, then went to the fridge. "Terrible," she said. She got herself a pineapple White Claw, then handed a blackberry to Katie and a mango to Jane.

"Why are all of the dates you go on terrible?" Jane said. "You need to be better at filtering out weirdos."

"What happened?" Katie asked.

Liz opened her drink and took a long sip before answering. "I thought we were getting along. Then, at the end of the date, she said she's sorry, but she just doesn't think she can date a Leo right now."

Jane and Katie made identical sympathetic expressions, which only confirmed the suspicion that had crept into Liz's brain about halfway through her subway ride home: Her date had just been letting her down easy.

"Well, personally, I think you're dodging a bullet." Jane turned off the burners on the stove and joined them at the breakfast bar. "Astrology people are always weird. Remember that girl who told you that your souls had connected in a past life?"

Liz made a face. "True. That was creepy."

"Aww," Katie said. "I thought that was kind of romantic."

"Why? Do you feel like your soul and Lydia's connected in a former life?"

Katie looked down, twisting the pull tab off her can, and didn't reply. Liz wished she hadn't said anything—teasing

Katie about her unrequited love for Lydia, their fourth room-mate, felt too mean.

"Sorry, Katie," Liz said. "I shouldn't have said that. I'm just in a bad mood because I've been on, like, forty failed dates this year. Forgive me?"

"It's okay," Katie said. "At least you've been on dates. I haven't redownloaded Tinder since that guy told me Dominican girls 'just taste better.'" She rolled her eyes and then laughed. Liz laughed along, grateful for her friend's easy forgiveness. She promised herself for the hundredth time that she was going to think before speaking from now on.

"How bad do you think this party is going to be tonight?" Liz said.

"I mean, the food's going to be fantastic," Jane gestured over her shoulder toward the stove. "But everyone's going to be depressed and sulky during the first half, then get wildly drunk and self-destructive in the second."

"I guess there's not really any other way for a 'you're all going to be unemployed next week' party to go," Liz said. All four roommates worked at the *Nether Fields*, a magazine for queer women, nonbinary people, and trans people. Living with three of her coworkers had originally sounded like fun, but now that they were all losing their salaries at the same time, Liz had to admit there were some flaws in the plan.

Jane sighed. "I just can't believe the magazine is really closing," she said, shaking her head. "I wanted to stay there forever. I mean, focusing specifically on trans issues at an all-queer magazine run by a woman of color? It's the literal dream."

"You're an incredible journalist, Jane," Katie said. "*Buzz-Feed* or *Autostraddle* or somewhere will snatch you up, and you'll be totally fine."

"Yeah, but it won't be the same." Jane looked like she might cry.

Liz chugged some of her drink, feeling guilty—both for bringing up the subject and for what she wasn't saying: As devastated as Liz was that the *Nether Fields* was closing, part of her was also glad. Unlike Jane, who covered the serious beats, Liz wrote the sex, relationship, and advice columns: dildo reviews, overviews of queer dating etiquette, the annual "Is scissoring a thing?" article (answer: Sure, if you're absurdly flexible). It had been fun when she joined the magazine right out of college, but after four years it was getting old. Liz wanted to do something more with her life. And now that the magazine was closing, she had a plan to make that happen. She just hadn't shared that plan with any of her friends yet.

Luckily, the door banged open and the tension broke as Lydia tumbled inside, heaving two cases of hard seltzer and several bags full of tall bottles.

"We have got to move to an apartment with fewer stairs," Lydia said, breathing hard. "I'm sweating all over my cute outfit." They gestured to their clothes: tight silver spandex shorts and a billowy button-down shirt that was mostly unbuttoned. Lydia was stick-thin, white, and androgynous, with a shaved head and a confident swagger that allowed them to pull off even the most ridiculous looks. Katie got up to help them with their bags.

"Is that hard liquor?" Jane said. "Are you trying to kill us?"

"Maybe!" Lydia said cheerfully. "It's the last-chance dance! We all need a little liquid courage to finally make moves on our work crushes."

Katie looked up from trying to cram the seltzers in the fridge.

"Don't worry. I got us something special." Lydia dug into one of the shopping bags and pulled out four tiny Fireball shooters. Everyone immediately started protesting.

"I don't want to hear it!" Lydia said, cutting off Jane's excuse that she was too old, Liz's excuse that she couldn't handle shots, and Katie's excuse that Fireball was disgusting. "Our lives are about to change. Who the hell knows what we'll be doing after next week? We need to mark this moment as coworkers, as roommates, and as best friends."

Lydia prodded them all into a tight huddle, then solemnly distributed a Fireball shooter to each of them.

"We're not just losing a job next week," Lydia said, glancing around the circle. "We're losing a friend. The *Nether Fields* may be just a small online magazine that never turns a profit, but it's also a badass queer space that helped a ton of people. So tonight, we're going to celebrate its life."

"Hear, hear," everyone echoed.

"This magazine meant a lot to so many people," Jane added, her voice shaking a little. "It helped queer people feel seen. We should be proud of that."

Katie's eyes filled with tears. Lydia cleared their throat. Liz's stomach twisted. Lydia and Jane were right—the *Nether Fields* was one of the few media outlets where queer people could see themselves. Losing it after almost two decades of operation was a huge blow to the community. How selfish was Liz, feeling relieved and even excited at a time like this?

"To us, for the work and love we poured into this magazine," Katie said, raising her tiny bottle.

"To our readers," Lydia added, raising theirs.

Everyone looked at Liz, waiting for her contribution. She couldn't think of anything to say. She suddenly felt like she had jinxed the magazine with all those nights she'd spent at her desk, racing to complete an article she hated and wishing she were anywhere else.

Katie put a hand on Liz's arm. Everyone gave her sympathetic looks, apparently assuming that she was overcome with emotion.

Jane raised her shooter. "And to every queer or trans kid who found our website and felt just a little bit less alone."

Katie let out a sob. Lydia's free hand balled into a fist as they tried to stay composed.

"To the *Nether Fields*," they all said. They clinked their tiny bottles together and tossed them down. The others all made faces, but Liz could barely feel the whiskey over the guilt already burning in her stomach.

■   ■   ■

After their toast, Jane strong-armed Liz into cleaning the living room as penance for being late. First, though, Liz ran into her room to change into black jeans and a V-necked teal T-shirt that she had stolen from Katie, pausing to stare despairingly into the mirror. At the moment, her brown hair was shaved into an undercut on one side and long on the other, flopping down into a swoosh over her pale skin. She had liked it at first, but today the length felt overly femme. She could never seem to get the style quite right. When she got a masculine cut, she felt like a little kid playing dress-up, trying to seem tough. When she got a feminine cut, she felt itchy and confined, like she was fading away into a role she didn't want. It didn't help that her budget rarely included going to an actual barber, so the quality of her haircut varied wildly, depending on which of her roommates had cut it and their level of sobriety at the time.

Luckily, she didn't have time to spiral into an identity crisis. Jane shouted from the kitchen that guests were coming soon, so Liz shrugged at her reflection and went back out.

The living room and the kitchen occupied one large room, separated by a breakfast bar. They had filled the living half with two couches, a cozy armchair, and one beanbag, all in extremely bright, contrasting colors. It would have been a nice space if the four of them hadn't treated it like their collective second closet.

On the other side of the breakfast bar, Jane was putting the finishing touches on the food. She had pulled her long braids back into a ponytail, which showed off the several long necklaces she had layered over a loose red dress. The combination made her look even more gorgeous than usual.

Liz and Jane had met when Liz started at the magazine. Jane, two years older, had seemed unbelievably cool and knowledgeable. Jane had shown Liz the ropes at the magazine, but they hadn't become true friends until Christmas, when Jane had gone to upstate New York to stay with her then-girlfriend's family. Jane and the girlfriend had ended up getting into a huge, relationship-ending fight on Christmas Eve, and when she messaged the *Nether Fields* group chat to see if anyone knew the best way to get back to the city without a car, Liz had driven three hours to pick her up and bring her to her parents' house in Massachusetts. Jane spent the holiday with them instead, helping Liz's mom bake and impressing Liz's dad with her Boggle skills. After that trip, they became friends, and when a room opened up in Jane and Katie's apartment six months later, Jane offered it to Liz. She had gone home with Liz for Christmas every year since.

Jane and Katie, meanwhile, had met at a conference for young journalists of color, back when Katie still worked at *BuzzFeed,* and instantly hit it off. Jane had encouraged Charlotte, the founder of the *Nether Fields,* to poach her to be their media reporter. Shortly after, Katie had decided that she couldn't stand to spend another year living with her parents in Jackson Heights, so they had banded together with two other reporters to find the apartment in Crown Heights, a neighborhood they loved for being both commutable and not majority white. The other roommates had eventually moved out of the city, leaving room for Liz and Lydia to move in. Liz had lived there for three years now, and she loved it—even if the living room was always disgusting.

Liz gathered up jars of body glitter in assorted colors (Lydia's), a pile of embroidery string (Katie's), a vegetarian cookbook (Jane's), a pair of TomboyX underwear (Liz's), and a crumpled can of White Claw, which she threw out before shoving the rest into the hall closet.

"Shit, have you seen the serving plate?" Jane asked, banging open drawers.

"On top of the fridge," Liz said without looking up. "You left it there after making cookies last week."

Jane was a talented reporter and an excellent cook, but she definitely was *not* organized—she just had too many good thoughts to pay attention to where she put down her phone or keys. Luckily, Liz had a weird knack for keeping track of things.

She was just picking up the final pieces of debris (a scattering of Bananagrams tiles and a succulent that had withered to death in its pot) when the buzzer rang, making her jump. It then rang three more times, each ring longer than the last.

"Jesus fucking Christ," Liz muttered, buzzing them in, knowing that anyone ringing the doorbell that obnoxiously was almost certainly one of their coworkers. A minute later, someone pounded on the door, and Liz opened it to find Charlotte Liu, the founder of the *Nether Fields*. Charlotte was a short, stocky Chinese woman in her midforties with a buzz cut. As usual, she was wearing a black T-shirt and black jeans.

"You're early," Liz said, surprised. "No die-ins at city hall today? No Dyke March committee meetings?"

Charlotte ignored her, strode across the room, and started banging on Katie's door.

"Katie!" she yelled. "Get the fuck out here. And where's Lydia?"

The door opened. "Well hello to you, too." Katie had exchanged her towel for a white short-sleeved button-down shirt, and she was holding an eyeliner pencil in one hand.

Lydia came out of the bathroom. "What are you doing here? You're, like, actually on time."

Charlotte took off her vegan-leather jacket and threw it at Lydia. "I have an announcement to make," she said. "One that will seriously affect this party."

"Oh no. Don't you dare try to cancel the party," Jane said, putting down a roll of aluminum foil and coming over. "I don't care how sad you are, I've been cooking all afternoon."

"Trust me," Charlotte said. "This is an announcement you want to hear." She gave them all a maniacal grin. "I should probably wait until everyone else gets here. But you're my favorites anyway, so . . ." She paused for dramatic effect, taking in their confused faces, then balanced her weight on Lydia's shoulder and climbed up onto the coffee table.

"What are you doing?" Liz said. "Take off your shoes and get off our furniture." She tried to push Charlotte off the table, but Charlotte avoided Liz's hands with surprising nimbleness for someone wearing combat boots. Lydia cackled.

"Ladies and gentlethems," Charlotte said, raising her arms like a preacher. "We are saved."

"Seriously, Charlotte," Jane said. "If you don't get off our table, you are banned from this apartment."

"Are you drunk?" Liz asked.

"Nope," Charlotte said, wagging a finger in Liz's face. "But we're all about be. Because the *Nether Fields* isn't closing."

"What?" Liz said.

Lydia clapped their hands to their face like the kid from *Home Alone.* Jane covered her mouth with one hand, as if afraid to speak.

"How is that possible?" Katie said.

Charlotte held up her phone and shook it at them. "I got an email this morning. We've been bought."

Everyone stared at her in stunned silence, Jane still holding one hand over her mouth, while Charlotte launched into a dramatic reenactment of her day—getting the email, not believing the email, following up on the email. She then read the entire chain out loud, even though it included the exact information she had just told them: Heather Media, their parent company, had accepted an offer from a private individual to buy the magazine.

"I didn't even know a person could just buy a magazine," Liz said. "That seems so—weird."

"Who bought it?" Jane asked.

"I bet it was a celesbian!" Katie said eagerly. "Like Kristen Stewart!"

"Kristen *Stewart?*" Lydia sneered. "Why would she buy a magazine?"

"It's no one famous," Charlotte said, putting a hand on Lydia's head for balance as she stepped off the coffee table. "It's some rich lesbian I've never heard of."

"Well, maybe she bought it *for* Kristen because Kristen didn't want anyone to know," Katie suggested. Katie ran a surprisingly successful queer meme account on Instagram and, at least twice a year, she released an updated version of a list called "Queer Celebrities I Would Die and/or Murder For." Kristen almost always snagged the top spot.

"Don't be ridiculous," Lydia shot back at her. "Why wouldn't Kristen want anyone to know?"

"Who is it?" Jane said, cutting them off. "Did they give you the name?"

Charlotte sat down on the couch, taking her time settling into the cushions around her, clearly enjoying letting the anticipation build. "Her name," she finally said, "is Bailey Cox."

Lydia immediately pulled out their phone. "Got her!" they said a second later, flicking their thumb impossibly fast across their phone screen. Lydia always claimed that their phone was why they were so good in bed—extra finger strength from all that texting. "Bailey Cox. Went to Smith College—figures. Grew up in New York. Lives in Manhattan. Works in real estate. On the board of a bunch of different charities and shit. *Aaaand* here. A picture."

They all clustered around Lydia's shoulders to peer at the screen. It was a headshot next to a bio on a company website. The picture showed a white woman, probably in her early thirties, with red-brown hair and a cheerful smile. She was wearing a women's blouse and her hair reached her shoulders, meaning most people would read her as straight, but there was something about her face that absolutely screamed "lesbian." It was the strong jawline, probably, or the confident way she held her shoulders.

"Huh," Jane said. "She looks nice."

"She looks like someone you would see at a wedding and spend the whole night trying to figure out if they're gay or not," Liz said.

"She's cute," Lydia said.

"I'd bang her," Katie said.

"Well, someone has to." Lydia waggled their eyebrows at the group.

"What are you talking about, Lydia?" Jane asked, taking Lydia's phone so she could study the photo closer.

"Think about it." Lydia leaned back against Katie, who put her arm around them. "Why else would a wealthy lesbian in her thirties buy a queer magazine?"

"To support journalism?" Jane said. "Especially at a queer magazine run by a woman of color?" She looked meaningfully at Charlotte, who winked at her cheerfully.

"No," Lydia said. "Clearly, she has bad dating luck and figures buying the magazine is a great way to meet, like, twenty eligible bachelors at once. Where else would you find so many queers in one place?"

"A queer bar? A lesbian cruise? Tinder?" Liz said, ticking the options off on her fingers and sitting down on the edge of the coffee table.

"Yeah, sorry, Lydia, but that's nuts," Charlotte said. "No one would buy an entire magazine to meet girls."

"Hey, if you have billions of dollars, why not?" Lydia said. "*Billions?*" Liz said.

Lydia grabbed their phone back from Jane and bent over it again, swiping through search results.

"Okay, it looks more like a few million," they said with disappointment, sinking onto the couch next to Charlotte. "Definitely not billions."

"Oh my God, millions?" Liz said. "That's not enough for you?"

"Be practical, Liz," Lydia said with a condescending shake of their head. "If she had a billion dollars, the *Nether Fields* would be a little pet project. But if she only has a few million, then she needs the magazine to make money. Which means either she's going to make a ton of changes until it turns a profit, or it won't make money and she'll try to sell us again. And then when she realizes that there's no market for failing dyke mags, she'll have to shut us down for good."

Everyone stared at Lydia in silence.

They shrugged. "It's just the truth."

Katie flopped down into the armchair with a loud sigh. Jane, still standing, put a soothing hand on her shoulder.

"Don't you dare ruin this for me," Charlotte said, hitting Lydia with a throw pillow. "This is huge! We're not shutting down. We're all still employed. And now the magazine will be owned by actual queer people instead of Heather Media. But"—she took a breath—"you do have a point. One of us has to sleep with her."

Liz laughed.

"Really, that's the only way to keep her invested enough in the magazine. Someone has to seduce her to keep the rest of us employed."

"I'll do it," Lydia said nonchalantly. Katie looked up as if she was honestly worried that Lydia might run off with a millionaire magazine owner.

"What's important is that the NF is clinging to life for a little bit longer," Charlotte said. "Which means this is no longer a goodbye party. It's a Get Shitfaced Celebration."

"Hell yeah!" Lydia shouted, hopping to their feet and running into the kitchen to grab a bottle of liquor. "We should do shots."

Everyone shouted Lydia down. Grudgingly, they put the vodka aside and started passing out hard seltzers instead.

"We should text the group chat," Jane said, opening her drink. "And let everyone know."

"I'll do it!" Katie said, moving her seltzer to the crook of her arm while she took out her phone.

Jane shook her head, a smile growing on her face. "Oh my God," she said. "Oh my God. This is *amazing*." She crossed the room and threw her arms around Liz. "Isn't this amazing?"

"Yeah!" Liz said, trying to sound equally excited. "It's incredible! Excuse me just one second."

Liz got up and went over to the bathroom. Still clutching

her hard seltzer, she locked the door behind her, pulled aside the Pride flag shower curtain, and stepped into the tub so she could lean against the tiny window and breathe in some fresh air. On the other side of the door, someone started blasting "Stayin' Alive." She felt her phone buzz in her pocket—Katie telling everyone the news—followed by more buzzing as the rest of the *Nether Fields* staff texted back.

Liz put her phone on silent and stared out at the dark alley between the apartment buildings.

The *Nether Fields* wasn't closing. Liz should be happy. She still had a job. Her friends still had jobs. Charlotte wouldn't have to give up the publication she'd been running for almost two decades. The magazine would live to see another day.

But this meant the end of Liz's plan. The plan that had formed the second Charlotte announced the closing. With the combination of her severance payment and unemployment, Liz would have been able to afford not to work for at least three months. Which would give her the time and energy to focus on what she'd always wanted to do—write a novel.

When Liz had accepted the *Nether Fields* job out of school, she'd been ecstatic to find a career that would let her write for a living. She'd assumed that she would work there during the day, then use the evenings to write a moving, prize-worthy novel about growing up queer in a small town. The kind of book that Liz had desperately needed when she was figuring out her sexuality in high school, feeling overwhelmed and alone.

But that plan had never turned into reality. After hustling to make deadlines all day, Liz didn't have the time or energy to write something profound. Over the years, the only writing she'd actually managed was a blog called *Confessions of a New York Dyke,* centering on a fictional lesbian called Colby. It was partly inspired by Liz's real life (Colby went to a surprising number of places that Liz liked to frequent) but mostly it was wish fulfillment: Colby was hot and confident, the kind of girl who told off homophobic strangers on the subway and couldn't walk into a queer bar without getting passed a phone-numbered napkin. Liz had updated the blog almost weekly when she first moved to New York and managed to build a decent following, but gradually it had started to seem more and more pathetic to write about Colby's many romantic adventures while Liz continued to have none of her own.

Over the past four years, Liz's excitement for both her blog and her job had faded. Her posts had gotten less and less frequent. Now she thought about Colby only when she got a notification that someone had commented, begging for an update. But the idea of posting again made her feel the same way she felt every time she turned in an advice column on how to tell if your straight best friend is in love with you: frustrated and stuck.

The magazine shutdown was supposed to be her golden ticket. An opportunity to focus on her dreams. Without the layoff money, there was no way Liz could afford to write full-time.

She hadn't told anyone about her plan. Telling her parents was out of the question—her dad was a carpenter and her mom was a first-grade teacher, and while she'd had a fairly privileged childhood, money had always been tight, and the last thing she wanted to do was stress them out about her financial future. She hadn't even told Jane or Katie. She was afraid that her friends might think that listicles and sex advice columns were all she was good for—and even more afraid they might be right.

But now she would never get a chance to find out.

She heard the buzzer ring, signaling the arrival of more guests. Liz took a deep breath, opened the hard seltzer, and chugged it as fast as she could. Then she crumpled the can, pulled the moldy rainbow curtain back into place, and headed back to the celebration.

2

Even though Liz lived with three of her coworkers, she almost always went to work alone. Jane tended to get to the office at least an hour early to drink tea while wearing a colorful shawl (knitted, very poorly, by Liz as a Christmas present two years ago) and reading her way through five different newspapers. Katie and Lydia, meanwhile, usually stumbled into work around ten, often still with glitter on their faces and stamps on the back of their hands from whatever club they'd been to the night before. Which left Liz to brave the Midtown crowds of grim-faced businessmen and oblivious tourists on her own.

The Monday after the party was a particularly brutal one: They were out of coffee, Liz hadn't done laundry in weeks, and she woke up to a classic text message from her mom: *Any new ladies in your life? Your father and I certainly wouldn't say no to a grandkid or two!* Her only clean clothes were cargo pants and a bright blue T-shirt from college that said EVERYTHING I KNOW ABOUT RUGBY I LEARNED FROM YOUR GIRLFRIEND. She looked at herself in the mirror and sighed. She knew she shouldn't wear it to work, but she couldn't bring herself to care. This was supposed to be her last week at the *NF.* Instead, she was going back in for a normal Monday out of what would now possibly be an entire lifetime of normal, boring, frustrating Mondays.

Liz was planning to spend the first few hours of her day drinking coffee and not talking to anyone, but minutes after she got to the office, Charlotte came over and sat on top of her desk.

"You're blocking my computer," Liz said with a grumpiness that was only half-feigned. "How can you expect your employees to be productive under these conditions?"

"Oh, please." Charlotte put her feet on one of the arms of Liz's rolling chair and started pushing Liz back and forth. "Like you'd do anything but take *BuzzFeed* quizzes for another hour anyway."

Liz rolled herself out of range. "Excuse you. Keeping up with competitive media is an important part of my job. What are you doing here on time?"

Charlotte, while extremely dedicated to the magazine, preferred to start her day around eleven so she could stay up late most nights, either working with one of the many activist groups she was part of or attending the kind of exclusive queer parties that Liz could only dream of getting invited to.

"Never went to bed." Charlotte winked. "I was at the opening of an underground burlesque ballet in Bushwick and then ended up at House of Yes. Made a few new friends." She winked again.

"You know, most humans require sleep to function." Liz hoped her voice sounded teasing-snarky and not jealous-snarky. When Liz had started at the magazine, Charlotte, who had grown up in Flushing, had been an indispensable guide. She'd taught Liz how to navigate the subway and given her a crash course in being young and broke in the city: how to budget, which bars did two-for-one happy hours, which email newsletters advertised the coolest free events. Liz didn't know if she would have lasted in New York without Charlotte's guidance. But now, four years later, she sometimes felt like she was still trying to convince Charlotte to see her as a real adult. Liz didn't want to be Charlotte's mentee anymore. She wanted Charlotte to take her to secret burlesque ballets.

"Sounds boring. What are you wearing, by the way?" Charlotte said, running a hand through the short bristles of her shaved head. "You look like you're about to through-hike the Appalachian Trail."

Liz rubbed her eyes. "I haven't been able to motivate myself to go to the laundromat in weeks. Everything is dirty."

"How do you have enough underwear to go that long without laundry?"

Liz looked at Charlotte over the top of her fingers. "I don't."

"Gross," Charlotte said, holding up a hand to stop her. "I don't want to know. But you might regret that outfit choice in two hours."

"Why?"

Charlotte drummed her hands on the desk with a little flourish. "The new owners are coming in today to inspect their merchandise."

Liz groaned. "Stop talking like that. It's creepy," she said. "Wait, what do you mean, owners? I thought it was just the one."

"Apparently there's a minority investor, too. Some woman named Daria."

"Great. More rich people."

Charlotte laughed and jumped off the desk. She cast a significant look at Liz's T-shirt before heading back toward her office. "I'm sure you'll make a great first impression."

A minute later, Liz's computer dinged with a calendar invite from Charlotte to all the employees with the subject line *Time to bend the knee.* The body of the email added only *Try not to act like your usual sloppy selves.* Liz looked down at her laundry-day outfit and closed her eyes.

"Shit," she whispered. Of all the days.

■   ■   ■

At noon, the entire *Nether Fields* staff assembled in the largest conference room, the Rosie Room. Named, of course, after Rosie O'Donnell.

By twelve fifteen, Charlotte and the new owners hadn't shown up yet, and everyone had devolved into a mild state of panic. In the seat next to Liz, Jane kept smoothing and resmoothing her floral skirt, until Liz finally reached out and grabbed her hand to make her stop. Jane looked up, startled.

"Literally everyone loves you," Liz said. "I don't think I could name a single person who knows you and doesn't like you. So, of everyone in this room, you have the least to worry about when it comes to making a good first impression."

Jane smiled. She smoothed her skirt out again, but then caught herself and sat on her hands. "I can't help it. How are you not nervous?"

"Luckily, I don't have to worry about making a good impression, because I have a zero percent chance of actually making one."

"What are you talking about?" Jane said. "You make a great first impression."

"Jane," Liz said slowly. "Look at me. I am wearing *cargo pants.*"

Jane looked down at Liz's pants and grimaced. Even she couldn't argue with that.

Before the meeting, Liz had debated running out and buying a new pair of pants, but a quick glance at her bank

account had put an end to that idea. She'd also considered
going home to raid Katie's closet, but there was no way she'd
make the deadline for her advice column if she spent two
hours on the subway. The best she'd been able to do was
borrow an old cardigan from the head of finance. She hoped
it made her look more professional, but it probably just
made her look even more like she'd picked her clothes out
of a middle school's lost-and-found bin.

Jane was clearly still struggling to come up with something encouraging to say about Liz's outfit when she was
spared by a shriek from Lydia. "They're here!"

Everyone arranged themselves into respectable positions.
A moment later, Charlotte entered the conference room followed by the two new owners.

The first person, who bounced into the room like she
couldn't control her excitement, was obviously Bailey Cox.
She wore a blue women's blazer over a creamy white scoop-
necked shirt and dark jeans, accessorized with sensible
women's loafers and a thin gold necklace. She smiled at
everyone as she came in, but Liz's eyes immediately moved
past her to the person lingering in the doorway. This had to
be the other rich woman Charlotte had mentioned, the minority investor. Unlike Bailey, she didn't look friendly and
excited. She looked . . . *sexy*.

She was white and butch, with a thin frame and strong
cheekbones. Her short, dark hair looked just slightly gelled
and was combed into a sharp, precise part. She was wearing
a tailored navy suit with a thin light blue tie and a matching
pocket square. She looked like a Brooks Brothers ad, if
Brooks Brothers had suddenly gotten very gay.

Liz's cheeks flushed, and she pulled her cardigan tighter
even though she suddenly felt overly warm. Why had she
decided to wear her most hideous outfit *today* of all days?

"Hi, everyone," Charlotte said once they'd all reached the

front of the room. "This is Bailey Cox and Daria Fitzgerald. The new owners of the *Nether Fields*."

Bailey beamed. Beside her, Daria nodded curtly in ac-knowledgment.

"So, uh," Charlotte turned to Bailey, looking a little flus-tered. "How would you like to do this?"

Bailey smiled again and pulled out a chair for herself.

"I think we can keep this short," she said, sitting down and leaning her elbows on the conference table. "We just want to introduce ourselves and let you know how excited we are."

Charlotte turned to offer Daria the other seat at the table, but Daria waved her off, leaning against the wall behind them with her arms crossed. Liz didn't mind, since she was able to stare covertly at Daria, admiring her tightly tailored pants and her long, agile-looking fingers, while appearing to look at Charlotte and Bailey.

"I'm Bailey Cox," Bailey said, looking around the room as she spoke. "I've been a huge fan of your magazine for years now, so when I heard it was going to close, I knew I had to do something. There are only so many media outlets where people like us can see ourselves represented. And luckily, I was able to convince my friend Daria to join me."

On Jane's other side, Liz saw Lydia mouth the word *friend* at Katie and elbow her in the ribs. *Were* they just friends? Did "just friends" suddenly decide to go in on purchasing an entire magazine together?

"We're not here to make a ton of changes," Bailey con-tinued. "Charlotte is an incredible leader, and you all know this magazine far better than we ever will. So we'll do our best not to get in your way. But we also want to be more sup-portive and involved than Heather Media was."

Daria Fitzgerald cleared her throat. "There will be *some* changes," she said. Her voice was low and smooth and un-

nervingly hot. Liz crossed her legs. She felt very conspicu-
ous all of a sudden, worried her face might be broadcasting
her singular focus on Daria.

"Right, of course," Bailey said, waving a dismissive hand.
"We'll be looking at all the financials and logistics in the
coming months as we try to figure out the best way to disen-
tangle ourselves from Heather Media."

The magazine was already "we" to Bailey. Liz looked
around, trying to see if anyone else found that weird. Five
minutes ago, none of them had met Bailey Cox, and now
they were all one unit, fighting together for their survival?

"But really, we're here to help you guys," Bailey said. "And
develop practices that will put us in the best position to stay
open for years to come. Daria, do you want to add anything?"

"No thanks." Daria shifted her weight to lean more fully
against the wall.

"All right then," Bailey said, with another smile. Though
Liz had expected her to have a car-salesman vibe, she
couldn't help feeling Bailey's eagerness was genuine. "Next,
we'd love to come around and meet you one on one."

With that, she turned to the person next to her and held
out her hand. Everyone stared uncomfortably for a bit,
watching in silence as Bailey asked what they did at the
magazine. Then, slowly, soft conversation started to break
out around the room.

Liz turned to Jane and raised her eyebrows. Jane raised
hers back, but Liz couldn't tell if it was a reaction to what
Bailey had said about the magazine or to Daria's hotness. Liz
glanced back at Daria. She and Charlotte were now following Bailey around the room, shaking hands with people as
they went. Oh God. Liz would have to shake Daria's hand.
Were her palms sweaty? She wiped them as discreetly as
possible on her pants.

"Here they come," Jane whispered, smoothing out her

skirt one more time. Liz tried to take a deep breath, but breathing suddenly felt very difficult.

"This is Jane Wilson, our head writer," Charlotte said as she, Bailey, and Daria approached. "She covers our political beats."

Jane stood up to shake Bailey's hand. "It's so nice to meet you."

"I'm actually a huge fan," Bailey said as they shook. "Your writing is one of the reasons I love this magazine so much. That piece you wrote last month about homeless trans youth? It was incredible. Everyone on my timeline was sharing it. It was just . . . beautiful, moving, and important."

"Oh! Thank you." Jane looked both pleased and flustered. "Thank you so much." She looked down, seemed to realize they were still shaking hands, and quickly took her hand back.

"And this is Liz Baker, our sex, relationship, and advice columnist," Charlotte said.

"It's so nice to meet you." Bailey shook Liz's hand with a smile. Over Bailey's shoulder, she saw Daria taking in her outfit with a frown. Her stomach lurched.

"I guess you probably won't compliment me on the beautiful, moving, and important article on butt plugs I wrote last week," Liz said, regretting the joke before it was even halfway out of her mouth.

Everyone stared at her, blank-faced. Liz swore she felt her heart stop. She tried not to look at Daria.

Bailey recovered first with a quick laugh. "You know, I must have missed that one. I'll have to look it up."

Liz tried her best to look like a normal, functioning member of society, but accidentally released her death grip on the cardigan, revealing her offensive T-shirt. "You should. Very good advice if you're in the market."

There was a second, longer pause, and then Bailey said, "And this is Daria, my business partner."

"Nice to meet you," Liz said weakly, then shut her mouth before she could say anything else. Daria nodded at her but made no attempt to shake her hand.

Bailey turned back to Jane and said, "Well, it was so nice to meet you. We should get lunch this week. I'd love to hear more about your vision for the features side of the magazine."

"That would be great," Jane said.

"And this is Mary St. James, our head of finance," Charlotte said, moving the group along.

Liz leaned over to Jane and whispered, "Let's go." They made it halfway down the hall before Liz pulled her into one of the smaller conference rooms, the Laverne Room. Named after Laverne Cox, of course.

"Please tell me I didn't just make the biggest fool of myself in front of our new boss."

Jane grimaced and shut the door. "Well, you didn't make the *best* impression."

"I basically told her she should buy a butt plug. Within seconds of meeting her."

"Yes." Jane nodded slowly. "You did."

Liz sat down at the table and put her face in her hands. "I don't know what happened. I was nervous, and Daria is, like, so hot, and she was wearing that incredible suit and I got overwhelmed and it just came out!"

Jane rubbed Liz's back with one hand. "It's okay. You'll have plenty of opportunities to impress them later."

"If they don't fire me immediately for being a pervert."

"They're not going to fire you," Jane said gently. "Especially not once they read the article and end up with the best butt plug of their lives."

Liz uncovered her face long enough to roll her eyes.

"Seriously," Jane said. "You're great at what you do, and your articles drive, like, half of our traffic. They're not going to fire you. You just got nervous!"

Liz moaned. "Well, at least you made a good impression."

"Do you think so?" Jane asked, looking down and turning the gold bracelet she always wore around her wrist.

"Um, yes. She basically said that you're the entire reason she bought this magazine."

"She did not say that." Jane couldn't hide a small smile.

"You already have a lunch date set up. You're in, Jane."

"I like her," Jane said, fiddling with her bracelet again. "She seems really nice."

"I don't know," Liz said. "It's just so . . . weird. They come in from out of nowhere and now they're in charge, so we all have to suck up to them."

"Just give them a chance, Lizzie," Jane said.

Liz sighed.

"I'll try," she said, standing up. "Now I need to go finish my advice column or I'll miss my deadline."

"Maybe you should give advice on making a good first impression," Jane said as she opened the door.

"*Way* too soon, Jane."

Jane laughed and Liz followed her to their corner of the office. The other staff writers were back in their cubicles, which meant the introduction session must have ended.

Liz went to sit down, then groaned when she realized she'd left her water bottle in the conference room. She made her way down the hall to the Rosie Room but stopped a few feet from the door when she heard Bailey talking. Clearly, she didn't realize that the doors in the office were far from soundproof.

"—think it went well. It's an adjustment for everyone, I'm

sure, but they all seem very nice, and there's some real talent in the group."

Liz took a deep breath and prepared to knock. Maybe this would be a chance to improve her terrible first impression.

"It's not too late, Bailey," said a second voice—Daria's. "Call this whole thing off while there's still time."

Liz stepped back.

"I'm not calling it off," Bailey said, sounding annoyed. "I've told you that a hundred times. The world needs magazines like this."

"Yes, but why do they need them from *you*?" Daria said. "Someone with no journalism experience who's never had any interest in running a magazine before?"

This definitely wasn't the kind of conversation Liz wanted to walk into. She should turn around. She should go back to her desk and get her water bottle later. Instead, she pressed herself against the wall, then took out her phone and tried to look like she was casually texting, in case anyone walked by.

"Because I have the money to keep this magazine from closing, which is something that very few people have, especially in the lesbian community. I have the opportunity to actually make a difference here."

"You're going to lose that opportunity," Daria said. She spoke quietly, and Liz hesitantly took a step closer to the door. She was definitely going to hell for this. "When you run out of money, the magazine is going to close. And you won't have the opportunity to put that money somewhere it might actually matter."

"This place does matter," Bailey said. "This is a queer magazine founded by a woman of color that's been running for almost two decades. We can't just let it close."

"Maybe so." There was the sound of a chair shifting. "But if this magazine was providing a service that people actually wanted, then it would be making money. Not losing readers every month."

"So they're a little outdated," Bailey said airily. "They're writers. You and I, we're business oriented. We can help them streamline things, increase revenue, leverage data analytics, maximize readership."

Daria scoffed. "You don't know how to do any of that, Bailey."

"So we'll learn," Bailey said. "Or we'll hire an expert. This place just needs a little tinkering."

"Tinkering's a nice euphemism for laying people off."

Liz took another step toward the door, her heart beating so loudly she worried she'd soon have trouble hearing them.

"Daria." Bailey's voice went hard. "We are not coming in here and immediately laying people off. I told you that. I want to *help* the queer community, not take away their salaries. We need to spend a few months getting to know the business first. Then we'll decide how best to cut costs."

"You know what the best way to cut costs is," Daria said. "And it's not going to be any easier once you've had a few months to make friends."

"There are some really talented people here," Bailey said. "Jane Wilson is probably the top transgender rights journalist in the country."

"Okay, sure," Daria said dismissively. "But one good reporter doesn't make this a worthwhile investment. Have you looked at their home page recently? It's all 'Twenty-five vibrators to heat up your spring' and 'A comprehensive ranking of every queer kiss on television so far this year.' It's absurd."

Liz let out a loud breath, then froze, worried they'd hear her. She knew she shouldn't be eavesdropping like this. But how dare they talk about her coworkers, her magazine, her own articles, like that? Liz wasn't sure that she wanted to keep working here, but still. They'd barely spent thirty minutes with the team.

Bailey laughed. "If you hate this so much, then why are you investing at all?"

There was a pause. "You know why."

"I'm perfectly capable of doing this on my own, Daria." Bailey sounded markedly less patient now. Daria didn't reply. After a few seconds, Bailey sighed.

"I know this isn't the most corporate environment. But it's a creative field. Just give these people a chance."

"I'll give you a month," Daria said. "And then we're laying off as many people as we need to. Starting with that asinine fluff-piece writer who kept babbling on about butt plugs."

Liz felt like she'd been punched in the gut. Before she could stop herself, she flung open the door to the Rosie Room with such fervor that it hit a nearby chair with a loud bang that reverberated around the room.

Bailey, who seemed to have been leaning back in her chair with her feet on the table, nearly fell over. Daria scrambled to her feet, staring at Liz with an expression of indignation.

"Oh," Liz said, making only a small effort to look surprised. "Sorry. I didn't realize anyone was still in here. Left my water bottle."

She walked across the room, trying to look cold and dignified, and picked up her plastic Nalgene covered in King Princess stickers.

"Well. It was *so* nice to meet you both." She knew that her clipped, aggressive tone would give away the fact that she had been listening in, but she couldn't seem to help herself. "I just can't wait to get to know you more." She crossed back to the door. "See you later."

"Bye," Bailey said weakly.

Liz slammed the door behind her. Then she went straight

to the Bechdel Bathroom (named, of course, after Alison Bechdel) and slammed the stall door, too. She thought briefly about punching it, but that seemed like overkill.

Those rich assholes. How could they come in out of nowhere and talk so casually about laying people off? Didn't they have any conscience at all?

That asinine fluff-piece writer who kept babbling on. Sure, she had said more than she'd meant to. But it hadn't been that bad. And Daria had just stood there, looking at Liz condescendingly, as if deliberately trying to make her nervous. Why was Daria even here? Why had she invested God knows how much money in a magazine that she thought was a waste of time?

Liz's mind buzzed with angry retorts. She should have given Daria and Bailey a piece of her mind.

No, she shouldn't have gone into that room at all. She should have walked away as soon as she overheard their first words.

She tried to hold on to her anger, but it was no use—she could feel it draining away, replaced by humiliation and dread. What had she been thinking? Surely they would guess she'd been eavesdropping. Which meant she'd pretty much sealed her fate as the first employee of the *Nether Fields* to get laid off. She'd be lucky if she even lasted a week.

Well, maybe that wouldn't be a bad thing. She'd get the severance payout she'd wanted and could focus on writing, just like she'd planned. But she didn't want things to end like *that*. It was one thing for the magazine to close. It was another to be sent packing by two rich assholes while the rest of her friends stayed employed, happily working there without her.

Liz unlocked the stall door. They hadn't kicked her out yet. Until they did, she was going to write fluff pieces so incredibly fluffy that they would go viral. She would make herself impossible to fire. She would be professional and confident and tough. She wouldn't care what anyone thought about her. Especially Daria.

Liz went to the sink to splash water on her face. She was going to do all of that. But first, she was going to find Jane, tell her what had happened, and cry.

3

Two days after the introductory meeting, Bailey and Daria officially moved in to the *Nether Fields* office. They took over the Janelle Room (named, of course, after Janelle Monáe), and let Charlotte know that they'd be coming in a few days a week to "get to know the magazine."

Liz had imagined that Bailey and Daria would have a hands-off approach to running a magazine, the way Heather Media had. Unfortunately, they turned out to be *extremely* hands-on. Apparently rich-people jobs came with a lot of flexibility, because Bailey started coming in almost every afternoon. She followed Charlotte around like a chatty puppy and sat in on every meeting so she could "observe without disrupting." When she wasn't observing, she walked around the office, having long conversations with whoever she ran into in the Kiyoko Kitchen (named, of course, after Hayley Kiyoko) and leaning over cubicle dividers to ask people questions about their jobs. She was, in short, an extremely enthusiastic nuisance.

Bailey's overeagerness was infinitely preferable, however, to Daria Fitzgerald's approach. She came in for exactly two hours, three days a week. The first day, she showed up at eight A.M., and Jane, who was the only other person there that early, told her roommates that Daria had stomped repeatedly around the empty office, glaring and checking her watch. Once Charlotte arrived, Daria complained to her that, in finance, all of the dedicated employees showed up early, and Charlotte reminded her that, in finance, people actually made decent salaries.

After that incident, whenever Daria came in, she holed herself up in the Janelle Room and sent emails. She asked Mary, their head of finance, to pull together a series of extremely detailed budget reports. She asked Lydia, who ran ad/promo, to put together an overview of their click-through rates for every ad from the last three years. She asked Tara, who ran their social media, to email her updated statistics on their engagement ratios and follower gains every week.

It was all fairly reasonable, until Daria crunched all of these reports into a series of graphs and charts full of declining lines, negative symbols, and angry red fonts, which she then emailed to the entire staff with the subject line *The State of Your Magazine Today.* In response, Lydia (disgruntled about the extra work putting together those reports had taken) texted the staff group chat a series of unflattering memes called "The State of Your Ass Today," which caused Katie to fall into such hysterics that she had to excuse herself to take a walk around the block. When Daria began updating and resending her depressing report every week, however, the situation started to seem a lot less funny.

Apparently Daria wasn't satisfied with picking apart only the big-picture issues, either. One morning, three weeks after Bailey and Daria had bought the magazine, Liz was in the Kiyoko Kitchen, waiting for coffee to brew and talking to Finn, a tiny Black queer person with short hair and a love of bow ties, who ran the magazine's website. Liz had originally

walked to the kitchen with Jane, but Bailey had been passing by and snagged Jane to "pick her brain" about the writing
process. Since that first week, Jane had become firmly Team
Bailey. She'd returned from their lunch together full of excitement about all the ways Bailey was going to optimize
their processes and update their systems. Jane and Bailey
were still standing in the hall just outside the kitchen, and
Liz could hear occasional bursts of laughter.

Finn was telling Liz about a fight they were having with
their parents over whether to keep inviting their homophobic cousin to family events. Listening to the story, Liz felt
extremely grateful for her own family. She didn't have any
weird conservative cousins, and her parents had always been
supportive, even when she came out. Liz chalked it up to
being an only child—her parents thought everything Liz did
was wonderful, even if they couldn't understand why she
had moved to the most expensive city in the United States
to write sex-toy reviews, which Liz had made them promise
to never read.

The coffee maker was moving into its final stage of sput-
tering groans when Daria came into the kitchen, carrying a
notebook. She wore a black suit with a skinny black tie. Liz
tried not to let her eyes linger—she *wanted* that outfit. She
could picture herself heading to a glamorous artsy party, hair
gelled high and the skinny tie contrasting with a bright pink
pocket square, dressed down with some Doc Martens. She'd
look like a sexy queer boy-band member. But she didn't even
want to *think* about how much a tailored suit like that might
cost.

"Good morning!" Finn chirped at Daria. "I love your tie."
Finn tweaked their own green bow tie at Daria and winked.

Daria nodded at Finn without smiling, then glanced at
Liz, who did her best not to blush—this was the first time

they'd been in close proximity since her little outburst on the first day.

Liz scowled at the coffee machine as Finn resumed their story about the unhinged rants their cousin kept posting to Facebook. She felt very aware of Daria lurking beside her. Daria was scanning the kitchen with her brow furrowed, as if she had never seen one before. After a few seconds, Daria walked over to the counter and leaned in to examine the coffee maker. Behind her back, Finn quirked an eyebrow at Liz.

Then Daria started counting the stack of disposable cups—out loud. Finn bravely tried to persevere with their story, but next Daria started pulling open the drawers to inspect their contents and write something down in her notebook. With each yank of a drawer, Finn's words came slower and slower. They shot a confused look at Liz, who shrugged. The coffee maker was almost done now, but neither of them moved toward it. They were too mesmerized. Finally, Daria crouched down to stick her head into the cabinet under the sink, and Liz couldn't help herself anymore.

"*What* are you *doing*?" She maybe let a little more exasperation into her tone than she should have, because Daria jerked in surprise, hitting her head on the cabinet. Liz winced as Daria turned around to glare at her.

"I'm taking stock of our supplies," Daria said, rubbing her head. Then she turned back around and continued inspecting.

"Is there a hurricane coming that we weren't warned about?" Liz said. "Upcoming nuclear war that we need to be prepared for?"

Finn stifled a snort in their fist. Daria finished whatever she was doing under the sink and then stood up. She opened a drawer and gestured to the boxes of plastic silverware inside.

"Do you know what this is?" she said.

Finn and Liz exchanged a glance.

"Cutlery?" Liz said.

"No." Daria slammed the drawer closed. "It is an unnecessary expense. And do you know what this magazine's budget cannot support right now?" She paused dramatically. "Unnecessary expenses."

She frowned at them both as if this thirty-second conversation had been a colossal waste of time, then walked into the hall, where Liz heard her yell, "Bailey! Get over here!" A few seconds later, Bailey scurried past the kitchen after her.

Liz and Finn gaped at each other.

"Wow," Finn said. "She is such a dick."

Liz laughed and shoved their shoulder. "Finn! I've never heard you say a mean thing about anyone!"

Finn laughed, too, but shook their head. "She deserves it."

Liz felt vindicated as she poured herself a cup of coffee and headed back to her desk. Even Finn thought Daria was a dick. Which meant Liz didn't have to feel the tiniest bit guilty that she had already told everyone in the office what she'd overheard in the conference room on the first day.

Originally, Liz had planned to tell only Jane so there wouldn't be an office-wide panic about layoffs. But she hadn't been able to resist telling Charlotte. And then she'd accidentally mentioned something about it to Lydia, who'd pestered her until she told the whole story. At which point, so many people found out that she figured there was no point hiding it anymore, so she'd given in and allowed herself the pleasure of dramatically recounting the event to anyone who would listen. As a result, the whole office now knew that Daria Fitzgerald wanted to slash costs and fire as many people as possible, if she couldn't convince Bailey to shut down the magazine altogether. Between that, the charts, and the fact that she stomped around the office without ever saying hello to anyone, the entire staff had concluded that she was an arrogant asshole and the worst possible thing that could have ever happened to the *Nether Fields*.

Lydia had done a deep internet stalk on Daria's background and, unsurprisingly, it turned out that Daria worked as an investment banker. A snooty, asshole career for a snooty, asshole person. She had grown up in Boston, where her mother was a local politician and her father was a prominent real estate agent, and she'd graduated from Smith College like Bailey. Based on her family and her job, Lydia estimated that she was even richer than Bailey.

Liz sat down at her desk. So what if Daria didn't like her? Daria was controlling and condescending and didn't like anyone else, either.

Two minutes later, Liz's inbox dinged with a new email from Daria, announcing that everyone would need to bring reusable mugs and forks from home, since disposable ones would no longer be provided. To emphasize the point, she included a detailed projection of how much money the magazine could have saved per year if it hadn't purchased disposable cups and silverware, and signed off with a suggestion that employees return to their desks while their coffee brewed, to increase efficiency and "avoid unnecessary time wasting."

4

Liz was starting to hate short-sleeved button-down shirts. Particularly ones with patterns.

That Friday night, as they did most weeks, Liz, Katie, and Lydia left work at four thirty to go to happy hour at Scissors, a tiny lesbian-owned bar in the East Village that had rainbow flags plastered onto every surface. Usually Charlotte and Jane joined them, but this week Charlotte had a date and Jane was meeting with TWOCs and Ewoks, her *Star Wars*–themed D&D group for trans women of color who were also giant dorks.

Once they'd gotten their first round of drinks, Lydia and Katie immediately began indulging in their new favorite hobby: complaining about Daria. Plastic silverware and re-usable cups weren't the only things that had met their ends over the past week. In the name of reducing "unnecessary costs," Daria had switched all of their subscriptions to digital only, emailed around strict new expense guidelines, and even password-protected the color printer to prevent "frivolous use" (Lydia swore this was just petty vindictiveness

after Daria had found one of Lydia's memes taped up in the
bathroom).

Liz, who didn't want to think about Daria any more than
she had to, tried to tune them out while she scanned the
crowd. Usually, Liz started a Scissors night full of hope that
maybe, just maybe, this would be the night she'd finally
meet someone. But tonight, she felt defeated. Now that the
weather was warm, it seemed like every single person in the
bar was wearing either a sundress or a short-sleeved button-
down. That morning, Liz had put on her baggier jeans and a
men's polo shirt she'd found at Goodwill. She'd felt casually
handsome as she walked to work, catching glimpses of herself in store windows. But now the loose fit of the clothes
made her feel frumpy and self-conscious. Maybe if she'd
worn something more femme, one of the short-sleeved
button-downs would be talking to her. Maybe if she had
whimsical, boyish shirts, she'd be buying a drink for someone in a sundress right now.

In an ideal world, Liz would look androgynous, mixing
genders in a sexy, dazzling way. Unfortunately, that type of
clothing was expensive and seemed to be made only for
stick-thin people with flat chests. It was hard to look androgynous when you had curves, especially when you had a
new-clothing budget of roughly zero dollars.

Some days Liz made up her mind to throw out her dresses
and skirts. But a week later, she'd long to feel feminine and
glamorous and show off her body. Then the pendulum would
swing the other way and for a week she'd double-layer sports
bras to make her chest flat under a dress shirt. The result
was far too many clothes to fit in her small closet and a ha-
tred of dating sites that encouraged you to select labels. Was
she a soft butch? Futch? A tomboy? A ChapStick lesbian?

"Looking for prospects?" Lydia said, leaning in and slinging their arm around Liz's neck. Liz wriggled away so no one would think they were together.

"Maybe."

"What about that person?" Lydia said, her breath hot against Liz's ear. "Blue coveralls in the corner. They look like your type."

Liz turned to the corner, trying to look casual about it. Lydia was right: Blue coveralls *was* her type. They were tall and androgynous looking, with a shaved head, standing in the corner and looking at their phone, apparently alone.

"You should go say hi," Lydia said.

"No, don't," Katie said. "Popping up beside someone and saying hi is weird. Try to make eye contact first."

Liz liked that idea. She liked any idea that didn't involve her going up to a hot stranger and potentially getting shot down. As Katie and Lydia started chatting about some new celesbian drama, Liz kept her eyes on the stranger, hoping they would look up.

And then they did. The person lowered their phone and glanced around the room. Liz tried to make it seem coincidental, like she'd just *happened* to look up from her drink at that exact moment, but blue coveralls must have caught her staring because their gaze jumped to Liz almost immediately. A wave of adrenaline buzzed through Liz's chest as they locked eyes, and she attempted a flirty smile.

The stranger didn't smile back. Instead, they made a show of continuing to scan the room, as if they'd just been taking in the scenery, and then fixed their eyes firmly back onto their phone.

"Ouch," Lydia said, cackling. "That was brutal."

Katie winced sympathetically. Liz could feel her face getting hot.

"Oh, shut up," she said. She drained the rest of her beer and stepped away to put the empty bottle on the bar. What had she expected? Liz didn't know why she kept doing this to herself. Coming to the bar, going on app dates, getting her hopes up. But she couldn't help it. She wanted to find love. She wanted to find her *person*, the one she'd be with long term.

Lately, though, it was hard not to feel like that might never happen. Because whenever she did meet someone she liked, they would ghost after the first date or send a vague message saying they "hadn't felt a spark" or "weren't in the right place for dating after all." Liz might be good for a one-night hookup, but she never seemed to be good enough for a second date.

"Lizzie," Katie said, grabbing her arm and pulling her over to where Lydia had started chatting with a stranger. "Stop pouting and get another drink."

"I don't want to get wasted," Liz complained.

"Yes, you do," said the person talking to Lydia. "Otherwise, why would you be in this crowded bar on a Friday night?"

"Maybe I just want to socialize," Liz said back.

"I'm Weston. She/her," the stranger said, holding out her hand. Liz shook it. Weston was white, probably a year or two older than Liz, and had dark hair down to her shoulders. She was wearing a black denim jacket over an artfully torn black-and-white T-shirt and a layer of long metal necklaces. The outfit was fashionable, if maybe trying a little too hard, but she was definitely cute. Real long-haired butch energy.

"Liz. She/her."

Weston raised an eyebrow and turned back to Lydia. "I think your grumpy friend needs a shot."

"Yessss!" Lydia and Katie said together. Liz's mouth curled into a smile in spite of herself.

"Fine," she said. "But just one. And not Fireball."

Weston leaned over the bar, trying to get the attention of

the bartender, who was deep in conversation with a butch in the corner. Lydia waggled their eyebrows at Liz over the stranger's back and mouthed, *Cute, right?* Katie looked away.

"Okay," Weston said, turning around to distribute tiny plastic shot glasses to each of them. "Cheers, queers."

They touched their glasses together, spilling tequila over one another's fingers. Katie and Lydia slammed their shots back. Liz hesitated, then drank hers. It was terrible. She made a face, gagging over the burn.

"God, I hate shots," she said. Weston winked at her, then tossed hers back.

"Show-off," Liz accused, but she felt herself smiling.

"So how do you all know each other?" Weston asked. Liz assumed she was fishing to see if any of them were coupled up.

"We work together," Lydia said, slinging their arms around Liz's and Katie's shoulders. "At the *Nether Fields*. We basically run it."

"Oh?" Weston said. "What's that?"

Lydia slumped. Liz understood why—you'd think, at the very least, people at a lesbian bar would know the magazine. Maybe their readership really was getting dire.

"It's the number five queer women's online magazine in the U.S.," Lydia said.

"Oh, cool." Weston picked her beer up off the bar and took a sip. "Like *Autostraddle*?"

"Yes," Liz said, grimly. "Like *Autostraddle*. Except smaller. And less profitable. Excuse me, I need another drink."

She extracted herself from Lydia's arm (on Lydia's other side, Katie was still holding on tight) and went to get the bartender's attention, which brought her closer to Weston, who was leaning against the bar.

Liz found she didn't mind the proximity, and because it was loud and crowded, she had every reason to put her lips an inch from Weston's ear when she leaned in to ask what Weston did. She moved back after she asked, but not all the way.

Weston smiled at her, a genuine grin this time instead of a flirty smirk. It looked a little goofy and made Liz like her more. "I do social media marketing for BYond."

"The gender-neutral clothing company?" Katie said, leaning over. Weston nodded.

"I've been in there a few times, but all their clothes are like a hundred dollars and made for skinny twinks with no hips," Liz said, then grimaced, wondering if that had been too insulting. Why couldn't she keep her damn mouth shut?

Luckily, Weston laughed. "Yeah, exactly. Plus, it's all rainbow or, like, a crop top that says BE GAY DO CRIMES."

"I need to go to the bathroom," Lydia said abruptly. They pulled Katie away with them, casting Liz a significant look over their shoulder. Liz turned back to the bar to hide her smile.

"Do you like working there?" Liz said. Weston stepped a little closer now that it was just the two of them, under the pretense of needing to hear her better. Their arms pressed together on top of the bar.

"Not really." Weston laughed. "It's boring."

The bartender came over then, and Liz ordered two rum and cokes. She could feel the shot working, making the level of noise in the bar more tolerable.

"How long have you been in New York?" Liz asked as she counted out crumpled cash from her pocket.

"A while now," Weston said. "Since after college."

"Where'd you go?"

"Smith, of course," Weston said. "Like a good dyke."

"Oh God," Liz said. Their drinks arrived, and she took a big gulp, deciding to lean in to getting drunk.

"What do you have against Smith?"

Liz rolled her eyes. "I've just been dealing with a lot of Smithies lately."

"Well, that might have something to do with the company you keep." Weston grinned. "Where in the city do you live?"

Liz started telling Weston about their apartment in Crown Heights and how she'd moved to the neighborhood right after college, despite never having heard of Crown Heights or even realizing that there were neighborhoods in Brooklyn other than Williamsburg. Weston was a good listener— cracking jokes, acting interested, adding but not interrupting. As they talked, Liz could feel her stomach humming with the thrill of flirting with someone new. It had been a long time since Liz had felt like this—like she was matching wits with someone, trading banter back and forth. She felt sexy, like she was getting taller and smarter and more confident with every quick retort and sip of her drink. She couldn't believe Weston was still there talking to *her,* out of everyone there.

Over Weston's shoulder, Liz saw Lydia watching her from across the room. Apparently, they'd had no success prowling tonight, because they were pressed against Katie, who was kissing their neck. Liz wished Lydia would stop doing that— hooking up with Katie when they were bored just filled Katie with false hope. Lydia pointed at Weston, gave Liz a thumbs-up, then flipped her off. Liz rolled her eyes.

She turned back to Weston, leaning closer than she needed to, letting her lips almost touch skin as she spoke, feeling a delicious jolt from her stomach in response. "My roommate will never forgive me for stealing you away from them."

Weston smirked with half her mouth in a stereotypical dreamy-dyke way that Liz had practiced in front of a mirror but could never quite pull off. "Well, if it's any consolation, I'm happy to have been stolen."

"Good to know," Liz said, holding eye contact over her drink as she took a sip (another move she had practiced in front of a mirror at least once, but with more success, which was why she was able to pull it off without spilling).

"So where are you stealing me to?" Weston asked. "All the way to Crown Heights?"

Was this really happening? Weston was attractive. She was funny. She hadn't made any offensive jokes. She had asked for no straw when she ordered drinks, for environmental reasons. It might not lead anywhere beyond a one-night stand, but still. Why the hell not?

"All the way to Crown Heights," Liz said.

She put her arms around Weston's shoulders. She let her body press against Weston's slowly, drawing out the moment because the anticipation was almost always better than the thing itself. Then she finally brought her face closer to Weston's, hesitating for just a moment before Weston closed the space between them. A few moments of lips, a second of tongue, then—

"Come on," Liz said, pulling Weston toward the door. "Stealing time."

5

————

Liz was still glowing on Monday morning. Normally, she didn't get giddy, but this was an exception. Weston was smart and sexy and *fun*. Liz could visualize them spending nights in together, cooking and watching TV. She could imagine them taking the train up to visit her parents, where Weston would charm them by helping in the kitchen and making witty jokes. She could practically smell the salt air of their seaside honeymoon.

But first, Liz had to figure out how to make the next move.

Weston had taken her number before she left Liz's apartment Saturday morning, and texted Liz not long after: *that was fun lets do it again sometime*. No caps, no punctuation, but there *was* a winky face at the end.

Liz had spent thirty minutes trying to decide if it was good that she'd texted so quickly (she couldn't wait to talk to Liz and wanted to make sure that Liz knew she'd had fun) or bad (she didn't care if Liz saw the text as desperate, she was just bored on the subway). Eventually, she'd decided on good and sent back *Yes please* and the sly winky face.

The only hitch in her long-term fantasy was that Weston

still hadn't responded. Liz wished she'd said something con-
crete and confident, like *Yes please. Thursday?* But now she
couldn't double text without looking like a loser. Or maybe
she *should* double text, to show she was nonchalant and
didn't care about looking like a loser?

Liz asked Jane to come to the weekly writers meeting fifteen minutes early so she could talk through her dilemma in
the privacy of the Laverne Room before anyone else got there.
But Jane seemed less than focused as Liz proposed a dozen
different response plans, possibly because they'd had the
exact same conversation the night before. Jane sat sideways
in her chair, swinging one leg and alternately pulling her
braids into a ponytail and taking them down, clearly changing
her mind every few minutes about which looked better.

"Jane?" Liz said, interrupting the ponytail process. "Are
you listening? I need a sex-life intervention here."

"Just wait until Friday," Jane said, checking her reflection
in her phone camera. "Then ask if she wants to meet up. It
will seem casual."

"But what if she already has plans for the weekend by
then?"

Jane shrugged. She seemed to decide that her hair looked
better back today and put her phone down. "Then you make
plans for the next weekend. Have you seen my gold D20
necklace, by the way? I couldn't find it this morning."

"Katie borrowed it last week. She probably still has it," Liz
said. "Also, I don't want to wait that long! I want to see her
tonight."

"Okay, definitely don't tell her that," Jane said. "Do you
need me to take your phone away?"

"I won't, I won't," Liz groaned. She slumped down so far
in her chair that her chin disappeared below the conference
table. "It's just . . . exciting to be excited about someone, you
know?"

"Yeah," Jane said, twisting the gold bracelet on her wrist. "I know."

At that moment, the door opened and Bailey Cox walked in. Liz quickly sat up to a normal height.

"Oh, hi! You two are early!" Bailey took the seat next to Jane. "I loved your last article, Jane. I think you're absolutely right that we need to follow the lead of queer people of color in the charge for environmental sustainability."

Jane beamed, asking if Bailey had read a recent article in *The Wall Street Journal*. Bailey had, and they started comparing notes. Liz, who never read *The Wall Street Journal*, was completely lost. Bailey and Jane didn't seem to mind— they leaned toward each other, punctuating their conversation with eager hand motions.

Liz stared at them. Jane was smiling. She let out a high-pitched, tinkling laugh. When Bailey gave her another compliment on her article, Jane glanced down at her hands then back up at Bailey through her eyelashes.

Oh shit.

Suddenly, Liz didn't know how she'd missed it. She'd seen Jane and Bailey talking in the Kiyoko Kitchen several times, and she knew their lunch had made a big impression on Jane. But she hadn't put the pieces together.

Why hadn't Jane told her? Liz was briefly furious, before realizing exactly why: because Liz would have tried to talk her out of it.

Liz stared at Jane, trying to mentally convince her to stop flirting, when Daria walked in.

Liz looked up, surprised. Daria had never attended a writers meeting before.

As usual, Daria was wearing an impressive suit. This one was gray with a light blue shirt and no tie. It was tailored a little more tightly than usual, as if begging Liz to imagine

what her body looked like underneath. But then Daria
dropped her briefcase on a chair with a bang, bringing Liz
back to reality. It was truly unfair that someone so hot could
be such an asshole. But maybe it was better that way. If
Daria had been that good-looking *and* had a good personality, Liz might have been in the same predicament as Jane.

Daria settled into the chair next to the one holding her
briefcase. Liz glared at her—was she really going to take up
an entire chair for her bag? Did she not realize other people
were coming to this meeting?

Liz's silent condemnation was interrupted by Charlotte's
arrival, the other writers trailing behind her. Once everyone
settled in, Charlotte called on each writer in turn so they
could pitch their ideas for the upcoming week. It was usually a casual meeting, but since Bailey had started attending,
it had become much less relaxed. This week, Daria's presence ratcheted up the tension, and each writer presented
their pitches in stilted, formal tones. Bailey chimed in here
and there, mostly with encouragement, but a few times with
surprisingly insightful ideas that the writer in question
would diligently mark down. Daria said nothing. She had an
unpleasant look on her face, as if she could smell something
rotting, and kept checking her phone. A desperate note
started to enter some of the writers' tones as they attempted
to capture her interest.

When it was Katie's turn, she pitched an interview with
an activist in Astoria who ran a pop-up lesbian bar that was
also a community pantry. Charlotte, Jane, and Bailey gave
their enthusiastic approval. Technically, Katie was the TV
and media writer, but she was becoming the rising star of
the magazine, successfully pitching herself for a wider range
of articles. She also had a growing social media platform
thanks to her meme account and the podcast that she co-

hosted called *¡Pussy Putas!* If Katie ever decided to leave the magazine, she'd be able to work pretty much anywhere she wanted.

Liz stared at her list, wishing she had something more exciting to share. She should have put more effort into her pitches this week. She should have found an angle that would let her write a more substantive article. Then she'd be able to wipe that condescending frown off Daria's face and prove she was more than just a fluff-piece writer.

"Liz?" Charlotte said. "Your pitches?"

Liz looked up. Everyone was staring at her. Daria had one eyebrow quirked, as if Liz was confirming her decidedly low expectations. *Shit.*

"Um. Okay. Let's see," Liz said, quickly scanning her list. "An advice column on what to do when you still live with your ex. A vanilla person's guide to spanking in the bedroom."

Liz glanced around. Daria was staring at her, looking unimpressed. Liz's face warmed.

"Three quizzes," Liz continued. "Which *L Word: Gen Q* plot hole are you? How many celesbian icons can you identify? What queer song should you bang to? And, um, a listicle about how good Kristen Stewart looks lately."

Daria scoffed. A very small, very quiet, but extremely dismissive scoff. Liz whipped her head over.

"Yes?" she said before she could stop herself. "Daria? Any feedback?"

"Oh no," Daria said, leaning back in her chair. "This Kristen Stewart article will change the world, I'm sure." The room went very quiet. Liz willed herself not to look at Jane or Charlotte.

"It's not meant to change the world," Liz snapped back. "It's meant to provide one fleeting moment of pleasure for people who work long days in an exploitative economy on a planet that's falling apart."

"Ah," Daria said. "So the Kristen Stewart listicle is a humanitarian mission. My mistake."

Liz opened her mouth to retort, but Charlotte cut her off. "Those are solid pitches, Liz," she said. "Daria, Liz's articles bring in some of the highest traffic the website sees. People love her quizzes."

"I look forward to finding out what plot hole I am," Daria said, her eyes back on her phone. Under the table, Liz dug her nails into her palms. She knew exactly what kind of hole Daria was.

They moved on to Amy, whose articles consisted mostly of recapping and commenting on any pop culture event from the past week that had even a tiny whiff of queerness to it. Liz ground her teeth. People kept glancing at her, out of either concern or secondhand embarrassment, so she tried to keep her face blank, but it was hard. Did Daria think she wasn't aware that her articles were a little silly? What did she think kept the lights on at this magazine? People wanted sex advice, not more depressing political articles. If anything, Daria was proving how little she knew about how to keep the *NF* alive.

"All right, everyone, I think that's it," Charlotte finally said, and they all filed out. In the hall, Jane looked like she was trying to catch Bailey's eye, but Liz took her arm.

"Jane? Can I talk to you for a minute?" Liz said, pulling her into the Lena Lounge (named, of course, after Lena Waithe) without waiting for Jane to answer.

"I know that was uncomfortable," Jane said as they closed the door behind them. "But it's not personal. Daria just doesn't understand how the magazine works yet."

"Don't you dare make excuses for her," Liz said. "Did you

hear her? She acted like only imbeciles would read my articles! She was insulting our fans."

"Liz, you complain about writing listicles all the time," Jane said.

Liz crossed her arms with a huff. "I'm *allowed* to complain. I have to write the damn things. Doesn't she understand that these articles make money?"

"Look, Liz—"

Liz cut her off. "That's not what I wanted to talk about. I want to talk about how you're totally in love with Bailey."

Jane sat on the couch and crossed her arms. "I am not in love with Bailey."

"But you're into her."

Jane narrowed her eyes.

"I mean, she's nice," she said. "And smart. And interested in journalism. And funny."

"You do realize you're listing reasons why you're into her."

Jane was quiet for a moment before relenting. "She just— gets me. And you know older white women with Aubrey Plaza style are my kryptonite! I wish she was some random person I just met somewhere."

Liz felt a pang of sympathy. "I get that. But she's not."

Jane fiddled with her bangle. "Would it really be that bad? To date her?"

"Welllll," Liz said, drawing the word out. She didn't want to crush Jane's hopes, but she also thought they could use a little crushing. "I mean, you work together. So that could be awkward. Plus, what's up with her and Daria? Are they involved? Because they're always together."

"They're not involved. Bailey told me," Jane said. "They're always together because they co-own the magazine."

"I guess," Liz said doubtfully. "But Daria totally sucks, which really calls Bailey's taste into question."

Jane abandoned the bangle in favor of inspecting her

nails, which were currently gold. "I just—I really like her, Lizzie," she finally said. "A lot."

Liz's heart sank. Jane hadn't felt that way about someone in a long time. She plopped down next to Jane on the couch.

"I'm sorry, Jane."

"I think she likes me, too."

"Well, duh," Liz said. "She's always talking to you, she's always looking at you, and she's always going on about how great your articles are. Plus, you're hot as shit."

Jane smiled but didn't say anything. "You know," she said finally, "tonight's Margarita Monday."

Liz groaned. "I am not going to Margarita Monday," she said. "I need this liver."

Jane turned to face Liz. She took a deep breath. "It just seems like a good excuse to invite her to join us for a drink," she said carefully. "I've worked way too hard to get here to throw it all away on some crush. But—I really think this could be something. And I just want to see. What it's like to spend time with her outside the office. Somewhere she isn't my boss. See if we still click."

"She's still your boss outside the office," Liz said.

Jane stuck her tongue out at her. Liz stuck hers back.

Liz was pretty sure that spending time with Bailey in a dark bar would make Jane more into her, not less. And she was pretty sure that dating your boss was guaranteed to end in disaster.

Still, how many bad romantic decisions had Liz made that Jane had warned her against? And it *was* fun to have a crush, even if it wouldn't go anywhere. Plus, the dive bar that hosted Margarita Monday was in the same neighborhood as Weston's office. Which made it a convenient excuse to casually text Weston and see if she wanted to meet for a drink.

"Fii-*iii*ne," Liz groaned. "We'll go to Margarita Monday."

6

Liz, Jane, Katie, and Lydia left the office at five to meet Bailey at the Board Room. They hadn't been able to convince anyone else from the *NF* to join them—apparently everyone wanted to stay alive for the beginning of Pride in two weeks. Liz had texted Weston, though, in what was hopefully a casual, spontaneous tone, saying she should come say hi if she was nearby. Her stomach swooped pleasurably when, a few moments later, Weston replied that she would try to be there.

The Board Room was the kind of place they would normally avoid: one of those dark, below-sidewalk-level establishments in Midtown that mostly attracted former frat bros from the surrounding offices. It also had an inexplicable board game theme: Paintings of Monopoly pieces and Candy Land monsters covered the dirty walls, and there was a shelf full of sticky games in the back, which were impossible to play since the bar was lit exclusively by red lightbulbs. But the Board Room did have one single redeeming quality: On Mondays they served two-dollar margaritas.

It was already packed by the time they got there. Leading the way, Liz had to turn sideways to move through the crowd toward the back corner, where she could see Bailey looking dubiously at a salacious mural of Miss Scarlet from Clue. It wasn't until she got close enough to shout a hello that Liz realized Daria was skulking by Bailey's elbow.

"What are you doing here?" Liz said, only half regretting how aggressive it came out.

"It's office bonding drinks," Daria said grimly. "I'm here to bond." She had her hands in her pockets, and her shoulders were up around her ears. Liz rolled her eyes.

Bailey went to get the first round, and Jane quickly offered to help her carry them. Daria's eyes followed Bailey across the bar; she clearly wasn't listening as Lydia launched into a story about the time they'd won a beer pong tournament here. Liz had a feeling that she'd only come out tonight to keep Bailey from getting too friendly with the employees Daria wanted to lay off.

After a few minutes, Bailey and Jane pushed back through the crowd, hands full of plastic cups. They distributed them, and Jane raised hers up. Bailey had gone for a Coke instead of a margarita, Liz noticed—possibly Jane had warned her in advance.

"Cheers!" Jane said. "To Margarita Monday!"

They all touched cups and drank. Liz watched expectantly as Daria took a sip. Her eyes widened and she made a disgusted face. Liz cackled.

"Oh my God. This is the worst thing I've ever put in my mouth," Daria said. She looked around, as if they might all be pulling an elaborate prank on her. "Why do you drink these?"

"Because they're two dollars," Liz said.

"It's really only the first two that burn like that," Katie said. "After that, they go down like juice."

Daria tilted her head slightly at Katie, as if trying to figure out whether she was joking.

Bailey laughed. "Another cheers," she said, holding up her cup. "To the *Nether Fields*. Thank you all for welcoming us to your team."

They all said cheers, Liz with more enthusiasm than she really felt. She kept drinking and didn't say much as the group chatted about the magazine. She noticed that Daria didn't say anything, either. She just stuck aggressively close to Bailey's side. Every time Jane leaned over to say something to Bailey, Daria was right there, listening in. Jane shot Liz a pleading look.

Ugh. Liz looked up to scan the bar for Weston, but she wasn't here yet. Maybe she wasn't coming. At least Liz was used to being ghosted.

"I'll get the next round," Liz said, hoping to distract herself. "Daria, can you help me carry them?" She made significant eye contact with Jane, who mouthed a silent *Thank you* in response.

Daria looked around, startled. Liz turned and pushed her way through the crowd without checking to see if Daria was following. As she leaned over the bar, she noticed that the man next to her was eyeing her chest. That morning she'd put on a flowy black shirt that was more low-cut than usual. All day, it had made her feel hot and powerful, like she was inhabiting the persona of some badass businesswoman, but now Liz tugged it up, wishing she'd worn something more butch. In masculine clothing, she was practically invisible to straight men—which pissed her off in different ways but was definitely preferable. Figuring out her presentation would be so much easier if Liz had only herself to think about. But what she wore changed how people treated her, and then things became so confused that Liz couldn't tell if she was reacting to her own feelings or reacting to everyone else's reaction.

Liz ordered and the bartender placed six drinks in front of her. She paid and turned around to find Daria lurking behind her, looking uncomfortable.

"Here." Liz handed Daria three of the cups. Their hands brushed as Daria took them, and Liz felt her cheeks heat up. She wasn't sure if it was from the skin contact or the humiliation of the words that echoed in Liz's head every time she saw Daria: *That asinine fluff-piece writer who kept babbling on.*

Liz looked away. She didn't want to give Daria the satisfaction of seeing her blush.

She pushed back through the crowd to their little circle, where she handed drinks to Jane and Bailey and then stood a little in front of them, subtly boxing them out from the conversation. It was all the encouragement they needed to drift away and lean their heads close together as they chatted. Liz might not approve, but she was still Jane's friend.

Daria, who seemed to have had more trouble navigating the tight crowd, finally emerged into their little corner, passing drinks to Lydia and Katie. Without saying thank you, Lydia pulled Katie into the crowd to help them coerce people into attending the Sock Hop, the roving club night they did promotion for. It took place in a different bar every Saturday, started at midnight, and was generally filled with people on a lot of drugs. Lydia always carried promotional cards and had an annoying habit of pressing them on anyone they met.

Liz was so focused on wingmanning for Jane that it took a minute to realize that she'd been left alone with Daria, who was leaning against the ice machine next to Liz, saying nothing. She had taken off her blazer and hung it on the hook behind her, rolled the sleeves of her light blue shirt up to the elbow, and undone the top two buttons of her shirt. Liz tried not to stare at the little triangle of collarbone the shirt revealed.

Liz decided she wouldn't speak first. If Daria wanted to lurk in silence in the corner, let her. But then she noticed that Daria's eyes were lingering on Bailey and Jane, keeping close tabs as Jane leaned forward and touched Bailey's arm.

Shit. Whatever Daria was thinking, it couldn't be good.

"Have you been here before?" Liz said, taking a step toward Daria in a strategic way that blocked her view of Jane and Bailey.

"No," she said. "Never." She cast a significant glance at the group of men playing flip cup at a nearby table.

"It is pretty terrible," Liz said, clutching at anything to say to keep Daria's attention off Jane. "We usually go to Scissors, but you can't beat two dollars for a cocktail. Do you go to Scissors much?"

"Never been."

"*What?*" Liz didn't want to give Daria the satisfaction of seeming interested, but a queer woman who had never been to Scissors? That was unheard of. "That was, like, the literal first place I went to when I moved to the city. I was so excited that a lesbian bar even existed."

Daria shrugged. Her entire body was angled away from Liz. "I've never really felt comfortable in bars."

An awkward silence grew between them. Liz felt desperate for an escape, wishing Weston would pick this moment to show, but she was nowhere in sight. Liz took out her phone and texted Katie and Lydia *Come back!!!!*, angling the screen away from Daria.

"How long have you been at the magazine?" Daria asked.

Liz looked up from her phone in surprise. Daria had actu-

ally asked her a polite—or at least neutral—question. "Four
years."

"And you . . . like working there?" Daria said.

"Yeah," Liz said. "I do."

"Doesn't it get boring, though, writing that kind of article
over and over again?"

There she was again, the judgmental Daria Liz knew so
well. She forced herself to take a deep breath before speaking. "And what kind of article is that?"

Daria took a sip of her drink without responding. Liz noticed Daria was holding her plastic cup so tightly that the
rim had started to buckle.

"Why did you invest in this magazine anyway?" Liz said
with a little too much salt in her voice. "You clearly don't appreciate it, and you seem to hate every minute you spend at
the office."

"Because Bailey insisted on throwing all her money into
this bottomless financial pit you call journalism, and the
only way to ensure she didn't completely ruin herself was to
make sure I had some control over the situation," Daria said
in a rush.

Liz huffed loudly. "What does it matter? Isn't Bailey rich?"

"She's not 'single-handedly support a magazine' rich,"
Daria said, glowering at Liz. "Your magazine has been losing money for years, and Heather Media has just been footing the bill. Probably to avoid the bad PR of shutting you
down."

Liz felt what little self-control she had leaving her body.
"Our magazine might not make money, but that doesn't
mean it's worthless," she said, her voice getting louder as she
spoke. "Not everything has to be about capitalism. Some
things have intangible value. Like a website where a college
kid who has no idea how to be a lesbian and thinks she's a

complete *freak* can read a guide to having gay sex instead of having a panic attack before her first date because she never got queer-friendly sex ed. Or dumb quizzes that let her see the fun in queerness instead of feeling like it's something shameful. Or articles that reassure her that she could actually have a happy life and fall in love with a woman and not, like, die of dysentery or burn at the stake like in every lesbian movie ever."

Daria raised her eyebrows. Liz flushed. She hadn't meant to say that much. But she was *right,* dammit. Even the advice columns and the dildo reviews mattered. Because where else could their audience get reliable, trustworthy advice on these topics? The *Nether Fields* made a difference in queer people's lives, just like it had for Liz when she'd read it as a lonely college student. And for most of her four years at the magazine, Liz had *loved* working there—she'd learned so much about journalism and she'd made lifelong friends with people she probably would never have met otherwise. The magazine was important, to readers and to Liz.

Even if Liz had kind of forgotten that lately.

Daria sipped her drink, looking uncomfortable.

"How can you spend so much time at the magazine anyway?" Liz said. "Don't you have a real job?"

"I do," Daria said, rattling the ice cubes in her cup. "It's almost summer, so things are quiet right now, but I'm still missing a lot of work. But I owe it to Bailey."

Liz fought the urge to roll her eyes. "Why is it your job to protect Bailey? She's an adult."

Daria sighed and shook her head, shifting her weight away from Liz and their conversation. "Bailey and I have a lot of history. We look out for each other."

Okay, there was *no way* they hadn't dated at some point. Two lesbians who "had a lot of history" and "looked out" for each other? Liz had to talk Jane out of pursuing Bailey.

Clearly there was some weird star-crossed-lover angst going on here, and getting in the middle of it could only lead to Jane getting hurt.

"No fucking *way*, bro!" One of the men from the flip cup game stumbled away from his table, yelling. He backed into Daria, crushing her up against the ice machine and knocking her drink to the ground.

"Hey! Watch it!" Daria said, shoving him away.

The guy turned, looked Daria over, and rolled his eyes.

"Whatever, dyke," he muttered, turning back to his table. His friends cracked up.

"Are you okay?" Liz said to Daria, who was swiping splashes of margarita off her pants.

"Yup. No big deal," Daria said, but her voice was strained and she was clenching her teeth. "I'm just gonna leave."

"What? You can't let that asshole run you out," Liz said. No matter how much she disliked Daria, there was no way she could let this guy just get away with that. Daria shook her head, avoiding Liz's eyes.

In one fluid movement, Liz stepped back toward the guy, lifted up her margarita, and emptied her cup down his collar.

"What the hell?" the guy yelled, slapping at his back.

Liz spun around, covering her mouth with a hand. "Oops!" she squealed. "I am so sorry! My little dyke hands slipped!"

"Are you fucking kidding me?" the guy shouted. He took a step forward. "You did that on purpose!"

Liz clutched her chest, as if shocked at the accusation.

"I would never!" She stared into the guy's eyes, trying to look like she was daring him. *Go ahead,* she wanted her gaze to say. *Go ahead and try to fight a girl in the middle of a bar. Make a scene and let everyone find out what you called us.* Her heart shuddered in her chest and her brain screamed at her to run, but she forced herself to stand her ground.

"Fuck you, bitch," the guy spat, but he let his friends pull him away.

Liz took a deep breath. She could feel her legs starting to shake from the adrenaline, but she felt incredible. Powerful.

"Do you have a death wish? What the hell was that?"

Liz turned around to see Daria staring at her, mouth open. "I thought we were going to *die*," she said. "I can't believe they just walked away. How did you do that?"

"Guess I'm pretty scary," Liz said, with far more casual bravado than she felt.

"That was so reckless," Daria said. "That was . . ." she trailed off, shaking her head, then locked eyes with Liz. "That was amazing."

Liz laughed. Her hands were shaking, but she felt high on her victory. It had been foolish for sure, but God, it felt good—all her nerve endings prickling and her pulse so fast she could feel it in her fingertips.

To Liz's surprise, Daria started laughing, too. She ran her hands through her hair, ruffling the precise part. Then she shook her head again, and some of her now-messy hair fell into her eyes.

"Seriously," she said, taking a deep breath and looking into Liz's eyes. "Thank you."

"Oh." Liz had never noticed how green Daria's eyes were. "It's no big deal."

Daria laughed again. "Do you make a habit of fighting straight guys in bars?"

Liz grinned. "Only when they need to be put in their place."

"Let me get you another drink," Daria said. "As a thank-you for sacrificing yours to defend my honor." She smiled at Liz. The rush of their encounter seemed to have relaxed her. She looked almost like a different person now, with her hair out of place and her shirt splashed with alcohol. As Liz followed her to the bar, she noticed that Daria moved a little more loosely, too, leaning against the bar with one arm instead of hunching with her hands in her pockets.

Liz leaned next to Daria while they waited. Her fingers still tingled with adrenaline, and she felt a euphoric rush in her chest, like she could do anything.

Daria signaled to the bartender for two more and then turned to face Liz. They were very close together, Liz realized. If she shifted her weight, their arms would touch.

"Don't you work in finance?" Liz said. "Aren't you used to jerks like that?"

Daria looked down at the bar. "I should be," she said, so softly that Liz had to lean in to hear her. "But whenever people say things to me, at work or in bathrooms or whatever, I freeze." She grimaced a little. "And then I spend the rest of the day thinking of devastating comebacks, of course. But in the moment? Nothing."

The bartender put two drinks down, and Daria paid. She handed one of the drinks to Liz, and their hands brushed again. This time, Liz didn't bother looking away to hide her blush.

"Maybe you think too much." Liz shifted closer. They were inches away now, and Liz was finding it a little hard to breathe.

"That's definitely true." Daria held up her cup. "Cheers. To not thinking."

"To not thinking," Liz echoed. They touched their cups together, holding each other's gaze. It was suddenly hard to remember why she'd decided Daria was unlikable when Daria was one small step away, gazing at her like Liz had just stopped a runaway train with her hands.

Daria opened her mouth to say something else. But someone grabbed Liz's waist from behind. Liz whirled around, ready to fight, but it was just Weston.

"There you are!"

"Oh my God!" Liz squealed, in a far higher pitch than she was comfortable with. "You scared me on purpose!"

"I totally did," Weston said, slipping an arm around her waist.

"Sorry about that," Liz said, turning back to Daria. "This is—" but she stopped when she saw Daria's face. She had frozen in place, glaring at Weston, her face twisted with anger. Liz felt Weston tense.

"Daria," Weston said, with a small nod. "Good to see you."

"Weston," Daria said, her voice curt. Her eyes dropped, briefly, to Weston's arm around Liz's waist, then she turned away.

"Enjoy your evening," she said to Liz, and stepped past her.

Liz watched her navigate through the crowd. She picked her blazer up off its hook, folded it neatly over one arm, and walked over to whisper something to Bailey, who whipped her head back toward Liz. Bailey said something to Jane and then, within seconds, Bailey and Daria were both up, pushing through the crowd and walking out the door. Through the front window, Liz could see them power walking down the sidewalk without turning back. Jane looked after them, her mouth slightly open, and Katie hurried over to her side.

"Okay." Liz unhooked Weston's arm from around her waist. "What the hell was that?"

Weston bit her lip, looking toward the door. "How do you know Daria?"

"She's my boss. How do *you* know Daria?"

"She's your *boss*? Doesn't she work in, like, finance?"

"Yeah, but she and Bailey have tons of money, so they bought our magazine for shits and giggles."

"Jesus," Weston said, turning to the bar. "I need a drink."

Something clicked into place in Liz's memory. "Wait. Smith. Were you there at the same time?"

"Yup. Daria and I were roommates freshman year," Weston said, managing to get the bartender's attention. "Two margaritas, please."

"*Really?*" Liz took a closer look at Weston. She had thought they were about the same age—because of Weston's energy, her way of talking, her skater-boi fashion—but if she had graduated the same year as Daria, that made her about thirty-two.

"Really. Here." Weston handed her one of the drinks.

"Thanks." Liz took a sip. "Okay, spill. Did you date? Are you former rugby rivals? What's going on there?"

"It's a long story," Weston said. "And I don't want to say anything bad about your boss to you."

Liz's curiosity spiked. "Well, we didn't exactly get off on the right foot to start with."

Weston looked at her, then back at her drink. She seemed hesitant.

"Of course, you don't *have* to tell me. If it's personal," Liz added, although she would have to do some serious internet stalking when she got home if Weston didn't tell her.

"Well, at first we were friendly," Weston said, leaning against the bar. "But once Daria found out I had an on-campus job and couldn't afford to go out to dinner with her, she decided she was better than me and found rich friends to hang out with instead. Like Bailey."

"That's terrible!" Liz said. Daria had seemed so nice for a minute there, but Weston's description certainly matched the impression Liz had gotten at the magazine.

"I dodged a bullet," Weston said, shaking her cup so the ice cubes rattled. "Bailey was totally in love with Daria. And Daria would always lead her on, give her just enough that

Bailey would think there was hope and rush to do whatever she said."

"I knew it," Liz said, feeling vindicated. "I *told* Jane there was something weird going on there." As they spoke, Liz could feel herself changing her body language: pushing her chest out a little more, sinking her weight to one hip, lowering her voice, looking up through her eyelashes. Acting more feminine, to complement Weston's masculinity. As soon as she noticed, she tried to stop and just stand normally, but she suddenly couldn't remember what normal standing looked like.

Weston moved a little closer to Liz and drained her drink. "God, I haven't thought about Daria in a long time," she said. "She completely ruined my life."

"By being a bad roommate?" Liz moved back from Weston, just a little, to give herself some space to breathe. She didn't like how feminine she was acting. It felt wrong. Fake. She wished she knew how to flirt without acting like a stereotype of a straight girl crushing on a football player.

Weston sighed and raked a hand through her hair. "This isn't something I like to talk about, because I'm not proud of it, but I actually didn't graduate. Daria got me kicked out."

"She *what*?"

Weston ran a finger along the rim of her drink. "So, my sophomore year, I started hooking up with Bailey." She looked up and made an apologetic face at Liz. "It was only a couple times, but Daria found out. She showed up at my room and screamed at me to leave Bailey alone or else I'd regret it. And I told her to go fuck herself."

"Good for you," Liz said. She decided not to process the fact that she and Bailey Cox had hooked up with the same person. "I can't believe she screamed at you."

"Yeah, well. I kind of wish I'd just listened. Because the next day, campus police showed up and searched my room."

"No way," Liz said. "For what?"

"Well, Daria knew I smoked weed. Which should have just been a citation. Except, I used to buy it in bulk, because it was cheaper that way, and I'd just bought some. And my dealer had offered me some coke, too. And I thought, why the hell not? It's college, I should try it. So when campus safety searched my room, they found a decent amount of weed and a little bit of coke. And"—she raised her hands in a faux-casual shrug—"that was it. I got expelled."

"Oh my God," Liz said. "Just like that?"

"Yup," Weston said. "Daria's family gave a ton of money to the school, and they had hard evidence and wanted to crack down on drugs. So I was out."

"Holy shit. I'm so sorry."

Weston nodded, her lips pursed. "I lived with my parents for a while and tried to go to community college, but they were furious with me. Eventually I just gave up. Moved to New York, tried to start over. But it's been hard finding jobs without a degree."

Liz felt a rush of fury on Weston's behalf. How messed up did a person have to be to ruin someone's life out of jealousy over a girl you weren't even dating? She didn't know what to say, so she put her hand on Weston's arm, trying to be comforting. Weston leaned in to her touch, her skin warm under Liz's fingers.

Weston put her cup down and placed her hand on Liz's waist, casually, almost as if she didn't notice she was doing it. Liz felt her heart rate pick up. "The worst part is I don't actually know if that was what she meant to do. She might have just thought I'd get a citation. But she definitely never apologized for it."

Weston's fingers curled around one of the belt loops on Liz's jeans, tugging her a little closer.

"Did Bailey ever say anything about it?"

Weston shook her head, shifting forward, her hand slipping to Liz's back. Liz could feel the heat through her shirt.

"I never spoke to her again," Weston said. "I tried to call her, but she blocked my number. Daria's doing, I'm sure." Her touch grew firmer on Liz's back, moving Liz forward so their faces were only a few inches apart.

"Wow. That's so messed up. She definitely knew, then." Liz's voice felt more breathy than usual. She hoped what she was saying made sense.

"Yup," Weston said, cocking her head to one side and giving her that practiced, one-sided grin. "So, do you still think I'm sexy now that you know I'm a college dropout?"

Liz smiled. They were both leaning forward, half inch by agonizing half inch.

"What makes you think I thought you were sexy before?"

Weston laughed, so close now that her lips brushed slightly against Liz's as she said, "You did. Admit it."

And then, before Liz could agree, Weston closed the last piece of air between them and pressed her lips softly against Liz's, moving her hand across Liz's back, bringing them closer together and sending goosebumps down Liz's arms.

Holy shit. Now this was a kiss.

7

———

iz Baker had a date. A *third* date, if you counted both times she and Weston had been at bars together as dates, which Liz did. They were just meeting up for drinks after work, but Weston had been the one to suggest plans. It hadn't been spontaneous, either. Weston had texted two days in advance. Two days! Two days of warning meant Weston officially liked her.

Liz smiled to herself as she got ready in the office bathroom. She couldn't even remember the last time she'd gone on a third date, let alone one with someone she was this excited about. She smoothed out her hair, put on deodorant, and dotted cover-up over the red spots on her chin. Then she assessed her reflection, debating whether to put on eyeliner. She'd been feeling more masculine lately and hadn't worn eye makeup in a month or two. Weston seemed like the kind of person who might like a girl in eyeliner, though. But if she put it on, was she putting it on for Weston or herself?

Liz shook her head. Of course she wasn't putting it on for herself. Whenever Liz went on a date with someone mascu-

line of center, she found herself acting more feminine—
holding on to the crook of their arm as they walked down the
street or letting them open doors for her. When she was the
more masculine one, she found herself standing taller or offering to open jars. The truth was, she liked both versions of
herself. She just wished she didn't feel like she always had
to pick one.

Fuck it. Liz put the eyeliner on. She wasn't trying to figure out the essence of her soul tonight, after all. She was
trying to go on her first third date in years.

Liz checked her phone. She still had twenty minutes to
kill if she wanted to arrive a casual four minutes late.

She would have spent those twenty minutes strategizing
with Jane about the best ways to make Weston fall in love
with her, but Jane was Otherwise Occupied. On the way to
the bathroom, Liz had seen her standing in the hallway talking with Bailey so intently that neither of them even noticed
her passing by.

Liz had hoped that the Margarita Monday disaster would
convince Jane to give up on pursuing Bailey. She'd pulled
Jane into the Lena Lounge the next day and recounted
Weston's story in vivid detail, but Jane had shut her down
when Liz had argued that it was a bad idea to get between
Bailey and Daria's toxic codependency. Jane had said that
their time at Smith was ten years ago. They were adults now,
and so was Jane. Daria might be an asshole, but Jane believed Bailey was not. And Liz should keep out of it, because
it was none of her business.

So, Liz was keeping out of it.

She gave herself a last once-over in the mirror: eyeliner
even, hair nicely gelled, her denim jacket looking good over
her black V-necked T-shirt, even though it was definitely too
warm for it. Weston was always so stylish. But this denim

jacket, which she'd spent the past few years adorning with
an array of queer patches and pins, starting with the rainbow flag pin Liz's parents had given her when she first came
out, always made Liz feel cool.

She left the bathroom before she could second-guess her
outfit. She desperately needed something to distract her.
Because if she thought about how long it had been since
she'd gone on a third date, she would get extremely nervous.
And if she showed up to meet Weston in that state, she
would start talking uncontrollably, say something weird, and
ruin it.

Liz could *not* ruin this.

She walked over to Charlotte's office and peered through
the glass door, but Charlotte was on the phone and waved
Liz away. Scanning the cubicles, she was disappointed to
see that Katie and Lydia had already left to get ready for a
queer fashion show they were going to. Changing tack, Liz
headed to the Kiyoko Kitchen instead. She would eat dinner. That way, she would have less of a chance of getting
drunk and embarrassing herself.

Congratulating herself on her forward thinking, Liz took
one of her frozen Trader Joe's meals out of the freezer. She
was about to pierce the plastic with a fork when she heard
someone enter. Turning, she found herself face-to-face with
Daria.

"What are you doing here?" they said at the same time.

"I work here," Liz said.

"Well, technically, I do, too." Daria was wearing a light
purple button-down shirt with the sleeves rolled to her elbows and gray dress pants. She put her briefcase on the
kitchen table, opened it, and took out a Tupperware container.

"Why are you here so late?" Liz said. It came out sounding very sullen. It was the first time they'd crossed paths since Monday night, and all Liz could think about was what Daria had done to Weston.

"I thought this would be a good time to go through the month's expense reports in peace," Daria said, prying the lid off her container. Liz glanced at it—it looked like a chicken breast with rice and vegetables. A boring meal for a boring person. Liz stabbed her fork into the plastic covering on top of her meal and turned toward the microwave—almost smacking into Daria, who had already put her dinner inside.

The *nerve*.

"Aren't you going to cover that?" Liz snapped.

"What?" Daria glanced over her shoulder, her finger hovering over the start button.

"Your food. If you don't cover it, it will splatter all over the microwave, making it gross for the next person who has to use it. Which is me."

Daria crossed to the sink, pointedly ripped a paper towel from the roll, covered her food, and closed the microwave door.

"Happy?" she said, pressing start.

"Extremely." Liz crossed her arms, eyes on the timer.

"Why are *you* here so late?" Daria said, leaning against the counter.

"Fluff pieces to write," Liz lied.

"Anything good?"

"Don't pretend you think there's such a thing as a good fluff piece," she said, trying and failing to keep her tone light.

Daria turned pink. "Look," she said. "About the other night—"

Liz's heart squeezed. Liz did *not* want to talk about Weston. Both because she didn't want to get fired for yelling at her boss and because she didn't want to ruin all her fluttery pre-date feelings with the huge turnoff that was talking to Daria.

"I think I was a little harsh about the magazine. I was just frustrated because the magazine has been pulling me away from my actual job, which has been a lot to juggle. But I shouldn't have been so rude."

It took Liz a second to comprehend that Daria was offering her an apology. Or, at least, something resembling an apology, since the words "I'm sorry" had certainly not come out of her mouth.

Thankfully, the microwave dinged, which spared Liz from having to respond. She watched as Daria opened the door and examined her food. Daria *did* look rather tired. Her shirt was end-of-the-day wrinkled, and a few strands of her usually gelled hair had come loose, falling into her eyes. Liz resented how it somehow made her look like a carefully disheveled model instead of a sweaty mess.

Daria picked up her Tupperware, balanced the lid on top, and grabbed her briefcase with her other hand.

"Enjoy your food," she said to Liz on her way out of the kitchen. Liz watched her go for a moment before remembering that she was supposed to microwave her own dinner.

When it was done, Liz went back to her cubicle to eat and mindlessly scroll through Instagram. The posts were all boring—shots of her New York friends out at bars, shots of people from high school with engagement rings and babies.

Then a black-and-white photograph caught her eye. Three visibly queer women perched on a fire escape, holding bottles of beer. One of them was mid-laugh, another was looking away, and the third was eyeing the photographer with a steady, almost confrontational gaze. They all had short hair but didn't look butch. Their clothes were androgy-

nous, tight pants and loose T-shirts. On the gender spectrum, they looked somewhere in the middle. They looked
like Liz.

Liz read the caption. It was a post from the Lesbian Her-
story Archives attributing the photos to Moira Campbell, a
photographer who had documented the gay-rights movement in the 1960s and '70s. Liz scrolled through the other
pictures: a group of friends at a gay-rights march; a lover
lying naked in bed, her eyes on the photographer; the same
woman, now clothed, working on a motorcycle.

Liz googled Moira Campbell and found a couple more
photos. The people in them looked like Liz and her friends,
but in black and white, with sixties fashions. Some looked
directly into the camera: strong, vulnerable, unapologetic.
Liz felt something she couldn't quite name. She paused in
her scrolling to think. These photos made her feel like . . .
like she had a history.

Liz knew that life had not been easy for queer people during this time frame, but she found herself yearning to melt
into the photo and join this group of friends. She wanted to
hear their life stories. She wanted their advice. She wanted
them to tell her how to find the courage to be herself.

She couldn't befriend the people in the photo, but she
could at least keep them with her as a reminder that there
was nothing wrong with being your own thing. Liz saved the
photo of the women on the fire escape and made it her lock
screen background. When she held up her phone to admire
it, though, she noticed the time—she should have left ten
minutes ago.

Liz hustled all the way to the bar, risking getting sweaty to
avoid showing up too late. By the time she arrived it was ten
minutes past, but a quick scan around the room showed her
that Weston wasn't there yet. Which was lucky, because Liz
needed a minute to catch her breath. She snagged two stools

at the bar and tried to think calming thoughts. The bartender had just handed over her vodka cranberry when
Weston came through the door.

"Hey!" Weston said, sliding into the stool beside her and
giving Liz a side hug. She was holding a large paper bag with
BYond on it. "I got you a present."

"A present?" Liz stared at Weston, feeling a little overwhelmed by her sudden presence. She was wearing tight
black jeans and a black blazer over a white T-shirt with several long gold necklaces layered on top, which matched the
rings on her fingers. She looked put-together and sexy and,
oh God, Liz was getting nervous.

Liz took a deep breath while Weston ordered a drink.
Their knees pressed together under the bar, which didn't
help Liz's nerves.

"When you came over to my apartment last week, you
were talking about how you wished you had more masc
clothing but it's all really expensive, right?" Weston said.

"Right . . ."

Weston grinned at her. "Well, we're swapping out the
store for summer, and some of the clothes can't be returned
because of minor damage. So . . ." she trailed off dramatically and reached for the paper bag. "I snagged you this."

Liz took the bag, stunned. "Why?"

She regretted her question immediately. Liz should have
coolly accepted the bag as if hot girls brought her presents
all the time. Instead, she had revealed that she had low self-
esteem, that this wasn't a normal occurrence, that Liz wasn't
desirable, that she wasn't worth bringing presents for, that—

"Because you're cute," Weston said. "And I like you." She
winked.

Liz nearly dropped the bag. To avoid looking at Weston,
she focused on opening her present.

Inside the bag was a floral blazer. It was light blue and

shiny, patterned with large pink and white flowers. Liz held it up. It was tuxedo-style, but tailored to fit more tightly, cutting in at the waist instead of hanging straight down like a traditional men's blazer would. The fabric felt silky and fancy under her touch. Liz could tell immediately that it was more expensive than anything else she owned.

Liz was speechless. Her face must have conveyed what she was feeling, though, because Weston laughed.

"Try it on," she urged.

Liz shrugged off her jean jacket and replaced it with the blazer. The sleeves felt cool and smooth as she slipped her arms into them. The blazer was just about her size, too. Maybe a little big, but that was better than the alternative. Liz checked her reflection in the mirror above the bar.

It was perfect: bold, eye-catching, stylish, masculine and feminine at once. Liz barely recognized herself.

"I—" Liz started to say, then stopped. She took Weston's cheeks in her hands instead and kissed her, long and deep.

"Thank you," she said when she broke away.

Weston smiled at her. "You look great."

Weston started telling Liz about her day, and Liz nodded along, but she couldn't stop herself from sneaking glances at herself in the mirror—her cheeks were pink and her smile was absurdly large. She lost the thread of what Weston was saying over the chorus repeating in her mind: *She likes me, she likes me, she likes me!*

8

A week later, Pride began. Or, as straight people referred to it, June.

Unfortunately, the first Pride event was one Liz was not looking forward to: Bailey had invited the entire staff to a barbecue at her house in the Rockaways. Liz could think of forty ways she'd rather spend her Saturday, but the rest of the *NF* staff, Jane in particular, seemed excited.

Liz felt distinctly less giddy. She hadn't heard from Weston at all since their date the week before. It had gone *so* well, and then nothing. Liz had texted her earlier in the week, asking if she wanted to get a drink on Friday night, but Weston had never replied.

Liz had gone over the date a hundred times in her head, but she couldn't think of anything she might have said or done to ruin it. She kept trying to tell herself that Weston was probably just busy. Now that it was the weekend, Weston would probably be free again and text her to get a last-minute drink. But of course, if she was all the way out in the Rockaways, there was no way she'd be able to get back in time.

Jane, unfortunately, refused to let Liz skip the party for the chance that Weston *might* text. So, on Saturday afternoon, one of the cars that Bailey had arranged to pick everyone up at the subway dropped Liz and her roommates in front of an extremely ugly beach house: some sort of edgy modern design involving lots of gleaming metal and enormous windows. It looked like three glass boxes stacked on top of one another.

In the backyard was a large patio with an enormous pool surrounded by lounge chairs. Most of the *Nether Fields* staff were already there: swimming, sitting around, or playing volleyball on the lawn. Liz saw several people she didn't know mingling among the crowd—Bailey must have invited other friends, too.

The roommates piled their stuff on a free lounge chair. Lydia immediately took off their shirt and tugged Katie over to the pool. Liz left on her jean shorts and her Tegan and Sara T-shirt. Normally, she loved showing off her TomboyX bathing suit: a bright blue sports bra–style top with tight spandex-style bottoms that had been a giddy, extravagant purchase last summer. But she felt a little self-conscious wearing it here, at this fancy party. Was it too masculine? Did it emphasize her hips too much?

Looking around, she was reassured to see a few bikinis, a few one-pieces, but also a lot of bikini tops and board shorts combos or sports bras in place of swim tops—the classic queer beach attire mishmash. Liz surveyed the group, looking for Charlotte, but didn't see her anywhere. Jane was also scanning the crowd, twisting the strap of her beach bag in her hand as she looked around the yard.

"Looking for anyone in particular?" Liz said, stepping into Jane's sight line. "Someone rich and ginger perhaps?"

"Keep your voice down," Jane hissed. "I just want to find Bailey so I can thank her for having us."

"Thank her with sexual favors?" Liz asked, then jumped out of the way as Jane tried to stomp on her foot.

"I just think tonight might be a good opportunity to . . . get to know her a little better."

"In a biblical sense?" Liz said, and this time Jane succeeded in stomping on her. "Ow! Jesus! Where even is she?"

But when Liz turned to look, she saw only Daria, who was backing out of one of the glass doors, wearing black swim trunks with a short-sleeved white button-down shirt and holding two large bowls of chips. Squinting at the sunlight, she tossed her head back a little to get her bangs out of her eyes as she made her way over to a picnic table near the volleyball game.

As much as she was determined to hate Daria on Weston's behalf, Liz couldn't help watching as Daria set the bowls down, her eyes tracing the shape of Daria's bare legs. It was too bad—there had been a moment at the bar where Liz had thought maybe she'd been wrong about Daria. But no. Weston had confirmed that Daria was just as much of an asshole as Liz had originally assumed.

"Jane! Liz!" Bailey materialized in front of them so suddenly that Liz jumped. She was wearing a black tank top, white linen shorts, and gold aviator sunglasses. "I'm so glad you came!"

"Oh my gosh, hi!" Jane's voice had taken on a curious Valley girl–style inflection. "It's so great to see you."

Jane and Bailey made smiling eye contact for a moment too long. After a couple of seconds, Liz said, "This is quite the house."

"Oh, thank you," Bailey said, beaming. "It's so nice to get out of the city on weekends. Have you seen the view?"

She shepherded them over to the edge of the lawn to a hill overlooking the water. Bailey started asking Jane questions about her latest article, and Liz nodded along, trying to seem like she was participating. She couldn't think of a graceful excuse to get out of the conversation. She scanned the party, hoping someone would wave her over, but to her horror, Daria glanced up from adjusting knobs on an enormous metal grill and caught Liz's eye.

"Hey, Liz," Daria called across the lawn. "Would you mind helping me carry some stuff outside?"

Liz tried to think of a way to say no without looking rude. "Ummm," she said, shooting a desperate glance at Jane before heading forlornly in Daria's direction.

"I hope it's okay that I commandeered you," Daria said when Liz caught up to her. "You looked like you wanted an out." She started walking toward the house, and Liz fell in step behind her.

"Just through here." Daria held open the door so Liz could go through, then led her down the hall to a gleaming kitchen, where several wrapped platters of veggie burgers and hot dogs rested on the counter.

"Can you help me carry these out?" Daria said. "I'm going to start grilling soon."

"Sure," Liz said curtly, grabbing a platter.

A work-sponsored pool party was a terrible idea, Liz decided as she followed Daria back outside. It was just *asking* for boundaries to get blurred. And not just between Bailey and Jane, apparently, because as she walked behind Daria in shorts, it was impossible not to watch the tendons flex in the backs of her calves and the slight curve of biceps as she lifted the platter a little higher.

They reached the door, and Daria pushed it open with her shoulder, holding it for Liz. Liz's side brushed lightly against Daria's as she passed, sending goosebumps flooding across her upper arm.

"You can just drop that by the grill," Daria said. "Thank you for the help."

Liz was setting her platter down when someone walked over, calling Daria's name.

"Daria, please tell me you're not just going to lurk around the grill all afternoon, leaving me to fend for myself."

"Caroline," Daria said in a warning tone. "This is Liz Baker. She's a journalist at the magazine. Liz, this is Caroline Hillier. She's visiting from Boston."

"Oh." Caroline turned to Liz and gave her a very fake smile. "Hi. So nice to meet you."

Caroline was white, with long, perfectly blown-out blond hair and a French manicure. She was wearing a bikini top with a matching sarong wrapped around her waist and was so gorgeous it was unfair.

"Nice to meet you," Liz said. "How do you know Bailey?"

"I went to high school with Daria." Caroline didn't even bother to look at Liz while she replied. She rested a hand on Daria's back. "Daria, honey, there's no need to fire up the grill yet. Come hang out with me for a bit."

Liz stared at Caroline's hand on Daria. *Oh.*

Of course Daria wasn't single. She might have a terrible personality, but she still looked like a butch *GQ* model.

Liz smirked to herself. Caroline seemed like *exactly* the kind of person Liz would have pictured Daria dating: gorgeous, high femme, and with an enormous stick up her ass.

"It's a barbecue," Daria said, reaching for the platter Liz had carried and dislodging Caroline's hand. "The grilling part is kind of important."

Caroline's lips pursed, and it looked like they were about to argue, so Liz coughed loudly. "I'm gonna just—" She waved in the vague direction of the pool, raising her eyebrows as she turned around. Apparently, Daria was just as cold to her girlfriend as she was to her employees.

Jane was still chatting with Bailey at the end of the lawn. Liz could see Charlotte now, but she was standing by the bar, talking with a group of people that Liz didn't know. Not wanting to make small talk, Liz pulled off her shirt and got in the pool, where most of the *NF* staff had congregated.

Liz paddled around in the water, chatting with Finn about a date they'd been on last week and laughing along as Amy, the pop culture writer, filled them in on the latest celesbian gossip. Since Bailey and Daria had taken over, her colleagues seemed so much happier. Their jobs were as secure as jobs at a failing queer magazine in a struggling industry could be. It was summer, it was Pride, and it was nice outside. Everyone, from the head of finance, who was shotgunning a beer with Lydia in the grass, to Katie, who was reclined on an inflatable flamingo with a peaceful smile on her face, seemed to be having a great time.

Except for Liz, who couldn't stop pouting about the fact that Weston hadn't texted yet.

With a sigh, Liz got out of the pool and toweled off. She crossed her fingers before taking her phone out of her bag, but there was nothing. Not even an annoying notification from social media or a text from her mom reminding her to wear sunscreen (she checked the weather for New York daily and texted any time she felt like Liz might be unprepared).

Liz pulled her clothes on over her damp bathing suit and went to find Jane. She hadn't seen her since they arrived.

But after searching the whole party, she couldn't find Jane anywhere. She wasn't on the hill overlooking the beach or relaxing on a lounge chair or snacking at the picnic table. Liz wandered over to the far side of the lawn. There was a small grassy area that she hadn't noticed before, tucked behind the side of the house. Liz could see someone lying in a hammock that was strung up between two trees. She tiptoed up, hoping it was Jane.

It *was* Jane. But she wasn't alone. She was lying in the hammock with Bailey, their bodies intertwined, Bailey's arm under Jane's neck, Jane's head against Bailey's chest. Liz could hear them speaking in low voices. As she watched, Bailey reached out and tipped Jane's chin toward her. She leaned in. Their lips met.

Jane was kissing Bailey Cox.

Liz turned around and hurried away as quietly as she could. She went inside to find the bathroom, keeping her head down so no one could see her expression, leaving wet footprints on the cold tile floors.

What was Jane *thinking*? Liz ranted to herself once she'd locked the bathroom door behind her. She was kissing her *boss*.

Liz splashed water on her face and tried to take deep breaths. This was Jane's business. It was her mistake to make.

Pulling out her phone—still no new notifications—Liz decided to make a mistake of her own. *Hey, how's your weekend?* she texted Weston. It was a double text, but what did she have to lose, apart from her self esteem and sanity?

Liz wished she could leave, but she wasn't about to pay for her own Uber to the subway. She couldn't handle going back to the party, though. She needed a minute alone to feel sorry for herself.

She went outside and crossed the lawn to the wooden stairs that led to the beach, deciding to take a walk by the water and be petty for a while, then come back when she was ready to socialize.

The beach was mostly empty. Liz walked toward the waves and closed her eyes, taking a deep breath, feeling the breeze on her face. It was a little disconcerting, how different the air here tasted from the air in the city. How was it possible that you could spend so much of your time breathing what felt like normal air only to realize it was unclean the moment you left?

"Bored of the party?"

Liz lurched into an embarrassing half leap and almost tumbled ass-first into the sand as she whirled around. "Oh my God! What the hell?"

Daria Fitzgerald was sitting cross-legged in the sand under the wooden staircase.

"Jesus fucking Christ," Liz shouted. "Did you purposely sit in the most hidden spot so you could scare the shit out of people?"

"I'm sitting in plain sight," Daria said. "You're the one standing there with your eyes closed."

"What are you even doing down here?"

"It's a beach." Daria stood up and dusted sand off her legs. "What are you doing down here?"

"Fair point." Liz looked down both sides of the beach, which seemed fairly identical (waves, sand, big houses), and started walking in the direction that appeared more deserted. "Enjoy your lurking."

"You know, the beach ends about half a mile down that way. It just looks long because of the curve," Daria said, falling into step next to her.

"Noted. Thanks." Liz picked up the pace in the hope that Daria would take the hint. "I don't need an escort."

"I don't mind," Daria said. "I could use a walk. I don't really want to be up at the house right now."

"Why not?" Liz asked, surprised. "Are you hiding from your girlfriend?"

Daria was silent for a few seconds. "She's not my girlfriend, actually. We broke up last year."

Liz raised her eyebrows, her desire to be left alone warring with her desire to hear gossip she could share with Jane. "Does she know that?"

"Yes." Daria sighed, then kicked a lump of seaweed out of her path. "She just hasn't fully accepted it yet."

"If you broke up, why is she here?"

"It's complicated," Daria said. "We're still friends."

Liz laughed. "Classic. Queer women have no bound-aries."

Daria pursed her mouth.

So, Daria was single after all. Not that it mattered.

"The beach is surprisingly nice here. Everyone thought Bailey was nuts for buying a house in the Rockaways instead of the Hamptons," Daria said, startling Liz, who'd been ex-pecting them to trudge on in uncomfortable silence. "But it's a lot easier to get to, and it's less crowded during the high season."

Liz snorted. "I wouldn't know."

"You've never been?" Daria said.

"The Hamptons is a synonym for money. You know what I make at the magazine. Do you think I can afford to rent a house there?"

Daria looked away and said, in a slightly higher voice, "I don't know. Someone could have invited you, or   "

Liz snorted again. "I don't normally hang out with the kind of people who spend time in the Hamptons."

"I didn't mean to offend you," Daria said. "I wasn't trying to imply anything or—anything. I was just making conver-sation."

Liz was surprised by Daria's apologetic tone. She didn't want the conversation to veer into more earnest territory, though. She was afraid that if they started talking about any-thing substantive, she would bring up Weston. And yelling at her boss about a decade-old rivalry didn't seem like the best way to keep her job.

"Oh, you didn't offend me," Liz lied, still focusing on her footsteps. "I'm like one of those inflatable punching bags that keeps popping back up whenever you hit it."

"A what?"

"You know, one of those punching bags for kids that are shaped like clowns? And no matter how much you try to knock them down you can't, because they have, like, a heavy ball as a base? So they start out fun because you just get to push them but eventually it gets frustrating until finally you're convinced that it's mocking you and then you start to think maybe it's alive, and then you run screaming from the room, thus fueling a lifelong fear of clowns?"

"I've never had the pleasure," Daria said. "My parents didn't really believe in that kind of toy."

"The violent kind?"

"The tacky kind." She looked up. "I didn't mean—I'm sorry. That came out wrong."

Liz's instinct was to reply with something clever and cutting, but she was tired and it was the first time she'd actually heard Daria say the word "sorry." She decided to give her a pass.

"Are there any children's toys that aren't tacky, though? Aren't they all brightly colored monstrosities?"

Daria was quiet for a few seconds, and Liz thought she'd abandoned the conversation when she said, "American Girl dolls."

"What?"

"American Girl dolls aren't tacky. They're very distinguished, actually."

"Please. Have you *seen* Samantha's party outfit?" Liz had never owned one, but she had read all the books her library stocked and pored over the catalog every time it came, earmarking pages for her parents just in case they ever felt inspired to gift her a doll more expensive than her bike. "Tacky to the extreme."

Daria snorted. "You're right. Samantha always was a stuck-up bitch. Molly was infinitely superior."

"I'm so glad her dad made it back from the war okay."

Daria smiled at that, a real all-out grin that reminded Liz of the giddy moment they'd shared in the bar. The smile made her look younger, too. Daria wasn't that much older than Liz, really. Liz couldn't help smiling back. They held each other's gaze for a moment, sending Liz's stomach swooping.

This was dangerous. Clearly, Liz couldn't be trusted to stay objective around Daria. "Let's turn around," she said.

As they walked back, the space between her and Daria felt charged. A few times, their hands almost touched, but Liz managed to yank her arm away in time. She felt like she was walking stiffly, hyperfocused on where Daria's limbs were.

"So how did you end up working at the magazine?" Daria said, abruptly restarting the conversation.

"The *Nether Fields* basically got me through college," Liz said. "Reading it allowed me to imagine the kind of future I wanted: being in the city, having a big group of queer friends, falling in love. So, once I graduated, I sent heartfelt emails and cold-called Charlotte begging for a job until she finally said yes."

"Oh wow," Daria said. She paused for a moment, and then added, "Did you ever want to do anything else?"

Liz chanced a glance at Daria. She was focusing on the beach ahead, not meeting Liz's eyes.

"Why?" Liz asked, unable to keep the suspicion out of her tone. Was Daria hinting that Liz was about to be laid off?

"Oh!" Daria said. "It's nothing like—no, I just meant I—well, I read some of your writing."

"Did you finally find the perfect butt plug for your body type?"

"No, your blog," Daria said. "*Confessions of a New York Dyke.*"

Liz almost stopped walking. "How did you find that?"

Daria had the decency to look embarrassed. "I googled you."

"Why?"

"I was just curious about—about the reporters at the magazine," Daria said hesitantly.

Liz's heartbeat stuttered. Had she looked up all the reporters? Or just Liz? Her neck started to sweat. Was Daria . . . interested in her? Was that why she was down here walking with her, being normal and nice?

Then Liz remembered Caroline, with her blown-out hair and her matching swimsuit-sarong combo. If that was the kind of person Daria was into, then Liz definitely wasn't her type. Liz wasn't feminine or polished. Not skinny or fashionable. She was just . . . Liz. When she tried to imagine someone as masculine and put-together as Daria with someone as messy and in-the-middle as herself, she just couldn't do it. That wasn't how these things worked. Usually, people were butch-for-femme or butch-for-butch. Not butch-for-the-human-equivalent-of-a-question-mark.

Liz tried to imagine Daria reading *Confessions of a New York Dyke*. Her face burned. The blog was supposed to be fun, a lighthearted way for Liz to practice her writing skills, not an actual serious project. The most profound thing that happened in Colby's life was a fight with her roommate or a mistaken hookup with her ex. Reading it certainly wouldn't make Daria think of Liz as less of a fluff writer.

"It's kind of addictive," Daria said. "I binge-read the whole thing. It was hilarious."

"Oh. Thanks." Liz rubbed her neck uncomfortably. She hadn't reread her early blog posts in a long time, but she could only imagine how poorly they were written.

"Why did you stop updating it?" Daria asked.

Liz looked out at the water. "I don't know. Writing the blog was fun for a while, but I want to write something meaningful. Something that will help people process the experience of being queer."

"And you think the blog isn't that?"

Liz waved a hand dismissively. "It's all just friend-group drama, breakups, hookups. It's fun, but I want to write something . . . bigger than that."

Daria paused thoughtfully, watching the water. After a few moments, she said, "Maybe. But isn't there something profound about just capturing everyday queer life?"

Liz shrugged, resisting the urge to roll her eyes. She wasn't going to accept encouragement from *Daria* about this—she knew Daria's stance on fluff pieces.

"I mean, there are some moments in that blog that I've never seen anyone write about before," Daria said. "Like when she shops in the men's section for the first time and she keeps thinking someone's going to come up and, like, kick her out of the store? And even though no one says anything, by the time she gets to the dressing room, she's too on edge to actually like any of the clothes? Or when she goes home for Christmas and sees her high school friends and starts to feel oddly sad? Because their lives are so different now and it feels like they can't fully understand each other, even though they used to be best friends? I've felt that way before."

Daria cleared her throat a little, self consciously. "It was pretty validating, actually, to see someone write about those things. It made me think, hey, maybe I'm not just weird, maybe this is a common experience."

Liz stared at Daria. She didn't know what to say. No one had ever spoken about her writing like that before. Her roommates knew that she had a blog, but Liz had been so dismissive of it that they'd never paid much attention. And Liz had never mentioned it to her parents—there were way too many sex scenes for that. She'd gotten gushing comments from anonymous readers before, but it was very different when someone was standing in front of you, saying your words had affected them.

"Wow," she said finally. "That's—wow. Thank you."

Daria shrugged, but she looked at Liz and gave her a small, nervous smile. Liz smiled back.

As they reached the stairs to Bailey's house, Liz was surprised to find that she was disappointed. Walking with Daria had actually been pleasant. She was in a much better mood now than when they'd left. They started back up toward the house.

"So do you—" Daria started, then broke off abruptly as they reached the top of the stairs. Caroline was standing there, blocking their way, her arms crossed.

"Have a nice walk?" she asked.

"We were just—" Daria responded, sounding oddly nervous. "Just talking about, um, the magazine."

"Well, I am *so* sorry to interrupt," Caroline said. "It's just that this is a barbecue, and the grilling part is kind of important? But you know, I can absolutely handle it if you're too . . . busy." She gave Liz a scathing look.

"No, of course not," Daria said, leaning against the railing to brush sand off her feet. "I'll be right there."

"Are you sure?" Caroline said. "Really, I feel just awful about intruding. I noticed Bailey getting cozy with a staff member, but I had no idea that you two were also"—she paused—"intimately involved."

Liz's face burned. She opened her mouth to clarify that, actually, they had just run into each other on the beach, but Daria beat her to it.

"Don't be ridiculous, Caroline," she said sharply. "That's completely out of the question."

And without a backward glance, she strode off across the yard toward the grill.

Caroline gave Liz a pitying, faux-apologetic smile. Then she turned and followed in Daria's footsteps.

Liz watched them go, feeling frozen in place at the top of the steps. It shouldn't hurt so much that Daria had appeared mortified at the mere *implication* that she might be connected to Liz. But she'd thought they'd been having a nice time together, even if it had been slightly awkward.

Well, it was all for the best. Liz tried to be glad that Daria had shown her true colors again. Because now she could go back to believing in the uncomplicated truth: Daria Fitzgerald was a major fucking asshole.

9

t was official. Jane Wilson and Bailey Cox had U-Hauled hard.

It was the hottest gossip the *Nether Fields* had experienced in years: The entire staff was trading whispers about how Bailey had asked Jane to be her girlfriend a week after the Pride party and how they were already planning a trip to Paris for fall. They kept things professional in the office, but outside of work they were like middle schoolers: planning adorable surprise dates for each other, exchanging playlists, and spending almost every single night together at Bailey's apartment on the Upper West Side.

"It's like Jane's completely forgotten we exist," Liz said. She was sitting in the bathroom on a folding chair, facing the mirror and waiting for Katie to cut her hair. Katie gave the best haircuts out of her three roommates but took the most wheedling to consent to give one: She always complained that the possibility of destroying Liz's getting-laid potential for the month made her flustered. "She's literally never here."

"It'll pass," Katie said, running her fingers through Liz's

hair. Their plan was to shave both sides of Liz's head this time, leaving the top long, which Liz hoped would convey more androgynous energy. "She's just excited. Wouldn't you do the same thing if you were starting a new relationship?"

Liz sighed. She wished she knew. Weston had responded to Liz's texts after she'd gotten home from the pool party, and they'd made plans for Liz to go over to her apartment that week. It had gone well—Weston was charming and *very* good in bed. But in the three weeks since, they had seen each other only twice. Liz couldn't tell if this was because their schedules were mismatched, or if Weston preferred a slow pace, or if, worst of all, she thought of Liz as a casual hookup. Did casual hookups give each other thoughtful, "I completely see you for who you are and respect that" gifts? She was trying to be one of those cool, chill girls who was okay with whatever, but the amount of time she spent obsessing about Weston was definitive proof that she wasn't.

"How's your love life going?" Liz asked, changing the subject.

"Well, Lydia's out hooking up with someone right now," Katie said, not meeting Liz's eyes in the mirror.

Liz winced. "I'm sorry, Katie. That sucks."

Katie shrugged. "I'm used to it," she said, but she still didn't lift her gaze. "This guy I met while writing an article asked me out today, though."

"Katie! You're hot shit! Are you going to say yes?"

"I don't know. He's cute, but I'm not super excited about him." She busied herself with pulling down locks of Liz's hair, measuring their length.

"Maybe it'd be good for you to go out with someone else," Liz said sympathetically.

Katie shrugged again and turned on the electric clippers. "I know. But it doesn't seem fair to lead someone on when I'm still so wrapped up in Lydia."

Liz reached behind her and grasped Katie's free hand, giving it a squeeze.

"You know . . ." Liz said, suddenly inspired. "If Lydia's on a date, then they won't be using their Spotify."

Katie clicked off the shears. "Luke time?"

"Luke time!"

Katie cheered, and Liz ran into Lydia's room to grab their laptop. Last December, Lydia had been absolutely insufferable about their Spotify Wrapped. They still had a screenshot of their top five artists in their Tinder profile, to show off how perfectly cool and obscure their music was. As retaliation for having to listen to Lydia brag, Katie had come up with a brilliant idea: Screw with their Spotify algorithm. For the past six months, every time Lydia went somewhere they were unlikely to use their Spotify, Katie and Liz would play the most absurd, embarrassing song they could find, on repeat: Luke Bryan's "Huntin', Fishin' and Lovin' Every Day." At this point there was no way it wouldn't be Lydia's top song of the year.

Of course, they could easily have put the computer on mute while they played the song on loop, but that would have taken the fun out of it. Because the truth was that, by now, they both secretly loved it.

Liz set Lydia's laptop on the closed toilet seat, hands over the keyboard. "What's their password again?"

"Carabiner69."

"Your recall powers are scary," Liz said, typing it in.

"It's not my fault you guys are lax with your digital security," Katie said. "I mean, your password is literally 'ilove-janellemonae9' for everything. Do you know how easy it would be to steal your identity?"

Liz groaned. "Ugh, I *wish* someone would steal my identity. I could use a break from being me." She set Lydia's

Spotify to play the song on repeat, then settled back into the folding chair.

"Okay, that's a little too self-pitying, even for you," Katie said, turning the shears back on. "Is this just about Jane?"

Liz shook her head, then stopped when she remembered the proximity of the clippers to her ears. "No. Lately, I just feel . . . stuck."

Katie made a sympathetic noise, running the clippers over the back of Liz's head.

"Do you ever get bored of working at the *NF*?" Liz asked.

"Honestly? No," Katie said. "I mean, I wish we had more resources. But I love getting to write something new every week. Even if I'm just recapping a bad TV show, I love looking at the world through the lens of meaningful storytelling. Asking myself, how can I pitch this in a way that pulls people in and makes them care? How can I write this in a way that's entertaining and affirming to my audience?" Katie met Liz's eyes in the mirror, looking a little embarrassed. "I genuinely enjoy the process, you know?"

Liz closed her eyes, listening to the buzz of the clippers and Luke's exaggerated country twang. Hearing the passion in Katie's voice emphasized how starkly Liz didn't feel the same way. The process didn't bring her joy. Writing articles in a couple of hours and sending them out into the world . . . Liz wanted to sit with her ideas for longer, to build something that would last more than a week or two.

"I just feel a little lost lately, in every aspect of my life," Liz said, opening her eyes again. "Career-wise. Romance-wise. Gender-presentation-wise. I really have no idea what I want my future to look like."

In the mirror, Katie put down the clippers and took out a pair of nail scissors. Tongue poking out slightly from her mouth, she started trimming the longer hair on top.

"I don't know." Liz sighed. "I wish I could be content with where I am. I know I'm lucky to be employed."

Hoping for a distraction, she pulled out her phone to check if Weston had texted. She hadn't.

"What's your new background photo?" Katie asked, leaning over her shoulder.

Liz tilted the photo so Katie could see. "I found it on Instagram the other day." She explained more about Moira Campbell and how much she loved her photos.

Katie put down the scissors. "Are there more?"

Liz pulled up some of the photos on her phone: a butch mechanic with long, flowing hair; a trans woman asleep on a floral couch, her face relaxed and her mouth half-open; the photographer winking into a mirror as she held up the camera, her haircut fluffy and androgynous.

"These are amazing," Katie said, pinching open the screen to zoom in.

"Right?" Liz said. "I tried to find more online, but there's almost nothing. She seems to have been completely overlooked by history."

Katie scrolled back through the photos, taking another look. "Is she still alive? You should totally interview her."

"For the magazine?"

"Yeah!" Katie said, handing the phone back. "Why not? I bet she has a super interesting life."

Liz thought for a moment. Maybe Katie was right. Liz had access to a platform, after all. If the article got some traction, it could lead to Moira getting some of the recognition she deserved, maybe even getting her work displayed in galleries or museums. And if Liz was the one to make that happen, the one to unearth a hidden queer hero . . . well, that certainly wouldn't hurt her reputation as a serious writer.

"Katie, you're a genius."

Katie laughed. "I know. But am I huntin', fishin', and lovin' every day?"

Liz reached over and pumped up the volume on the computer. Over-the-top banjo chords filled the bathroom, just in time for the part of the song where Luke spoke in an earnest monotone about his love for wading in mud.

As they sang along, Liz felt infinitely better. She had a goal to work toward. Maybe this interview was exactly what she needed to shake things up and finally get herself unstuck.

10

Four days later, Liz met with Charlotte, Jane, Bailey, and Daria to discuss her article idea. Liz paused outside the door to the Laverne Room, rolling her shoulders back, trying to look confident and put-together. She was wearing a women's button-down shirt over tight black pants. The outfit felt uncomfortably femme, and Liz had been tugging at the collar all day, but she didn't have many formal masculine outfits, other than the blazer Weston had given her, which was more suited for a wedding than the office.

"Liz! How are you doing?" Bailey said cheerfully as Liz walked into the room. She was sitting next to Jane, who gave Liz a wide smile. As resistant as Liz had originally been to the Jane–Bailey pairing, she had to admit that Jane seemed absurdly happy lately.

"Good. How are you?" Liz took a seat next to Charlotte. Daria, who was sitting on the far end of the conference table, typing loudly on her laptop, didn't look up.

"Good, good," Bailey said, leaning over the table toward her. "So, tell us about this feature idea."

Liz explained what she knew about Moira Campbell, how

much more she thought there was to explore about Moira's role in the early gay-rights movement, and why she thought the *Nether Fields* audience would be interested in her story. Jane, Bailey, and Charlotte nodded along encouragingly. Daria stayed focused on her screen. She'd been added to the meeting only when Charlotte had heard there might be some travel expenses involved.

Liz had been thrilled to find out that the photographer lived in Boston. If she'd been in California or Montana or somewhere else that would require a flight, the magazine would never have sent her. But Jane had gone to Boston at least once for a story. Plus, Liz knew Boston. Her parents lived in a small town less than three hours away, and when Liz was growing up, they would sometimes drive in for the day to explore the city and eat hot dogs in the top ring of seats at Fenway Park.

"I emailed Moira and she agreed to be interviewed and show me more photographs," Liz said in closing. "And she's only a train ride away."

Bailey and Charlotte exchanged a mutual grimace.

"Can't you interview her over the phone?" Charlotte said.

Liz shook her head. "She said she's hard of hearing, so I'd have to come in person to talk to her. Plus, she has the actual photos at her house."

"Moira sounds incredible. And I know how excited you are about it," Charlotte said carefully. "But you know how tight things have been lately. We just don't have the budget to send you to Boston right now."

"I looked up bus tickets, too," Liz said. Jane gave Liz an encouraging nod. "It's only about fifty dollars round-trip, and I wouldn't need to spend the night."

"I'm sorry," Bailey said. "We're making it a policy. No travel." It sounded like the words were costing her all the courage and authority she could muster. If Liz hadn't felt so demoralized herself, she might have felt bad for Bailey. Beside her, Jane frowned, looking surprised. "I know fifty dollars may not seem like much," Bailey continued, "but we have to establish a firm no-exceptions policy, at least for the foreseeable future."

"I understand that," Liz said. She took a deep breath. "But Moira deserves to be recognized. She was one of the few people documenting the lives of queer and trans people in the 1960s and '70s. These are people who would have been lost to history without her. Who still might be lost to history if Moira doesn't get the chance to tell their stories."

"You're right." Bailey's face was grim. "She does deserve recognition. But we just can't make the exception."

"I'll pay my own way, then," Liz said quickly, even though she didn't have a spare fifty dollars lying around. She wished she'd discovered Moira Campbell at the end of last year, when her parents had bought her round-trip Amtrak tickets to come home for Christmas. She could have taken their car and driven to Boston.

"Liz," Charlotte said, shaking her head. "I respect your enthusiasm, but I can't allow you to spend your own money on travel for work. That's not a good habit to get into, and it's not a narrative we need out there, internally or externally."

Liz felt herself deflate in her chair, not even bothering to hide her disappointment. So that was it. Moira Campbell would fade into obsolescence and Liz would spend the rest of her career in listicle hell.

"I really am sorry, Liz," Bailey said. Liz had to focus on the table and bite the inside of her cheek to keep from tearing up.

She was about to stand up when Daria spoke from the other end of the room. "I can take you." Everyone's head turned in Daria's direction. She wasn't typing anymore, but she also hadn't looked up from her laptop.

"Sorry?" Charlotte said.

"I'm going to Boston this weekend for my aunt's birthday," Daria said. "So she can ride with me."

Liz's brain spun for a moment, not comprehending.

"The new policy isn't being announced till next week, right?" Daria went on, finally raising her eyes to meet Bailey's. "If a reporter organizes her own ride, at no cost to the magazine, before the policy change has been formalized, it's not technically breaking any rules."

"No," Bailey said, seeming taken aback. "I suppose it's not."

Jane shot Liz a puzzled glance. Liz shrugged slightly.

"Well," Charlotte said, clapping her hands together with a jovial finality. "I guess it's all settled, then."

"Wait," Liz said. "I don't—I'm not—" Jane kicked her under the table, and Liz broke off, wincing.

"Nonsense." Charlotte was already standing up. "You want to do this interview, and now you have a ride."

"I—when are you even going?" Liz said.

"Saturday," Daria said. "Just for the night."

Liz had loose plans to meet with Weston on Saturday. "Overnight?" she said. "I don't have anywhere to stay. So I don't think this makes sense." Liz *did* want this interview, but she also couldn't imagine being trapped in a car with Daria for several hours. Her palms started to sweat at the thought.

Daria shrugged. "You can stay at my aunt's, too. There's plenty of room."

Before Liz could invent an important conflict or sudden illness, Charlotte jumped in again, gathering her notebook in her arms. "This is great. Liz, this article will be a real opportunity for your career."

"I'm so glad this worked out," Bailey said, sounding relieved to no longer be the bearer of bad news.

"I'll email you the details," Daria said.

Liz wanted to protest, but it seemed decided. Slowly, she stood up and made to follow Charlotte out of the Laverne Room. "Um, thanks, Daria," she said on her way out.

Daria just nodded at her computer screen.

11

Daria picked Liz up at a truly absurd hour. An hour Liz had previously suspected might not even exist on Saturdays. It was still mostly dark out. Which was actually a blessing, because it allowed Liz to pretend that she was still asleep and this entire road trip was an elaborate nightmare.

A gleaming black car was idling in front of Liz's apartment when she went outside. It looked fancy. Daria opened her door and got out. She was wearing jeans and a black sweater over a white button-down shirt, the most casual Liz had ever seen her dressed. Of course, she still looked incredible, as if the clothes had been made specifically for her. Which maybe they had been. Liz didn't know how rich people clothes worked.

"Good morning," Daria said.

Liz made a noise that she hoped resembled a greeting.

"I see you've come prepared."

"What?" Liz croaked. It was the first time she'd spoken out loud since waking up.

Daria nodded toward Liz's bulging duffel bag and backpack. The previous night, rather than try to confront the complex web of her own identity, Liz had just packed two of everything—a tomboy version and a femme version. As a result, it looked like she was leaving for a month abroad.

"Oh." Liz wanted to come up with a witty reply, but her brain wasn't interested in supplying one, so she left it at that.

Daria took her duffel bag and put it in the trunk. "Backpack?" she asked, holding out her hand.

"No," Liz said, bringing it with her to the passenger side. She had stuffed her backpack with everything that she thought might make this road trip a little more bearable— her laptop, snacks, a homemade *L Word* trivia game from one of the parties Lydia had thrown last year, Carmen Maria Machado's latest book, even a coloring book she'd bought on Etsy from a trans comic artist. Anything to make the next five hours survivable.

Daria shut the trunk and they both got into the car, Liz barely managing to wedge her overstuffed backpack at her feet. The inside of the vehicle felt far too clean. Every surface was shiny and new looking, without a single smudge. Except for the two enormous cups of coffee in the cupholders.

"Coffee," Liz said.

"One of them is tea, actually." Daria turned to check the road before pulling away from the curb. "The coffee's for you."

"Oh my God, *bless* you." Liz cupped the coffee in her hands and inhaled the smell, relieved to find out she did, in fact, have the capacity to speak more than one word at a time. "You just saved my life."

Daria shrugged. "You strike me as someone who needs coffee in the morning."

Liz took a sip and immediately felt better. "This doesn't count as morning. The sun isn't even up."

"Yes it is." Daria stopped at a light and put on her turn signal. "The sun rose at five twenty-five and it's nearly six."

"Why do you know what time the sun rose?"

"I run three times a week with a queer running group called the Pride Runners, at either six A.M. or nine A.M." The light changed, and Daria turned onto the traffic circle in front of Prospect Park. Vendors were already setting up tents for the Saturday farmers market.

"Ugh, gross." Liz made a face.

"You have something against running?"

"I have something against the kind of person who wakes up before sunrise to run."

Daria laughed, then fell quiet as they merged onto the highway. Liz took advantage of Daria's concentration to look at her a little more closely. Maybe it was just the jeans, but she seemed more relaxed than usual. Her hair had gotten longer, and the front flopped down into her eyes. She tossed her head a little to get it out of the way, and the early morning sun caught highlights in it, lighting them up like tiny threads of gold.

Sitting in the same enclosed space as Daria, Liz felt self-conscious every time she shifted in her seat or made a small noise. But the blurring scenery gradually lulled her into a drowsy stupor.

She must have fallen asleep at some point, because she woke up with her neck at an awkward angle against the window and drool running down her chin. She wiped at it quickly, hoping Daria hadn't seen, and sat up.

"Jesus," she said. "What time is it?"

"Past nine."

Liz rubbed at her eyes. The seatbelt seemed to have left an impression across her right cheek. She took a sip of cold coffee. "Sorry I fell asleep."

"That's okay," Daria said. "You want to be well rested for your interview."

Feeling slightly disoriented by Daria's friendly tone, Liz checked her phone, hoping to see a text from Weston, but her last message was still *wow guess youd rather hang out with daria than me* followed by a long string of Liz's apologies and explanations. Liz could imagine how upset Weston might be, knowing that Liz was spending the weekend with someone who had ruined her life. But it was also a little frustrating that Weston couldn't see how important this was for Liz's career. It wasn't like she was hanging out with Daria for *fun*.

Liz's only new messages were a meme from Lydia and a photo from Jane: a selfie of her and Bailey on top of a mountain in hiking clothes. They were spending the weekend together upstate. Liz sent a stream of heart emojis back. Jane and Bailey were sickeningly cute. On the few nights Jane spent at home, she moved around the apartment humming and gazing dreamily out the windows like some sort of Disney princess. Truthfully, it was nice to see her so happy. One night, after a couple of drinks, Liz had even gone so far as to admit to Jane that she thought they made a good couple.

Liz read over her conversation with Weston one more time, then forced herself to put away her phone. She leaned over to rustle through her backpack. "You want some Goldfish?"

"Wow." Daria watched her open the bag. "I haven't had Goldfish since I was, like, twelve."

"I promise you they're even better than you remember."

Daria held out her palm. Not wanting to spill Goldfish all over the shiny car, Liz hovered her hand under Daria's as she poured in a small handful. Warmth radiated between their almost-touching skin, and the edges of Daria's knuckles brushed against Liz's palm as she pulled away. Daria glanced at her before tipping her hand to her mouth.

"Oh my God. These are so good."

"Right? Here, have some more."

Daria held out her palm, and this time Liz cupped it with hers. Daria's hand was soft and warm. Liz could see some Goldfish dust around Daria's mouth, which was the closest to messy Liz had ever seen her. It was surprisingly endearing. Still staring at Daria's mouth, Liz accidentally tipped the bag too far, and a small avalanche of Goldfish poured onto the floor.

"Oh shit!" Liz pulled back, startled. "I'm so sorry." She bent over, picking up as many as she could see.

Daria cleared her throat. "It's fine. Leave them."

"And waste perfectly good Goldfish? I don't think so." Liz popped some of the floor fish into her mouth.

"That's disgusting."

"Please," Liz said through her mouthful. "Your car floor could not be any cleaner."

Daria glanced at Liz, and the brief eye contact made Liz flush. The car felt very warm, suddenly. She tried to think of a way to change the subject.

"So, why did you go into investment banking?"

Daria let out a long breath. "Um. It's embarrassing, really," she said. "But in college, when I realized that I wanted to . . . look the way I look, I felt really lost. I knew that *this*"— she gestured toward herself with one hand—"was right for me, but I wasn't actually sure how to live like this in the real world. Now it sounds so ridiculous. You just live life however you want, right? But—back then." She paused, as if struggling to find the right words. "It's kind of like when you greet people at a cocktail party. The men shake hands with each other and hug the women. I'd never noticed that before, until I started dressing like this and suddenly men had no idea how they were supposed to greet me."

Liz resisted the urge to say that, actually, she never went to cocktail parties and certainly not ones with lots of men in attendance.

"I grew up knowing how I was supposed to act, what rules I was supposed to follow." Daria kept her eyes firmly on the road, as if not looking at Liz made it easier to talk. "But then I realized that all of those rules were gendered. There were no rules for people like me. I knew that I didn't want the path my parents had chosen for me. So, I followed the only other path I could see. If I didn't want to act like a woman, I'd act like a man." Her expression had hardened slightly, as if she had no sympathy for the younger version of herself who'd made these choices. "In short, I started behaving like my father. I chose a profession that I knew a lot of men went into. I decided to prove to my parents that I could be successful, in the way they measured success. By making a lot of money." Her eyes darted to Liz, back to the road, and then to Liz again. "Ridiculous, right?"

"No," Liz said softly. "Not at all."

Daria let out a hard laugh. "It was," she said. "I was walking around so focused on trying to seem tough that I wasn't acting like myself at all. Over time, I realized that just because I want to look masculine, I don't have to *act* masculine. That I can still be feminine in some ways and that's okay." She blew out a puff of air from her cheeks. "After that, I realized I probably would have been happier working at a nonprofit or something. But at that point, I was a couple years into my career. And I do enjoy the work. It's interesting. Plus, I figured I can probably do just as much good working there and donating money as I could working at a nonprofit. So, I stayed." Daria shrugged. Her face had gone very pink.

Liz studied Daria, who kept her eyes resolutely ahead. These were some of the thoughts that Liz had been trying to turn into words in her head for months. A different variation, yes, but the same theme. Hearing Daria say these things, when Liz had felt lost in these feelings for so long—inexplicably, embarrassingly, Liz wanted to cry.

"I know what you mean," Liz said, pitching her voice a bit lower so it didn't sound unsteady. "About feeling lost without rules to follow. Me, I feel like I go back and forth, back and forth, about how I want to look and act. Some days it's femme, some days it's masc, but it's never all one thing. Which makes me feel almost like I'm faking it or something, you know? If it changes based on the situation, if it's not consistent, how do I know that it's real?" Liz absentmindedly rubbed the seatbelt imprint on her cheek. "Isn't it sad that I write advice articles for queer people, and I can't figure myself out? I leave the house in femme clothes and feel small. I go out in men's clothes and feel like I'm trying too hard. I'm pretty sure I identify as a woman, but I'm not really sure what it looks like, to not be either of those things."

"I like your in-the-middle thing," Daria said softly. "It works for you."

Liz's entire body flushed. She felt like they were on the verge of something dangerous. She couldn't think clearly. The car was too small, too enclosed, too hot. Daria was too close. She'd rolled her sleeves up to the elbow and her forearms looked strong and competent, tiny muscles flexing as she made adjustments on the wheel. Liz couldn't take her eyes off them.

"Thank you."

"I wish—sometimes I wish I was bold enough to be more in the middle." Daria glanced over, as if nervous to see how Liz would react.

Their eyes met. Liz willed herself not to look away. "I bet you could be."

Daria smiled.

"That's actually part of why I want to interview this photographer," Liz said. "I mean, in addition to getting her some small bit of the recognition she deserves. Someone who's been out for more than fifty years? I feel like she'll have *some* advice, at least, on how to live your life when there aren't any rules for you to follow."

Daria looked at Liz again. "This seems like exactly the kind of article I could use in my life right now," she said, but her voice was so low and smooth that it almost sounded . . . flirty.

Liz turned to the window and pressed her face against the glass, hoping it would cool down her cheeks. She couldn't look at Daria anymore. But she also couldn't help smiling to herself as she watched Boston come into view.

*   *   *

Daria's aunt's house turned out to be an enormous light blue Victorian in the heart of Cambridge. Liz had never been to this part of the city. During their visits, her family had mostly stayed in Boston, visiting the aquarium or Fenway or the museums. The one time they had come to Cambridge, they had wandered around Harvard Yard taking touristy photos. They had certainly never ventured into this maze of streets lined with houses so large they were practically mansions. Liz felt a little guilty being in the same state as her parents without seeing them; she hadn't told them she was coming because she knew they'd want to come meet her, and she wanted to focus on the interview without distractions.

Daria opened the door with her key, and Liz barely had time to gape at the chandelier and the grand, sweeping staircase in front of her before Daria hustled her down the hall. Her aunt was probably in the back gardening, she said, so she would introduce them and then Liz could take the T to the photographer's apartment in Boston. Daria had offered to drop her off, but Liz had turned her down—she wanted to have a moment to herself to clear her head before the interview.

Daria led her through a kitchen that Jane would have lost her mind over and out onto a brick patio overlooking a small lawn lined with vibrant flower beds. Liz had expected to see an older woman in a large straw hat, holding a pair of gardening shears and bending over some rosebushes. Instead, Daria's aunt was sitting at a patio table under a large umbrella with her arms crossed, barking orders to a small woman crouched next to a bed of violently purple flowers.

"Happy birthday, Aunt Katherine," Daria said, stopping at the edge of the table. Aunt Katherine held a hand up to Daria, silencing her.

"For heaven's sake, Isabella, you're not stomping grapes for wine. Have some consideration for my poor vines."

"Yes, ma'am," Isabella murmured, seeming unaffected. She positioned the shears around a vine and then paused, looking up at Katherine for approval.

"Not that one. Do you have some vendetta against hydrangeas? The one to the left."

Isabella repositioned her shears, Katherine nodded, and the vine went. Only then did Katherine turn around. She looked to be in her late seventies. She was white, with gray hair pinned into an elaborate bun. She wore a creamy, expensive-looking scoop neck blouse with a string of pearls and a navy cardigan despite the summer humidity. Her face was stern, and Liz caught a strong resemblance to Daria in the line of her nose and the disapproving furrow of her brows.

"Happy birthday, Aunt Katherine," Daria said again. "Your garden's looking great."

Aunt Katherine sniffed. "It looks ghastly. Isabella's doing her best to strangle it, but I've been holding her back."

"Nonsense. You're doing a great job, Isabella," Daria said, waving.

Isabella waved back. "Great to see you again, Daria."

"Yes, the garden looks beautiful," Liz added, feeling like she should chime in, rather than just shift awkwardly behind Daria and wait to be introduced.

"Who are you?" Aunt Katherine said, shifting her focus.

"This is Liz Baker," Daria said. "The reporter I was telling you about from the magazine."

"Happy birthday," Liz said. "Thank you so much for letting me stay with you."

Aunt Katherine looked Liz up and down. "Well, I'm glad you didn't get dressed up on my account," she said.

Liz's face burned. She was wearing industrial-looking gray work pants and a black T-shirt with her black Doc Martens. It was more butch than Liz's usual taste, but the outfit gave her a bit of swaggering confidence that she thought would help with the interview. She hadn't considered that she'd be meeting Daria's aunt in her outfit choice.

"So you work at Bailey's magazine, do you?" Aunt Katherine said.

"Yes, I do." Liz had a strange urge to add a "ma'am" to her sentence.

"What a ridiculous decision," Aunt Katherine said. "I called Bailey myself to tell her not to invest. I told her to focus on real estate, not play pretend journalist and lose all her money. But did she listen? No."

"Oh," Liz said. "Well, we're very glad that she bought us."

"Yes, I suppose you are." Aunt Katherine peered at Liz suspiciously. "Well, dinner is at Rosings. Seven o'clock."

"Oh, I'm not—" Liz started to say, but Katherine interrupted.

"Make sure you change beforehand, dear. This place has a Michelin star."

Liz darted her eyes to Daria, hoping for help.

"I didn't mention dinner to Liz, Aunt Katherine. I'm sure she has her own things to do in the city."

"Nonsense," Aunt Katherine said. "You're staying with us, so it would be rude of me not to invite you and even ruder of you not to accept."

"Really, I don't want to intrude," Liz said. "It's your birthday."

"Seven o'clock," Katherine repeated, enunciating. "Different outfit. We'll leave here at six forty-five. Caroline's meeting us there."

"Caroline?" Daria asked.

"Yes, Caroline. I invited her."

"Why?" Daria said, and Liz heard an almost teenager-like whine in her tone.

"Just because you two can't figure yourselves out doesn't mean I have to stop spending time with her. You know very well that she keeps me company while you're living so far away. Isabella, *what* are you doing to my petunias?"

Daria looked like she was about to protest, but then sagged. "Aunt Katherine, I'm going to walk Liz out so she can get to her interview, okay?"

Aunt Katherine didn't respond. Daria held the door to the house open for Liz.

"Sorry about dinner," she said once they were inside. "It's a good restaurant, though."

"Can't you get me out of this?" Liz said desperately. "It's very nice of her to let me stay here, but I really don't think I should go to dinner."

Especially if Caroline was going to be there. Somehow,

Liz didn't think that her skewering Daria's ex-girlfriend with a salad fork would be very celebratory.

"Uh, probably not," Daria said, rubbing the back of her head. "My aunt can be a little . . . opinionated."

"Okay," Liz said, annoyed. "Well. See you at six forty-five, then. In a *different outfit.*"

Daria winced. "I'm really sorry about that. She's just a little formal." She opened the heavy front door for Liz. "Good luck with the interview."

Liz walked off without replying. Apparently, she was having dinner with Daria, Daria's aunt, and Daria's ex-girlfriend. If Liz managed to get through the night without at least one murder on her hands, it would be a miracle.

12

After the interview, Liz caught the T back to Daria's aunt's house in a daze, her mind spinning with everything she'd learned.

Moira Campbell lived in a small apartment in Jamaica Plain with her wife. Their home wasn't fancy, but it was comfortable and welcoming, with two orange cats lying across the furniture. And seeing Moira squeeze her wife's hand as she talked, both women in their seventies, had made Liz's heart ache with longing. On an intellectual level, she knew that queer people could have long, successful relationships that lasted to old age. But it was a very different thing to actually *see* it. To believe it.

Moira had dozens of photo albums, and she'd paged through them with Liz next to her on the couch, explaining where each shot was taken: on Christopher Street for the 1970 Gay Liberation Rally, in the hallway of her ex-girlfriend's East Village apartment, inside the kitchen of a women's rights conference. It had been obvious that some of the stories were hard to tell; Moira's fingers drifted across the pages, detailing the ways that so many of her friends had died too young.

"That's why I wanted to take their pictures," she said. "Because the world wanted to forget us. Even as we were living, they wanted to forget us. And I didn't want us to be forgotten."

"Does any part of you want to try to get the photos out there in a larger way, to make sure they're not forgotten?" Liz had asked eagerly, turning to face her. "To try to put them online or in a book, or see if any collections would display them?"

Moira had considered this for a while, stroking one of the cats around the ears thoughtfully. "I didn't take these photos for them to be in galleries. People would have seen them as a scandal, as spectacle. Curiosities at best, degenerates at worst. I didn't want to capture our world for other people." She gave the cat one last stroke and then turned to Liz. "I was trying to capture our world for us. My friends. My lovers. The strangers I met at all these rallies and conferences, who were fighting for a better world or just fighting to survive. I developed most of my photos in duplicate so that I could give my subjects their portraits. I think I wanted to show all of us that we were worth photographing. That we were beautiful." She smiled at Liz then. "And I loved taking them. Being the person with the camera allowed me to talk to a lot of people I otherwise wouldn't have met. It allowed me to see the beauty in everything we were doing. In everything we were. I barely scraped by, but I loved every second of it."

Liz turned those words over in her mind as she walked down the hot sidewalks of Cambridge toward Aunt Katherine's house. In the moment, she had felt slightly chastened. She had come here dreaming of getting Moira the gallery show she deserved, but Moira didn't need that from Liz. For her, it wasn't about showing the photos to the world. Taking the photos had been enough.

Liz couldn't stop thinking about the passion in Moira's voice as she talked about her photography. Moira had known she wouldn't find money or fame with her art, but she had done it anyway. She had *loved* it anyway.

Liz was always so worried when she wrote—that she wasn't good enough, that no one would want to publish her, that no one would want to read her work, that she wouldn't be successful. But maybe Moira was right. Maybe none of that mattered. Maybe it was enough just to love doing it.

Liz felt energized, buzzing with a renewed determination to write. She was going to do it, she decided. She was going to dedicate herself to writing the novel she'd always wanted to write. She would capture the queer experience like Moira had and make her art without caring about how the world would receive it. Starting today, Liz Baker was a novelist.

Unfortunately, however, she couldn't sit down and start outlining right away, like she wanted to. Instead she had to go to the world's suckiest-sounding birthday dinner.

After their car ride, Liz felt a little flustered at the thought of spending more time with Daria. This seemed to keep happening. Liz would talk to Daria and forget, temporarily, about all the reasons she had for not liking her. But then Daria would do or say something and the illusion would come crashing down, reminding Liz once again that she'd been right about Daria from the very beginning. Daria hadn't done anything hate-worthy on this trip so far, but Liz was sure it was only a matter of time.

At six forty, Liz went downstairs. She was wearing the most femme outfit she'd brought—tight black jeans and a button-down shirt. She had a feeling that Daria's aunt would have preferred a dress, but Liz hadn't thrown a lot of fancy dining options into her bag.

Liz went into the living room to wait for the others. Floor-to-ceiling bookshelves lined one wall, full of impressive-looking sets of matching leather-bound books. Liz sat down on a sofa with a curved back, trying not to displace any of the carefully angled throw pillows. A painting of a young girl hung over the fireplace. Liz stared at it for nearly a minute before realizing that it was Daria.

She stood up to get a better look. It was a large oil portrait. Daria was about eleven or twelve, wearing an elaborate, lacy white dress with a long sheet of dark hair over her shoulder. She wasn't smiling.

Liz heard someone coming down the stairs, and a very different Daria from the one in the painting walked into the room. This Daria was wearing a gray, tight-fitting suit with a white shirt and a red tie with a matching pocket square. It looked very, very good on her.

"Hello," Liz said. "I was just admiring your painting."

"God, I hate that thing," Daria said. She sat down in an armchair facing the opposite direction.

"Don't worry, you still look *very* masc. It's all in the eyes." Liz settled back on the couch.

"I look like a child bride," Daria said. "How did the interview go?"

"It went *so* well," Liz said, unable to keep her enthusiasm from spilling out. "She told me incredible stories. Her community faced so much persecution, from every side, but they just kept living. Dressing how they wanted, loving who they wanted, fighting for their rights, standing up to everyone who wanted to keep them down."

"Wow. That's so inspiring. I wish I could have met her," Daria said, smiling. "Did she give you any advice, as an older queer person?"

"Sort of," Liz said, leaning forward. "I asked her how she found the courage to live like that, when she had no role models and faced so many repercussions. She said she didn't feel that courageous at the time. Every step of the way, she imagined all of these things that could go wrong if she came out, if she went to a rally, if she lived openly."

Liz paused, trying to remember the photographer's exact words. She wanted Daria to understand how inspirational it had been. "And all of those things she imagined could go wrong? She said they all happened. Family rejected her. Friends turned their backs on her. People she loved got badly hurt. But she said that, as awful as those things were, most of them weren't as bad as she feared they would be. Living life as herself was so . . . so joyous and freeing that it made her strong enough to bear the terrible things." Liz swallowed. "She said that if she has any advice for younger queer people, it's to try to let go of the fear. You can spend a lot of time and energy waiting for bad things to happen, or worrying about what other people think. It's better to focus on the potential joy of living as yourself, rather than the potential pain."

"Wow." Daria blinked rapidly a few times. "That's—wow. I needed to hear that."

Liz smiled at her. This article was going to be incredible. If Moira's words had already moved someone as stoic as Daria, then they could move anybody.

They heard footsteps in the hall and Katherine came into the room, wearing a conservative turquoise dress with a gray shawl. She told Daria she looked nice and told Liz her outfit was "something of an improvement." Daria offered her an arm and they went outside, where they got into an Uber Black.

Caroline was waiting for them just inside the door of the restaurant, holding a large present with an absurdly ornate bow. She was wearing a silver dress that plunged at the neckline—Liz had to focus to keep herself from looking too closely at her cleavage. Her hair was blown dry, her makeup was impeccable, and her nails matched her dress. Liz hated her.

"Happy birthday," Caroline said, air-kissing Aunt Katherine's cheeks. "You look splendid."

"I hope that's not for me," Aunt Katherine said, gesturing to the box.

"Of course it's for you. How could I not get you a present on your birthday?"

"You know I hate presents," Aunt Katherine said, but she looked pleased. Then Caroline saw Liz, and her simpering expression slipped.

"What are you doing here?" she said.

"Liz is here working on a story," Daria said.

"Do you know each other?" asked Aunt Katherine.

"We met at Bailey's beach house," Caroline said. She still hadn't said hello, Liz noticed.

"Oh, you've been to Bailey's place?"

"Yes," Liz said. "It was very nice."

"Well, good for you for not hesitating to make use of your employers' houses," Aunt Katherine said. "Daria, go get the table."

Liz gaped.

"Yes, ma'am," Daria said.

"I'll come with you." Liz never thought she'd see Daria as the safer option, but she didn't want to be left alone with those two. She scurried off behind Daria to the host's stand.

"Good evening, sir," said the host, a tall man in a three-piece suit. "Do you have a reservation?"

"Fitzgerald. Seven o'clock." Daria's voice was clipped.

"Oh! I'm so sorry, ma'am," he said, looking flustered. Daria nodded but didn't reply. "Right this way, *ma'am*."

"Thank you." Daria motioned to Caroline and her aunt, then followed the host into the dining room.

At the table, he stopped and pointedly pulled out a chair for Daria. Daria grimaced but sat down. Clearly, he was overcompensating for his earlier mistake, but it also felt like he was trying to put Daria back into her proper place. Liz pulled out her own chair before the host could get to it.

Once they were all seated, a server handed out tiny card stock menus. Liz tried not to panic. She really hoped this wasn't a split-the-check kind of situation.

"Caroline, how are things at the law firm?" Daria's aunt asked.

"Busy," Caroline said. "We have a few big cases coming up."

"What kind of law do you practice?" Liz asked. "Corporate?"

"Human rights law, actually," Caroline said coldly, without looking at Liz. "We're working on a big case on behalf of asylum seekers from Colombia. It could reach the Supreme Court."

Liz frowned, determined to keep hating Caroline anyway.

Caroline turned to Daria. "Daria, do you want to split the shaved brussels sprout salad and the tuna tartare to start? I know you love both."

"Actually, I was planning to get the crab cake," Daria said, not making eye contact with her.

"We're getting the tasting menu," Katherine said. "It's my birthday, and I want to indulge."

"In that case, we shall." Daria set her menu down. "So how does it feel to be another year older?"

"Just one year closer to death," Katherine said. "But don't get too excited—I don't plan on dying anytime soon."

"Excited?" Daria said. "I don't think I could handle losing you."

"Well, I'm sure the house would be a great comfort." Katherine folded her hands together. "Elizabeth, dear, in nice restaurants, it's common practice to put your napkin on your lap."

Liz looked up from her menu. She glanced around the table and realized that her napkin was the only one still on the table in front of her. Turning red, she quickly unfolded it and spread it over her legs. Caroline smirked.

A server came over. Katherine told him that the whole table would be having the tasting menu.

"The five course or the seven, ma'am?"

Liz looked up, alarmed, as Katherine ordered the latter. *Seven* courses? They would be here for hours. She should never have agreed to this dinner. She should never have come to Daria's house in the first place. If this were a horror movie, the entire audience would be screaming at Liz to escape while she still could.

The server asked for drink orders. Liz quickly scanned the cocktail list and ordered the one that seemed like it had the highest alcohol content.

"It feels like forever since I've seen you, Caroline," Aunt Katherine said once the server had gone. "When you were kids, I used to see you practically every week. You were always so kind to Daria growing up. Didn't you once get suspended on her behalf?"

Daria chuckled. "She punched Annie Curtis in the face for calling me a freak. Thankfully, the tooth she lost wasn't an adult one or her mom probably would have sued."

Caroline shrugged. "I warned her that if she didn't leave you alone, I was going to deck her, but she didn't listen. I was just following through on my promise."

Daria and Caroline exchanged smiles. Liz wished she

could disappear. This dinner was clearly a setup to get Caroline and Daria back together. She asked herself for the hundredth time why she was here.

"You were Daria's little protector," Aunt Katherine said. Daria looked down at her plate and fidgeted uncomfortably. "I always told her that if she'd just try to fit in, the other kids wouldn't give her such a hard time. But did she listen? Of course not."

"Daria's always been an individual," Caroline said, turning toward Daria fondly, but Daria was studiously examining her fork.

Seeming to sense Daria's discomfort, Caroline changed the subject. "Katherine, I'm dying to see your garden. How are your petunias?"

Katherine launched into a detailed explanation of how her garden had been faring this summer. Liz tuned them out, looking around the restaurant at the heavy white tablecloths and the waiters in their matching suits. This couldn't be further from the way Liz's family had celebrated her dad's birthday last year: a backyard party with the neighbors, her mom's chili, and a few cases of beer. After dinner, they had played Spoons until everyone got too rowdy and they'd had to call the game off before someone broke an arm.

"Elizabeth," Katherine said suddenly, as the waiter placed drinks on the table. Liz unconsciously straightened her posture, then felt extremely silly.

"It's Liz, actually," Liz said.

"So, you're a journalist?"

"Let's toast," Caroline interrupted, lifting her cocktail, a dark-colored whiskey drink with an orange peel in it. "To another year of living with your wit and insight. Happy birthday."

Katherine nodded, accepting her praise, and they all raised their glasses. Katherine had ordered champagne, and Daria had gotten something lavender colored with a layer of pale foam. Liz had already forgotten the name of her drink, and almost choked as she took a sip—it was very strong.

"It must be hard to make ends meet," Aunt Katherine said, turning to Liz again. "I can't imagine they pay you much of a salary."

"No, not much." Liz looked at Daria rather pointedly. "But enough to get by."

"And in New York, too. Do you have roommates?"

"I do. Three."

"Three?" Aunt Katherine sounded appalled. "You must never get any privacy."

"Not really." Liz took a big sip of her cocktail. Why was she so on edge? She shouldn't care what any of these people thought. "I like it that way, though. It's kind of fun."

"Fun," Aunt Katherine repeated, as if she'd never heard of it. "Do you have debt? From college?"

"Uh," Liz said. "Yes. I do."

Aunt Katherine shook her head. "Student loans are vicious. The financial consequences can haunt you for decades. Thank goodness I was able to appreciate that fact more than your father could, Daria."

"I'm very grateful to you," Daria said. It looked like she was biting the inside of her cheek. Liz shot her a curious glance. She'd assumed Daria's entire family was ultra-rich. Was it just Aunt Katherine? Then she remembered what Daria had said in the car about proving herself to her parents.

Had they rejected her for being gay?

"And what's your long-term plan?" Aunt Katherine asked.

"Um," Liz said. "I don't know. I guess I've always wanted to give fiction writing a try." She reddened. She had to give Katherine some credit for her interrogation skills. She was getting Liz to admit things she hadn't even told her parents or Jane.

"Not profitable," Aunt Katherine said, her mouth pursing

disapprovingly. "I published several stories in the Radcliffe literary magazine in college. All my professors told me I was a great talent. But then I married Richard and it seemed a bit trivial, so I gave it up."

"Oh." Liz didn't know what else to add. Luckily, Caroline jumped in, asking Katherine if she had any copies of the literary magazine left, saying she would love to read her stories. Liz thought Caroline was laying it on a bit thick, but Katherine seemed to accept this level of praise as her due.

Liz was relieved when the food finally began to arrive. There was a crispy sweet potato with a green sauce that was probably the best vegetable she'd ever had in her life, and a tuna tartare dish that she could have eaten ten of. The courses were small, since there were seven of them. Liz switched to what Daria was drinking and tried to drink fast.

After a brief discussion of politics, in which Liz managed to offend Aunt Katherine several times in rapid succession before Daria changed the subject, they moved on to discussing when Daria would be moving back to Cambridge.

"I don't know why you insist on staying in New York," Caroline said, putting her hand on Daria's arm for emphasis. "It's so dirty."

"Well, I do work there." Daria reached for her drink, dislodging Caroline's hand. Liz wondered if it was on purpose.

"There are plenty of investment banks here," Aunt Katherine said. "And then you could see me every week, instead of every two months."

"I was here three weeks ago," Daria said.

"But only for two nights. And you're only staying one this time. At least stay for lunch tomorrow," Katherine said. Liz shot an alarmed look at Daria, willing her to say no.

"We have to leave early to beat traffic," Daria said. Liz nearly sighed in relief.

"I don't understand why you drove," Aunt Katherine said.

"Just return the car here and take the train back in the afternoon."

"You drove?" Caroline said, sounding shocked. "What, did you rent a car?"

Daria shrugged sullenly, and Liz thought she caught a glimpse of what Daria might have been like as a teenager. "I never get a chance to drive in the city. I wanted to make sure I don't forget how."

Liz studied Daria, but Daria avoided her eyes. Why had Daria rented a car when it was easier and faster to just take the train? Wanting to practice driving seemed like an excuse. Had she rented the car to help Liz? But if she had, did that mean—

"Excuse me," Liz said, standing up to find the bathroom. She needed to hide for a moment and think this over.

The bathroom was dimly lit with an enormous brass trough sink and a floor-to-ceiling mirror on one wall. Liz studied herself, trying to imagine what Daria saw when she looked at her. Could Daria really be interested?

Part of Liz's brain wanted to scream, *Definitely not!* She hadn't forgotten the way Daria had said it was "completely out of the question" at Bailey's beach party. But then she remembered the way Daria had looked at her in the car. Her hand resting softly on Liz's palm. How her voice had sounded, saying that she needed an article like Liz's.

Maybe she *was* attracted to Liz. It wasn't so unbelievable, was it? There did seem to be . . . something between them. Sure, they had almost nothing in common. But there was something a little sexy about the thought of hooking up with someone you didn't like.

Of course, it was only the thought that was sexy. In reality, hooking up with Daria would be a disaster. Daria owned the magazine. Daria's best friend was dating Liz's best friend. She had ruined Weston's life without remorse. And also she was kind of the worst. So no, Liz wouldn't be hooking up with Daria. Ever.

Liz turned in front of the mirror, examining herself. She was underdressed for the restaurant, but she looked pretty good, actually. Was it possible that Daria had rented the car just to help Liz get to Boston for this interview? She had to admit, the thought was flattering. She giggled at her reflection. She was tipsier than she'd thought.

She was washing her hands in the giant sink when Caroline walked in.

"Oh, hello," Liz said, her smile fading.

Caroline took a lipstick out of her clutch and examined her makeup in the mirror, turning her chin to inspect the sides. "You seem to be spending an awful lot of time with Daria lately."

"Only for work." Liz turned off the faucet.

"Really?" Caroline applied a layer of lipstick, then blotted her lips with a tissue. "Staying at Aunt Katherine's house, coming to her birthday dinner? That's for work?"

"I'm here for a story." Liz dried her hands.

Caroline capped her lipstick. "It's just interesting that both you and your best friend are spending so much time with the magazine owners. It's almost like it's part of some sordid plan."

"Oh please." Liz pulled open the door, but before she could leave, Caroline spoke again.

"Just leave Daria alone," she said, her tone harsher than before. "She's had a tough time, and she doesn't need to be taken advantage of, okay?"

"Don't you mean leave Daria alone because you're desperate to get her back?" Liz said scornfully, pausing on the threshold.

Caroline didn't respond. Liz smirked. "See you back at the table," she said, and let the bathroom door close behind her.

13

Finally, after seven endless courses, dinner ended. Daria paid the bill and called a car. In one Uber ride, Liz would be free.

When the car arrived, Caroline kissed Katherine and Daria on the cheeks and left without saying a word to Liz. This car was smaller than the last one, with only one row of seats. Daria gallantly climbed into the middle. Liz hesitated for a moment before sliding in next to her, so close that she could feel Daria's body heat against her side. They reached to buckle their seatbelts at the same time, and Liz's fingers bumped against the back of Daria's hand. She pulled back and let Daria go first.

"I wish you'd quit this nonsense and get back together with Caroline already," Katherine said before the car had even pulled away from the curb.

Daria sighed. "We're not getting back together," she said. "I wish you'd stop encouraging her."

"She adores you and she's perfect. I don't see why not."

"We're just . . . not right together."

Liz looked out the window, trying to fade into the background. It was only nine, but she was exhausted. She also couldn't remember how many cocktails she'd downed.

They turned left, and Daria's body slid into Liz's. When the car straightened, Daria didn't move away. Liz sat very still. She could feel Daria's shoulder against hers. Daria's leg, warm and solid, was pressed against hers from knee to hip. Was Daria trying to give her aunt plenty of space? Or was she leaning into Liz on purpose?

Tentatively, Liz let her right leg relax into Daria's. Daria didn't move away.

So, not an accident, then.

As Liz was debating whether she should try to make herself one with the car door or let herself slide closer to Daria, the car pulled up to the house. Liz got out quickly, grateful to have the choice made for her. It was the right decision, Liz told herself as she climbed the front stairs. Flirting with Daria was a terrible idea, even if Daria was flirting back—no, *especially* if Daria was flirting back.

Inside, Liz went to get a glass of water. She could hear Daria saying good night to her aunt in the hall. As Liz was filling her glass at the sink, Daria came into the kitchen.

"Good idea," she said, getting a glass of her own. "I always drink too much when I'm with my aunt."

"I wonder why."

Daria came over to the sink and filled her glass. "I'm sorry about dinner," she said. "Aunt Katherine can be difficult. But I owe her a lot." Daria leaned against the counter, staring into her water glass. She looked tired. Her hair was ruffled now, as if she'd run her hands through it.

Liz didn't say anything. Half of her knew that spending more time with Daria tonight was a bad idea, but the other half, the shamelessly gossipy half, was desperate to find out more.

"She's the only family I really have," Daria said. "My

parents—we don't talk. I came out in college. I cut my hair short and started dressing differently, and I couldn't exactly hide it anymore. So I told them. And they stopped paying tuition. They didn't want to pay for me to go to 'lesbian school.'" She drank some of her water. "I was going to take out loans, but my aunt stepped in. She paid for college and let me stay here during breaks. That's what she was talking about at dinner."

She looked up. The kitchen was dark, lit only by the moon shining through the window and the soft light from the hall.

"I'm so sorry," Liz said. "That must have been awful." Liz had always known that she was lucky to have a family who supported her no matter what, but she had never felt it quite as strongly as she did in this moment. She refilled her glass of water for something to do. Going to the sink brought her closer to Daria, though, who was still leaning on the counter. So close that Liz could have reached out and taken Daria's hand.

Liz should go to bed. She should say good night and rush up the stairs. She should brush her teeth or call Jane or scroll through Instagram. Anything besides staying in this dark kitchen, sneaking glances at Daria by moonlight.

At the very least, Liz told herself, she should take a couple of steps back, because she could feel herself and Daria shifting incrementally closer in a way that felt inevitable.

"It's okay," Daria said softly, still looking at Liz.

"It's not." Liz turned off the faucet. She didn't move away.

Daria shrugged. "No. I guess it's not. But what was it that your photographer said? Focus on the potential joy rather than the potential pain?" She gave a very small smile. "I'm glad you're here."

"I—thank you." Liz's heart was beating very fast. She held on to the edge of the sink, feeling a little dizzy. "Thank you for helping me get here."

"Any time," Daria said. "I mean it." She put her glass down on the countertop with a little clink, then straightened up. The kitchen started to feel rather small. She took a step closer.

The glass of water in Liz's hands felt slippery. Liz focused on holding on to it, staring at the condensation dripping down its sides. She could feel her pulse beating in her throat and a bloodless tingle in her fingers. She swallowed. In her peripheral vision, she saw Daria take another step closer.

"Liz," Daria said. Her voice was soft. When Liz looked up, their faces were inches apart. She set her water glass down.

Daria reached up and rested her hand against the side of Liz's cheek. Liz stopped breathing. Hairs rose on the back of her neck. She could actually feel the shiver travel through her entire body, ending between her legs.

Liz put her hands on Daria's shoulders. They felt reassuringly steady under Liz's shaky fingers. Slowly, she moved her hands to the back of Daria's neck, into her hair. And then she pulled Daria close and kissed her.

Daria kissed back, so softly that it made Liz's chest ache, so she opened Daria's lips with her tongue and pulled their bodies closer together. Daria pressed Liz against the counter. With one firm hand, she turned Liz's chin to the side. Her lips brushed lightly across Liz's neck. Liz dug her nails in and Daria bit down, hard enough that Liz moaned.

Liz was kissing Daria Fitzgerald. Arrogant, annoying, sexy Daria, with her dark eyes and sharp cheekbones and tailored suits. It was a mistake, Liz knew that, but the mistake was already made now, wasn't it? Liz might as well keep going. Especially because she didn't think she could bring herself to stop.

Liz pushed off Daria's blazer and let it drop to the ground. She put her mouth back against Daria's and started undoing shirt buttons and bra clasps. Their hips ground together. When Liz reached the last button, she pushed Daria back so she could take in the view: her slim hips and surprisingly large breasts and the visible curve of muscle in her upper arms. Somehow Daria was even sexier with her clothes off.

Liz raised a hand and ran her nails lightly down Daria's chest. Daria groaned—a small, involuntary sound of desire that turned Liz on so much she could actually feel herself getting wet. Liz tugged off her shirt. She hesitated, then took off her bra, too.

Daria's eyes traveled over her, and Liz's nipples stiffened. Her hips were wider and her stomach was softer than Daria's, but for some reason, she didn't feel self-conscious. Not with Daria looking at her like that, like she was starving and Liz was dessert.

Daria bent down and flicked her tongue across one of Liz's nipples. Liz gasped and buried her hand in Daria's hair, pulling her closer. With her other hand she reached down and opened the button of Daria's pants. Then she slowly unzipped them and slipped her hand inside.

God, Daria was wet. Liz ran her fingers lightly over Daria's clit, and Daria's entire body tensed. Liz kissed her hard while her fingers worked, slow and soft at first, then faster. Daria moaned into her mouth, sending a flush of pleasure across Liz's entire body.

"Take off your pants," Liz said. The confidence in her voice surprised her. Daria obeyed at once, pulling off her light blue boxer briefs too, and then pressed herself back against Liz, eager. Liz pushed her against the counter.

"Can I?" Liz asked, and when Daria nodded, Liz slid two fingers inside her, groaning at how hot and slick it felt, at the feel of textured ridges transitioning to smoothness under her fingertips as her hand sank deeper and deeper. Liz hooked her fingers and moved them back and forth, while using her thumb to circle Daria's clit. Daria arched backward, holding on to Liz's shoulders for balance as she rocked her hips against Liz's hand.

"Oh my God," Daria whispered. "Oh my God." She sounded completely undone, feral almost, her voice raw in a way Liz had never heard before. Liz kissed her, thrusting faster, and she felt Daria start to shudder around her hand. She kept going, and Daria shifted forward, digging her teeth into Liz's shoulder, her breath hot and wet on Liz's skin. Liz felt Daria clench around her hand again and again in time with their heartbeats and a wave of wetness slicked her palm.

Liz pulled back, breathing hard. Daria's eyes were wide and vulnerable, but as Liz watched, her expression shifted into something more like hunger. She reached for Liz's pants and roughly pulled them off, then lifted Liz onto the countertop. The cold sent goosebumps across Liz's exposed skin. Then Daria dipped her tongue between Liz's legs and Liz stopped caring about the cold counter. She stopped thinking. She stopped feeling anything except her back against a cabinet and Daria's tongue. She gripped Daria's head with her thighs, moving her hips forward and back, and Daria reached up to pinch her nipples. Liz took one of Daria's fingers into her mouth, then two, sucking hungrily to keep herself from screaming as she came.

When the orgasm subsided, Liz's legs were shaking so hard she worried she'd fall off the counter. But Daria stood up, tucked Liz's head against her shoulder, and put her arms around her, keeping them steady. Liz leaned into the embrace, breathing in the sea-breeze scent of Daria's cologne, feeling both of their heartbeats gradually start to slow. She felt strangely safe there. Protected. Cared for. Held.

And then the arms encircling her body slowly slid away. Daria took one step back, then two. She turned around and braced her arms against the sink.

Without Daria's arms around her, Liz suddenly realized that she was freezing. The countertop underneath her was absorbing all of her body heat, and her butt was absurdly uncomfortable. But she didn't move, afraid of breaking up the moment. She wanted Daria to come back and make her feel the way she'd felt five seconds ago: her body satisfied, her mind quiet, enjoying the warm comfort of another person pressed against her. She didn't want to deal with reality just yet.

Daria's hands gripped the edges of the sink so tightly they turned white. "Shit," she said.

So apparently Daria was not on the same page in regard to avoiding reality.

Daria yanked open the cabinet under the sink, crouched down, and started rifling through it.

"Are you okay?" Liz asked, even though she could tell from Daria's jerky movements that she wasn't.

Daria ignored her. She grabbed something and stood up. When she turned around, Liz could see that it was cleaning spray.

"Can you—" Daria said, gesturing with the bottle toward the counter.

"Oh," Liz said. "Yeah."

She jumped down and stood to the side, her arms crossed protectively in front of her bare chest. Daria sprayed the counter in a wide area around where she had been sitting, then held up the bottle to read the side.

"What are you doing?" Liz asked.

"It says let sit for thirty seconds before wiping."

"No, I mean—" Liz shook her head, trying to clear out the

intense, sexy feelings and catch up to what was going on. "Why are you disinfecting the counter right now?"

Daria's face flushed. "My aunt cooks *food* in here," she said. "And we just—" Her face turned an even darker red. "What if she'd come down? And those doors are *glass*. What if one of her neighbors saw us?"

She yanked a wad of paper towels off of the roll and started aggressively cleaning the counter. Like if she washed it hard enough, she could erase what they'd done. "What was I thinking?" she spat out, more to herself than to Liz.

Liz stood frozen. One part of her wanted to laugh, watching the usually polished Daria scrub a kitchen counter stark naked. The other part, though—a larger part—wanted to cry.

And Liz was *not* going to cry in front of Daria.

Desperately, Liz turned to the pile of clothes on the floor, trying to figure out what belonged to her. She put her shirt on, not bothering with her bra. She needed to get out of here. She pulled on her pants. Then she hesitated, her underwear balled in her fist. Daria was still scrubbing.

"Well," she said. "I guess I'll . . . go upstairs, then."

Daria didn't look up.

"You want to get up early tomorrow, right?" Liz said. "To beat traffic?"

Daria made a grunting noise. Liz took a tentative step toward the stairs.

"I'll see you at six thirty, then," Liz said. "Bright and early. Early bird gets the worm or whatever."

Daria still hadn't said anything. Liz took another step backward, waiting to see if she would stop Liz from leaving. But she just kept scrubbing.

"Great," Liz said. "Awesome. See you then."

And then, before the first tears could fall from her eyes, Liz turned around and fled up the stairs.

14

iz didn't sleep. She couldn't. Her brain was a tumbling vortex. Liz kept trying to get her thoughts in order, but all she could think about was the look on Daria's face as she'd scrubbed that counter. She had looked . . . furious with herself.

Well, was that so surprising? It wasn't like Daria had made any secret of thinking Liz wasn't good enough for her.

Except . . . Liz had felt like they'd shared a few nice moments. Their conversation after Liz had spilled her drink down that guy's back at Margarita Monday. The way Daria had talked about her blog on the beach. And on the ride over, sharing their thoughts about gender and self-doubt. Plus, she had rented the car so Liz could interview the photographer. Or at least, that's what Liz had thought. What if Daria really *had* just wanted to practice driving? What if this had all been a drunken mistake, and Daria wasn't even attracted to Liz at all?

With a cringe, she recalled Daria's bitter, cold voice when she'd asked herself, *What was I thinking?* It was a good question. What had *Liz* been thinking?

She hadn't been thinking. That much was obvious.

Liz's brain played her a helpful montage: Daria calling her an asinine fluff-piece writer; Daria scoffing when Liz pitched her article ideas; Daria's horrified face when Caroline implied that she and Liz might be together; Daria, looking like she wanted to punch Weston at Margarita Monday.

Oh God. *Weston.* How could Liz have done this to Weston? Daria had ruined Weston's entire life. How could Liz have looked past that and had sex with her? No wonder Weston didn't want to date seriously. Liz was a selfish, impulsive mess who couldn't be trusted. Wasn't Jane always telling Liz that she needed to think things through before acting? Liz could see Jane's judgmental, disappointed face now. How was Liz going to explain this to her?

Well . . . maybe Liz wouldn't tell her. Would that be such a big deal? It wasn't like this was ever going to happen again. It wouldn't even really change anything between Liz and Daria. They'd disliked each other before; they'd continue disliking each other now. Besides, Jane spent all her time with Bailey now, so why should Liz tell her every little thing that happened?

At four A.M., after hours of yelling at herself, Liz got up. As quietly as possible, she put her stuff back into her duffel bag. She couldn't spend five hours in the car with Daria today. She couldn't stand to listen to whatever excuse Daria would give to try to let Liz down easy.

Liz had been let down easy by too many people over the last few years. People who claimed that they weren't ready for a relationship, then three weeks later posted Instagram photos of their new girlfriend. People who ghosted after weeks of messaging on dating apps. People whose faces fell when Liz walked into the bar for their first date. People who said it wasn't Liz, it was them, and people who said Liz just wasn't what they were looking for, and people who said Liz was just *too much* for them and they couldn't handle it.

Liz was always too much.

Liz would have sent a text, but she didn't have Daria's number. She thought about writing a note, but she didn't want Daria's aunt to find it. Instead, Liz sent Daria an email: *Had to get back to New York earlier than expected today, so decided to catch a bus. Thank you for the ride!*

She hesitated before pressing send. She tried to imagine what Daria would feel, reading this in a few hours. Was the email too cold? Would it hurt Daria's feelings to wake up and find Liz gone?

Then Liz remembered Daria's face as she had scrubbed the counter. How horrified she had seemed at what had just happened. How she hadn't even *looked* at Liz, even though their bodies had been pressed against each other minutes before. Liz was being ridiculous. Daria's only emotion in the morning would be relief.

She hit send. Then, as quietly as she could, Liz gathered up her stuff and crept out of the house.

.   .   .

Liz spent the entire next week in a state of nauseous dread, panic zipping up her spine every time she heard the office door open. But Daria never showed. She hadn't responded to Liz's email, either. Clearly, Daria was avoiding her.

Liz tried her best to put the whole thing out of her mind. But it was hard. She'd be standing at the Page Printer (named, of course, after Elliot Page), and her traitor brain would suddenly drift into an image of Daria's head tilted back against a cabinet, her mouth open as Liz's hand moved inside her. Or she'd be in the Kiyoko Kitchen, waiting for coffee to brew and unnecessarily wasting time, and she would remember how it had felt to rest her head on Daria's shoulder, her body cradled in Daria's arms as their breathing started to slow.

She didn't tell any of her roommates what had happened, answering their questions about how bad it was to be stuck in the car with Daria by forcing out laughs and changing the subject. It wasn't difficult not to tell Jane, who was still at Bailey's almost every night. And Weston still seemed mad that Liz had canceled their plans to go to Boston and "hang out with Daria," not quite ghosting Liz but not quite *not*-ghosting her, either, which was just as well because Liz didn't know how to face her after what had happened.

To distract herself, Liz focused on writing. And not just her article on Moira Campbell, either. Liz was actually sticking to the vow she'd made after the interview to try writing a novel. She had written up a loose outline about a bullied queer teenager in a small town, who was waiting to turn eighteen so she could run away to New York, and she wrote a little bit every night. It was slow going—it wasn't like her articles or her blog, where Liz could just get into a groove and let words flow. Instead she had to focus on every word or her tone would start to slip, becoming flippant and casual. After years of writing fluff pieces, it felt like she'd lost her serious writing muscle. But she forced herself to keep working anyway. Surely, over time, with practice, the writing would get easier.

Unfortunately, Liz couldn't avoid Daria forever, especially since they had an all-staff meeting a week after the road trip. It would be better to get it over with, though, Liz decided. Once she saw Daria a couple times and it was clear that there were absolutely no romantic feelings between them, Liz would be able to stop obsessing about their night together.

On the morning of the meeting, Liz spent twice as long

getting dressed, finally picking out a professional-looking women's blazer over a tank top and black skinny jeans. It was an outfit that Liz *knew* she looked good in. A simple, easy, completely femme outfit. She didn't exactly feel like herself in it, but she figured it was more important to look hot in this instance. She was planning to ignore Daria, of course, but she didn't want Daria to look at Liz and feel like she'd made a colossal mistake.

In the Rosie Room, she sat with Katie and Lydia, pretending to listen to their conversation while her pulse leapt every time someone opened the door. What if Daria said something about what had happened between them, in front of everyone? No, of course she wouldn't do that. But what if Daria asked Liz to stay behind after the meeting? What if she'd been unable to stop thinking about that night, just like Liz? What if she saw Liz, in her professional outfit and makeup, and decided she had to have her?

The door opened, interrupting Liz's spiraling thoughts. This time, it was Daria. A wave of something painful— Nerves? Guilt? Regret?—swept over Liz, and her neutral expression slipped. But Daria stomped directly to the head of the table without looking at anyone and started connecting her laptop to the projector. Liz saw people exchange glances across the room: Daria seemed *pissed*.

She queued up a slideshow titled "State of the *Nether Fields*," then straightened up and looked around the room, frowning. When her eyes found Liz, her expression darkened into an unmistakable glare.

Liz blinked rapidly, willing her face not to turn red. Of course Daria hadn't spent the past week dreaming about Liz. Clearly, she was still furious with herself for what had happened. *Fine.* They'd go back to hating each other. That was perfectly okay with Liz. She crossed her arms as Daria began to present their latest numbers. She seemed to be taking out her feelings on her slide-changer button, sending an aggressive *click* through the room every time she showed them a new chart.

Despite Daria's gloomy presentation style, it turned out that operating costs were down, ad revenue was up, and audience numbers were growing. Liz's coworkers smiled at each other as Daria went through the stats. When Daria presented a slide listing how many new advertising partners they'd secured in the past month, the room even broke into a spontaneous round of applause for Lydia, who stood up and bowed.

Daria, however, didn't seem pleased by the magazine's change in fortune. Her face stayed stormy as she explained that the improvement was insufficient, because the magazine was still losing money every month. Everyone's smiles slowly faded as Daria outlined the projections of where their numbers needed to be in order to stay solvent.

"I know it's hard to hear that we're still in the red," Bailey said, joining Daria at the front of the room. "But the progress we've made in such a short time, thanks to your hard work, is outstanding. Which leads me to a very exciting announcement."

"Bailey," Daria said in an undertone. "We agreed that we needed more time before deciding whether or not to—"

"As the majority owner, it's my call," Bailey said, cutting her off. Liz's curiosity was piqued. She'd never heard Bailey disagree with Daria before. "I am thrilled to let you all know that we've been invited to apply for a Nielsen Independent Media Grant."

She beamed. Liz looked around to see if anyone had any idea what she was talking about. Jane looked encouraged and Charlotte was nodding thoughtfully, but everyone else looked confused. Behind Bailey, Daria scowled and sat down in one of the conference room chairs.

"This is a large onetime grant, meant to help a publication set itself up for long-term success by investing in new growth strategies. Now that the *NF* is owned by private individuals, not a large media conglomerate, we're eligible."

Behind Bailey, Daria disconnected her laptop from the projector and started putting it back in its case. Her lips were pressed so firmly together that the color was leaching out of them.

"Right now," Bailey went on, "we're paying Heather Media to continue using their operating systems, but this grant would cover the cost of building our own. It would also enable us to update our website to make our interface more appealing to readers, increase advertising opportunities, finance the kind of meaningful content we want to see more of, and most importantly, avoid layoffs. In short, we'd be able to set up the *NF* for a long, successful future."

The room broke out into excited murmurs.

"*Please* don't get your hopes up," Daria said, shoving her laptop case in her bag. "This grant is extremely prestigious and competitive, and the application is immensely time-consuming. Which is why"—she shot an annoyed glance at Bailey—"I don't think it's a good use of our time at this stage."

Bailey sighed. "Daria's a pessimist," she said. "But, I will say, between you and me"—she winked at them—"I spoke to a friend of mine who's involved with the organization, and he thinks we have a strong chance of winning."

Katie and Lydia nudged each other, grinning. Finn bounced eagerly in their seat. Charlotte was writing furiously in her notebook, probably outlining plans for the magazine's long, happy future.

"Daria is right about one thing, though," Bailey said, calling their attention back. "Applying for this grant will take a lot of work. Over the next four weeks, we'll need to put together a comprehensive proposal, including financials, content, marketing, ad plans, and creative vision, so I'll be calling on many of you for help. As for the rest of you, Nielsen will be keeping a close eye on the magazine, so now is the time to drill down even harder on the great work you're already doing."

Bailey dismissed them with a peppy "All right, everyone! Let's get to it!" while behind her, Daria looked murderous, and the staff started flooding toward the doors. Liz avoided walking next to anyone as she headed toward the kitchen.

It felt like the night of the closing party all over again, when Charlotte had burst into their apartment with the news that they'd been bought. Everyone seemed thrilled about this grant news. Liz knew that she should be, too. She wanted the next generation of queers to have the *Nether Fields* to look to for advice and guidance. She just didn't necessarily want to be the one providing that guidance.

She was pouring herself a cup of coffee when Lydia came in. They clapped Liz on the back, making her spill.

"Sorry!" Lydia said, giggling. "I'm just excited."

Liz sighed as she wiped up the coffee. "We haven't won the grant yet."

"Yeah, but you heard Bailey. We're shoo-ins. Besides, how could any foundation not want to support *us*?" Lydia struck a pose, framing their face with their hands. Liz couldn't help smiling.

"That should be our whole application," she said. "Fifty pictures of your face."

"Honestly, we would win." Liz rolled her eyes. "Cheer up, Lizzie," they said. "The *NF* is thriving. Our jobs are secure. All thanks to Jane and her powers of seduction. Just like we planned." They made devil horns with their fingers and cackled like some sort of supervillain.

Liz laughed. "Just like *you* planned," she said. "I want no part of your evil schemes."

"We should take up a collection, get her an Edible Arrangement or something. 'Thank you for securing our jobs with your pussy-eating skills. Someone had to do it.'"

"Ew, ew, ew," Liz said, holding her hand up to stop Lydia. "Too far. I am leaving." She took a sip from her coffee as she headed out of the kitchen. Unfortunately, she was so focused on not burning her mouth that she walked directly into someone as she rounded the corner, splashing coffee everywhere for the second time and stumbling. Two arms shot out to steady her. Liz looked up. It was Daria.

Of course it was.

"Oh!" Liz squeaked. "Sorry! These corners are such a hazard. I can't tell you how many times that's happened. Which, actually, maybe says more about me than the corners." The words were already out of her mouth before she remembered that she was supposed to be acting cold and aloof.

Daria looked like she was going to say something, but then her expression hardened and she dropped her arms. She stepped past Liz and hurried down the hall without a backward glance.

Liz watched her go, indignant. So they weren't even going to pretend to be civil with each other? Well, fine. Whatever. It didn't matter to Liz.

She stomped her way back to her cubicle. After all, she had asinine fluff pieces to write.

15

Over the next two weeks, the atmosphere in the office became increasingly frantic. Bailey had Jane, Charlotte, and Mary, the head of finance, working on the grant proposal almost constantly, which meant that everyone had to pick up extra work to cover their usual jobs. On top of that, Daria would only do the bare minimum to help with the application because she thought it was a waste of time, so Bailey kept having to ask Lydia, as the most tech savvy, to help them put together various complex budget reports. Daria's unwillingness to pitch in made her even less popular with the NF staff than before. Everyone assumed she was trying to sabotage their chances of getting the grant because she wanted the magazine to close. Personally, Liz couldn't help but wonder if Daria just didn't want to spend any more time than necessary near Liz and the constant reminder of the night she'd let her standards slip so low.

It wasn't only the grant proposal committee that was busy, either. Everyone seemed to be taking Bailey's words to heart and upping their game. Tara launched a brand-new social media campaign to capitalize on their increasing engagement rates. Daniela, their designer, designed snazzy logos and adorable graphics to spruce up their look, and Finn stayed late incorporating them into the website. Katie started a series of "What Does the *Nether Fields* Mean to You?" articles, cowritten with various readers, to activate and engage with their fan base. Everyone was on a mission.

No one seemed to need Liz's expertise for the proposal, however, so she focused on her article on Moira, which Charlotte wanted to run the first week of August, since it was usually a slow content month for them. Liz wanted it to be perfect. Even though Moira didn't feel like she *needed* recognition, Liz still hoped that if she did this article justice, it would get her some.

Liz started working longer hours than she ever had, trying to get every sentence right. By the time she sent the article to Charlotte for review, Liz felt like it was good. Really fucking good. She had agonized over every line, and she was sure it was the best thing she'd ever written.

On the day the article went live, Liz kept trying to distract herself so she wouldn't check her email and Twitter every five seconds. It took time for things to go viral, she knew that. But she couldn't resist. That entire week, she refreshed her inbox constantly, waiting for news that her article had been shared by some huge celebrity or that a museum had committed to displaying Moira's photographs for the first time.

A few notes did arrive—the kind of heartfelt emails that reporters dream about, telling Liz the article had made them feel seen and comforted. A few said that reading Moira's advice had given them the courage to finally take the leap into pursuing their own dreams. Liz read those emails over and over until her eyes got teary. She printed them out and pinned them to the wall of her cubicle.

But after a week, the emails stopped coming. The article didn't go viral or fire people up to support Moira. Instead, it got slightly fewer reads than Liz's average quiz. Like all of Liz's listicles, it was forgotten. Just like Moira would be forgotten. Just like Liz would be forgotten.

After two weeks, Liz stopped checking the article's readership stats every day. She tried to tell herself that it didn't matter, that Moira had never cared about recognition anyway. But she couldn't help wondering if another writer could have made the article work. She tried to distract herself by working more on her novel, but her heart wasn't in it anymore. Every time she reread a sentence, it seemed overwritten and pretentious. All she could see were all the ways her writing fell short. Liz was officially in a slump.

She wasn't the only one. As head writer, Jane was drafting most of the content for the grant proposal. She was reluctant to pass off her usual articles to anyone else, though, which meant she was trying to juggle her full workload, too. She started spending late nights in the office, and whenever anyone tried to talk to her, she would shout "No time!" without looking up. Liz often poked fun at Jane for losing things, but the more stressed she got, the more it seemed like her things went missing several times a day. One day she even spent five minutes searching all the meeting rooms for her sweater, which she turned out to be wearing. Liz wasn't sure how long Jane could last like this.

Jane came home one night, well past nine P.M., and walked straight into Liz's room to crash face-first on her bed, groaning loudly into the comforter.

"Yeah?" Liz said, putting her laptop on the floor so she could rub Jane's shoulders. She was glad for the interruption—she'd been trying to write, but she kept getting frustrated and opening Instagram instead.

"I'm so tired," Jane moaned.

"Jesus. Your shoulders are so freaking tense." Liz dug her thumbs into a knot in Jane's back.

"I feel like I haven't slept in weeks," Jane said into the bed.

"Well, the application goes in this week, right?" Liz said. "After that, things will calm down."

"Yeah." Jane turned her head to the side. "But also . . . I think something's up with Bailey."

"What do you mean?" Liz leaned against the wall and pulled her knees against her chest as Jane rolled over. She'd missed this. Just the two of them, best friends, talking in her bed.

"I mean, I've been spending all this time with her and the grant committee working on the proposal. But she hasn't invited me to her place once in the past two weeks. She keeps saying she's exhausted, between the grant writing and summer being the busiest season for real estate, and I am, too, but it's not just that. Sometimes it seems like she's avoiding me, even when we're in the same room—less eye contact, no hand squeezing under the table." Jane took a deep breath. "We've gotten dinner a few times after work, but she's seemed distracted. Even kind of cold."

Liz considered this, surprised. "Maybe you've been working together so much that it's hard to snap out of that mode and just be girlfriends."

"Maybe. Hey, why is my Harry pillow in here?" Jane picked up a throw pillow which showed gold sequins if you brushed it one way and Harry Styles's face if you brushed it the other.

"You left it here two weeks ago when we watched *Pariah*."

"Ah. Gotcha." Jane pulled the pillow into her lap and started running her fingers over the sequins. "Anyway, I'm worried something is up."

"Just talk to her," Liz said. "The application will be done soon, and you'll both be less stressed. Before you know it, you'll be having tons of hot sex and making heart eyes at each other across conference room tables again."

Jane rolled her eyes but said, "Okay, okay. You're right." She held up the pillow to show Liz her masterpiece—she'd brushed the sequins so that Harry's face shone against a background of gold. "Even if something is up, I'd rather know about it than tiptoe around like this. I'll text her now."

"There you go," Liz said, propping the pillow up in a position of honor at the head of her bed. "Just say you miss her and want to reconnect. You two have been all over each other for the past two months. There's no way you're breaking up now."

16

They broke up.

Liz was out with Weston, getting drinks at a bar in Bushwick, when she got Jane's text. She and Weston were being cute and flirty—pressing their knees together, touching hands across the table in between sips—and it felt incredible. Liz had decided to do her best to forget that Daria existed and, so far, she was succeeding. She'd avoided Weston's questions about the Boston trip, and things felt good between them again. She didn't want to ruin the moment, so she ignored her phone when it started to buzz in her pocket. But when Weston went to the bathroom, she saw two missed calls from Jane and a single text message: *We broke up.*

Liz read the message three times, not comprehending. At first, she didn't believe it. How could Bailey and Jane, the most U-Haul-y couple in New York City, have broken up?

But then it hit. What didn't matter was how they could have broken up or why. What mattered was Jane.

Where are you? Liz texted.

On my way home, Jane sent back. *She called me an Uber.*

Liz hated that, with every fiber of her being.

"I'm so sorry," she said to Weston when she returned from the bathroom. "I have to go. Jane and her girlfriend broke up."

"What? You're leaving?"

"I'm sorry." Liz grabbed Weston's hand and squeezed it. "Can we see each other again soon?"

"This was supposed to be our night," Weston said, pulling her hand back.

"I know, and I've had an amazing time, but Jane needs me. I'm really sorry."

Weston twisted her face into a pout. "I thought you missed me."

"I do! I have! So let's get together soon. Okay?"

Weston pursed her mouth to the side and didn't say anything. Liz kissed her on the cheek and left, feeling torn. Maybe she should have stayed. Maybe by leaving she had permanently ruined everything, and Weston would never want to talk to her again. But there was no way Liz wasn't going to show up for Jane in her moment of need.

When Liz got off the subway, she jogged home as quickly as her Doc Martens would allow, stopping at the fancy bodega for salt-and-vinegar chips, gummi worms, and mango White Claw. All of Jane's favorites.

She found Jane sitting on the ground, leaning against her bed. She wasn't crying, but she clearly had been.

"Oh, Jane." Liz dropped her bag of snacks and got on the floor, too, putting her arms around her friend. Jane leaned into her and started sobbing. Liz waited for Jane's breathing to settle before she asked what happened.

"I don't know," Jane said, her head still against Liz's shoulder. "I don't know." She breathed in with a wet sound, sat up, and accepted a tissue from Liz. "I texted her, saying I missed her and wanted to talk things out. And she said yes, to come over tonight. So, I went. And—" She blew her nose. "From the moment I walked in, I could tell something was wrong. She was all quiet." Jane took a second to breathe. "So, I was like, 'What's wrong? You're not breaking up with me, are you?' as a joke. And—"

Tears filled her eyes. Liz rubbed her back. "And she *looked* at me, with this horrified expression. And I knew."

"But," Liz said. "But. That doesn't make any sense. She's obsessed with you. She invites you over, like, every night. She texts you all day long."

"Not lately," Jane said, blowing her nose again. "Lately she barely responds at all. I should have seen this coming. I'm so stupid."

"No," Liz said fiercely. "You are not stupid. There was no warning at all. I mean, how did she explain herself?"

"She said—" Jane's voice hitched. "That I'm great but it was just—not right to be dating someone she employed. And she shouldn't have crossed that line in the first place."

"What the fuck? She's been our boss this entire time. Why would that start to matter now?"

"And." Jane took a deep breath. "She said she didn't think things were working out anyway, so it was better to end it now."

Liz stared, thunderstruck. "*What?*" she said. "You were literally planning a trip to Paris. That doesn't make any sense."

"You should have seen her," Jane said, fresh tears rolling down her cheeks. "She was like a completely different person. All cold and rehearsed. She barely even looked at me."

Liz put her arms around Jane again. She didn't know what to say. She didn't know how to make this better. Bailey and Jane had seemed so happy. Liz had thought this seemed like *it*. She didn't understand how or why it had all ended so suddenly. And, clearly, neither did Jane.

And then an idea started to form in Liz's head. A fiery parasite of fury, worming its way into her brain. Breaking up with a woman she seemed to adore, out of nowhere, coldly and without explanation? That didn't seem like Bailey at all. But it *did* seem like Daria.

Daria, who'd never thought buying the *Nether Fields* was a good idea. Daria, who was looking for every excuse to tear her friend away from the magazine. Daria, who had gotten Weston expelled out of jealousy over Bailey.

The more she thought about it, the more certain she felt. Daria had been meddling in Bailey's love life again.

Liz didn't mention this theory to Jane. Not yet. For now, the priority was cheering Jane up. Liz spent a while abusing Bailey for being an asshole, but Jane kept jumping in to defend Bailey, so she pivoted to giving a long pep talk instead, focusing on how wonderful Jane was and how she would find someone even better. Then she filled Jane with snacks and stayed in her room watching old *Fresh Prince* episodes until well past two A.M., when they both fell asleep in Jane's bed.

The next day, Liz felt exhausted, dehydrated, and greasy. Jane called in sick to work. Before Liz left, Jane made her promise that if Bailey was in the office, Liz wouldn't say anything to her. Liz promised with her fingers crossed behind her back. She had every intention of confronting Bailey at the first opportunity. This breakup made no sense, and Liz wanted to get to the bottom of it.

But Bailey wasn't in the office that day. Neither was Daria. In fact, neither of them showed up that week at all, now that the grant committee had finished up the proposal and sent it in. Which was something of a relief. Jane kept insisting that she was ready to see Bailey, but Liz was pretty sure she would immediately burst into tears.

Everyone at the *Nether Fields* knew about the breakup, of

course. Jane had tried to keep it quiet, but Lydia saw Jane crying in the apartment, and once Lydia knew anything, the entire staff did, too. Soon, everyone had assured Jane that they were on her side and now hated Bailey, which only made Jane more miserable.

By the following week, Jane had stopped crying at random times during the day. She still carried the general energy of Eeyore everywhere she went, but she seemed a little more resigned.

But Bailey didn't come in that week, either. Liz wished she'd grow up and act a little more responsible. She was the owner of the magazine, after all. What had happened to basic professionalism?

Daria, however, came in twice. The first time, she took several boxes of paperwork into the Janelle Room and barricaded herself inside for three hours. The second time, she met with Charlotte for fifteen minutes and then left. Both times, Jane was on edge, constantly looking up at the door to see if Bailey might be coming to join her friend. And both times, Liz spent the duration in a violent argument with herself, trying to decide if she should confront Daria.

In the end, Liz decided not to. She had no proof that Daria was behind this breakup, just a strong feeling. She also didn't want Daria to think that Liz was upset because Daria had pointedly ignored her after sleeping with her. Because she obviously wasn't. Instead, Liz focused on her articles during the day and on painstakingly trying to force out more of her novel at night.

Someday, though, Daria would get what was coming to her. Liz would find a better job or write a bestselling book and leave the magazine. And on the way out, she was going to give Daria the most epic exit speech she could imagine.

17

The magazine's fiscal year ended in August, which meant their annual review meeting was always in early September. Usually, Charlotte brought in doughnuts, told them exactly how much money they'd lost, then ended the meeting by encouraging them to keep up the good work. This year, though, Bailey and Daria were in charge. It was time for Jane to see her ex.

The afternoon of the review, Liz walked with Jane—who looked fantastic in the red pantsuit she wore to interview politicians—to the Rosie Room, where they sat on one of the benches lining the walls. A few people greeted Charlotte when she arrived, but she didn't say much as she settled at the head of the table. Liz watched her. She seemed . . . off somehow. Now that Liz thought about it, she'd barely talked to Charlotte the past few weeks. Liz felt a small twinge of guilt for not realizing how stressful the grant proposal process must have been for Charlotte and made a mental promise to get lunch with her soon.

When the door opened again, the whole *NF* staff looked expectantly at Jane. Liz frowned at as many people as she could, trying to shame them into looking away. Jane, however, kept her poker face on, head held high, as Bailey came through the door.

The same couldn't be said for Bailey. She looked miserable, Liz noted with satisfaction. There was a generally unkempt air about her, like she hadn't slept in days. Her eyes were red, her clothes were rumpled, and her posture was stooped. Her eyes immediately swept the room and found Jane. Normally, she bounced into every room with enthusiastic greetings, but today she didn't say a word, her footsteps slow and heavy as she approached the head of the table.

When she and Daria sat down, neither of them said anything right away. Instead, Daria shuffled through some papers, and Bailey looked at her hands. Finally, they looked at each other, and Bailey made a hopeless "you start" kind of face. An alarm pinged in Liz's brain.

Daria frowned at Bailey but spoke. "Thank you all for coming today," she said. "Normally, this meeting would be a review of the magazine's performance from the past year. Unfortunately, however, we have an announcement first." She glanced at Bailey, who nodded for her to continue. "The *Nether Fields* did not make it to the finalist stage for the Independent Media Grant."

A chorus of distressed *oh*s broke out across the room.

"Since *some* of us were counting on that grant money"—Daria side-eyed Bailey as she continued—"we worked it in to the plan for next fiscal year's budget. Without that financing, we won't have the cash flow to meet our operating expenses, let alone invest in updating systems.

"For that reason," Daria continued, looking at the stack of papers in front of her, "we have made the difficult decision to put the magazine up for sale."

Liz froze. Around her, everyone started exchanging

shocked glances. Charlotte looked at the table, not making eye contact with anyone.

"I know that's hard to hear," Daria said. "But this is a business decision based on numbers. So we're putting the magazine on the market for the next three months. At which point, if we haven't received an offer, the *Nether Fields* will be dissolved on December first."

"*What?*" Lydia said, interrupting. "You're shutting us down?"

Daria's face stayed hard and impassive. "No. We're taking ninety days to seek alternative investment opportunities."

Jane's hand found Liz's on the bench. They squeezed. Liz's heart was beating very hard.

"Bailey," Daria said. "You wanted to say something?"

Bailey swallowed, then said, "I am"—she paused, her voice hoarse and strained—"so sorry. I've loved every minute of working with you. You've all done . . . beautiful, important work. And you've worked so hard. It just—financially, we couldn't keep going. We want to, but we can't." She looked like she was fighting back tears, pleading with them to understand.

Liz wanted to scream at her. What good were her apologies when they were all probably going to lose their jobs?

Daria said a few more practical things—promising them all a severance package if no buyer materialized, explaining that they'd be able to prolong their health insurance while they were unemployed, if it came to that—and then she cleared her throat.

"I think Charlotte wanted to say a few words to you alone," she said, gesturing to Charlotte, who nodded. "But Bailey and I will be working in the conference room next door for the next hour. So please feel free to stop by if anyone has questions."

Was it Liz's imagination, or did Daria glance at her when she said that?

Daria stood. Bailey cast one last plaintive look at Jane, then followed her friend out the door. There was a brief silence as they shut it behind them, and then everyone started talking at once.

"I can't believe they would just—"

"How are we supposed to find a buyer?"

"Daria totally sabotaged our chances to get that grant! She never wanted us to get it."

"They've been here, what, five months? And they're already giving up?"

"We've been working our asses off, and now it's all for nothing?"

Liz stayed quiet, trying to process what was happening. Maybe it was seeing how hard everyone had worked lately, but she was surprised to find that, suddenly, the prospect of the *NF* closing filled her with panic. What were her friends going to do? What was *she* going to do? Sure, she'd written a few chapters of her novel, but her writing dream had seemed so much more doable before she'd actually started writing again. It wasn't like she was going to pull together some bestselling novel in three months.

"Everyone," Charlotte said over the chatter. They quieted down. "We've had a really good run. This magazine has lasted nineteen years, which is longer than anyone ever thought it would, including me. We're probably not going to find a buyer this time, but at least Bailey and Daria were able to give us a couple more months than we thought we had." She cleared her throat. "We've made a difference in people's lives. And, yes, this news is awful, especially when it seemed like things were just starting to turn around. But Daria isn't wrong; we won't be able to keep going without outside financing. I hope you're all proud of what you've done here. Because I know I am. We've shown queer people that they matter. Trans people and queers of color in particular. I hope you know how meaningful that is."

She cleared her throat again, and Liz was stunned to see Charlotte's eyes fill with tears. Liz had never seen Charlotte cry before. "I'm sorry I let you down," Charlotte continued, her voice breaking. "I'm sorry things are scary and uncertain and that we're going through this for the second time now. But I am so proud of every one of you."

Katie, who was closest, got up and put her arms around Charlotte. Finn followed, and soon everyone joined in, forming a massive, unstable group hug. Liz and Jane stretched their arms across the backs of the people in front of them. Then Lydia fell down and shrieked and the moment ended. Charlotte excused herself, saying she was going home for the night, and everyone broke off into groups, whispering and comforting one another.

"Did she do this because we broke up?" Jane said softly.

Liz shook her head. "If Bailey got rid of twenty jobs because she felt awkward after a breakup, then she's an asshole."

"She's definitely an asshole," Lydia said, jumping into their conversation. "They're only giving up because we didn't get that grant. Which Daria never wanted us to get in the first place. We can't just let this happen."

"What can we do?" Katie said. "Unless you know anyone with a couple million dollars to spare."

"We can fight this!" Lydia said. "We can tell our readers what's happening and get them invested. Maybe set up a Kickstarter campaign. We've all seen the numbers—our audience is growing. We have an opportunity now that we didn't have back in May."

"There's no way we'd raise enough money," Liz said. She didn't want to be a naysayer, but it seemed like a fantasy.

Their readers were young queer people trying to figure out how to survive in the world, not rich people with money to spare.

"So, let's start a petition!" Lydia said. "Raise awareness for the magazine and show potential buyers that we have a dedicated fan base supporting us."

"Why would people suddenly start caring now when they haven't this whole time?" Jane said. She sounded defeated.

"We're journalists," Lydia said. "We can *make* them care."

"We could write an article about the closing of lesbian spaces," Liz said slowly, warming to Lydia's enthusiasm. "And try to make it go viral."

Jane shook her head. "Lesbian spaces are always closing. They've *been* closing. That's not news."

"Well, what if we make it news?" Liz was getting excited now. "What if we write about how no one has given us a chance? How Heather Media tried to shut us down without actually trying to fix anything? How things were turning around under Bailey and Daria, and we just haven't had enough time to prove that there's a future here?"

"That could work," Lydia said. "We could use the article to pitch ourselves to potential buyers and put a link to the petition at the bottom." A couple of people nodded, looking thoughtful.

Jane seemed unconvinced. "We've been dumped by two owners in the past year. Who would invest now?"

"Come on, Jane," Liz said. "Let's just give this a shot. You're our head writer. You could do this better than anyone."

Jane crossed her arms. "I won't write an article criticizing my ex-girlfriend's management."

"Okay," Liz said. "That's fair. I'll write it."

"I don't want *anyone* to write it," Jane said.

"Let me at least draft something," Liz said. "I'll just talk about the history of the magazine and our impact on the LGBTQ+ community. You can read it and have veto power."

Others jumped in, volunteering to help with setting up the petition, making graphics for social, and finding advertising space. Eventually, Jane seemed to come around, even agreeing to reach out to some of the more high-profile people she'd interviewed over the years and ask if they would post about the petition.

"Okay," Lydia said, typing notes into their phone. "This is great stuff, guys. We can do this." They gathered everyone into a huddle like a soccer team, and everyone shouted, "*Nether Fields!*" as one.

Since it was nearly the end of the workday, everyone decided to continue planning at a bar nearby. Liz, wanting to get started on the article, returned to her desk, telling them she'd meet them later.

Liz's fingers flew across the keyboard. At first, she felt fired up by her coworkers' enthusiasm. Maybe Lydia was right. Maybe they had been too apathetic back when Heather Media put them up for sale in May, and they had more power than they realized. But the more she typed, the more a horrible, furious rage built inside her. Jane, Charlotte, Lydia, Katie, Finn—they all deserved more than being unceremoniously laid off like this. Daria's words played in a loop in her head: *This is a business decision based on numbers.* But this was affecting real people, not just numbers.

Liz smashed her fist down on her keyboard, sending a random spiral of characters across the page. She wanted to break something. Preferably a limb, preferably belonging to Bailey.

Liz stood up and kicked the corner of her desk with her Doc Martens. She took her sushi-shaped stress ball and threw it across the room. Then she sat back down on her chair so hard it rolled backward several feet and crashed into the wall of Katie's cubicle. She stayed there, head tipped back, her thoughts spiraling.

A sound came from the hallway. Liz started. She'd forgotten that Daria and Bailey were still here.

She stood up. *Don't go in there, Liz,* she told herself. *Don't be impulsive, like you always are.* She took a few steps toward the Janelle Room. What was the point in holding back now? Daria and Bailey could fire her if they wanted, and it wouldn't make much difference. After this, they would retreat into their expensive apartment buildings and their beach houses, and Liz would never see them again.

She was down the hall before she'd had a chance to think it over further. Through the glass door of the Janelle Room, Liz could see Daria sorting stacks of paper into different files and then adding them to large cardboard boxes. She looked like someone who was preparing to flee the scene of the crime.

Liz opened the door. "Where's Bailey?" She hadn't meant to shout the question, but she didn't care.

Daria looked up, a folder in her hand. "She left." She slowly put the folder down on the table. "I didn't realize anyone was still here."

Liz stepped inside and closed the door. It was the first time she'd been alone with Daria since Boston, she realized. The thought made her strangely nervous.

Daria's hair was ruffled, and the sleeves of her gray shirt were rolled up past the elbows. Liz wished suddenly that she'd thought to fix her hair before coming in here, but then squashed that idea. She didn't care what Daria thought.

Daria leaned against the table, waiting for Liz to say something. Now that Liz was here, she wasn't sure where to begin. In all her fantasies about this moment, Daria had been elitist and unrepentant, wearing a fancy suit and saying terrible things. Possibly even rubbing two gold coins

together like Scrooge McDuck. But this version of Daria—
exhausted, even defeated looking—was unsettlingly human.

"You," Liz said, trying to build up steam, "are an asshole."

She hoped Daria would say something rude back and give
Liz a reason to get worked up. But Daria just stood frozen
against the table. After a few seconds, she said, in a quiet
voice, "Oh."

"Oh?" Liz said, taking another step into the room. She
had imagined this moment feeling triumphant, but instead
she felt queasy. "That's it? You don't want to know why?"

Daria looked down at the cardboard box she'd been filling
with paperwork. "I guess—" she started to say, then cut off.
"I thought you came in here for something else."

"Something else? What—" Liz stopped abruptly. She'd
been about to ask what else she could have possibly come in
for when Daria looked up. Her eyes were wide, her face
dismayed, her expression unguarded.

Oh.

Liz put her hand on one of the chairs for balance. Unfortunately, it had wheels. Liz stumbled and Daria darted over,
putting a hand on her arm to steady her.

They stood there, frozen, Daria's hand on Liz's arm. Liz's
heartbeat seemed to intensify, becoming a shuddering bass
line. When Liz didn't pull away, Daria slid her hand slowly
down until their fingers wrapped together.

And then Daria kissed her. It wasn't like the kiss in Boston, when they'd pressed themselves against each other
hard and started immediately pulling at clothes. This time,
Daria kissed her slowly. She kissed Liz like she was trying to
tell her something. She kissed Liz like she was making a
promise.

Daria's other arm wrapped around Liz's waist, pulling
them together. Without conscious thought, Liz lifted her
hand to cup Daria's cheek, and Daria parted Liz's lips with

her tongue, letting out a soft moan that raised all the hairs on Liz's body. Liz hadn't been kissed like this in—had Liz *ever* been kissed like this?

And then, to her embarrassment, she felt tears well up in her eyes. It was too much. She pulled back, breaking off the kiss, then turned around and walked over to the window so she could wipe her eyes without Daria seeing.

The distance seemed to clear her head a little. It reminded her that they were in the office. The office of the magazine, which Daria was shutting down. The magazine where all of Liz's friends worked. Friends like Jane. Oh my God. Liz hadn't come into the conference room for *this*. She had come in here to confront Daria.

What was she *doing*?

"Don't say it."

Liz turned around, startled. "Don't say what?"

"Don't say whatever excuse you're about to give for why you can't do this." Daria was still standing where Liz had left her, hands in her pockets.

"I—" Liz was caught off guard. "I *can't* do this."

"Yes, you can," Daria said. "I know this"—she waved at the office around them—"isn't the best of circumstances. But I know you feel it, too."

Liz took a step back and leaned against the wall. She was afraid that if she didn't, she might fall—her legs were shaking underneath her. For once in her life, she could think of nothing to say.

"Liz," Daria said, approaching her. "Don't you know how into you I am?"

Liz stared. Daria stopped a few feet in front of her. "I think about you all the time," she said. "I can't stop wanting to know what joke you'll crack next, or what completely inappropriate thing you might say. I can't stop wondering how you manage to go through life not caring what other people think or what behavior they expect. Me—I think too much, all the time. But you're just *you*."

She reached out and took Liz's hand. "I go to sleep thinking about you. I wake up thinking about you. I walk around *talking* to you in my head, thinking of places I want to take you. And I can't help myself anymore." She swallowed. "I don't want to help myself anymore."

For a moment, Liz was actually tempted. It would have been so easy to fall into Daria's arms and not think at all. To let herself be kissed. To let herself be taken care of. Liz had wanted someone to feel this way about her for so long. She had wanted someone to look at her, to see all the different, messy parts of her, and still see something worth loving.

But this was *Daria*.

Daria, who was shutting down the magazine where all her friends worked. Daria, who had ruined Weston's life. Daria, who had broken up Bailey and Jane. Liz might be impulsive, but she couldn't give in to *this*. There was a line. At some point, she had to grow up and be a fucking adult.

She shook off Daria's hand.

"You must feel it, too," Daria said, searching her face.

"But—" Liz started to say. She hated that her voice was shaking. "In Boston. You acted like that was a huge mistake."

"I panicked," Daria said. Her face was pleading. "I didn't mean for things to happen that way. I mean, we work together, and my aunt was just upstairs, and I—I didn't think things through. I just needed a minute. To think. But then I woke up and you were *gone*." She shook her head. "I was so hurt at first. So *angry*. But I know you were just scared, too. I know that you feel more than you let on."

"Oh, I definitely feel more," Liz said, and something in her voice made Daria recoil. All the indignation and hurt that had propelled Liz into the conference room seemed to flood her nervous system at once. Daria's words brought her back to that horrible scene in Aunt Katherine's kitchen. The chill of the countertop on her bare skin as Daria's arms slid away from her. Daria scrubbing the counter, refusing to even look at her. Fleeing upstairs with her underwear in her fists. Lying awake all night, hating herself, feeling like this was just one more piece of humiliating evidence that she was never good enough for anyone.

Liz was sick of feeling not good enough. And she wouldn't do it anymore. This time, Daria wasn't good enough for *her*.

"I don't just dislike you," Liz said. "I *hate* you. Do you think I'd actually be interested in you after everything you've done?"

"Everything I've done?" The vulnerability in Daria's face vanished and her cheeks flushed.

"Shutting down the magazine. Sabotaging our chances to get that grant. Laying off all my friends. Stomping around this office, acting like you're better than everyone."

"We were *never* going to get the grant." Daria's fists clenched, and it sounded like she was struggling to keep herself in control. "That grant is meant for new media organizations, not magazines that have been floundering for twenty years."

"But you let Bailey convince you to add it to the budget?" Liz was practically shouting now. "Even though you were so sure we wouldn't get it? So, then, when we didn't, she'd have no choice but to shut us down?"

Daria looked away. The tendons in her neck flexed as she clenched her jaw. It was as good as a confession.

"And I know—" Liz's voice hitched. This was her chance to finally say everything she'd wanted to say for so long. She would *not* cry. "I know that you were behind Bailey and Jane's breakup. They were completely fine and then, all of a sudden, it was over. You broke them up so Bailey would agree to sell the magazine."

"No, I broke them up to protect my friend!" Daria said, raising her voice to match Liz's. "I heard you! I heard you and Lydia laughing about how this was your plan all along."

Liz had no idea what she was talking about. "Our plan?"

"In the kitchen! After that meeting about the grant. I heard Lydia talking about how Jane seduced Bailey so you could all keep your jobs."

Liz gaped at Daria. "What?" she said. "Do you seriously think we plotted a fake *seduction* to keep the magazine open? Do you think *Jane* of all people would actually do that?"

Daria's lips curled in a sneer. "I don't know what she would do."

"Jane was in love with Bailey," Liz spat. "It was the real thing. How could you not see that? She's heartbroken, and now Bailey is, too. Everyone is miserable because of *you*. Because you won't stop meddling in people's lives like you—" She paused for the briefest of moments, then recklessly plunged onward. "Like you did with Weston."

Daria went very still. "And what did I do to Weston?"

"She told me everything. How you couldn't bear to think that Bailey might be interested in someone besides you, so you went and got Weston kicked out of college. You ruined her entire life."

Daria's face twisted. There was no hint of affection in it now, no evidence of the person who had been kissing Liz moments earlier.

"And then you come in here," Liz said, still riding her wave of rage, "and you expect me to jump into your arms and run off to your fancy apartment with you, so you can fuck me for a few days and then call me an Uber back to Brooklyn when you get bored?"

"It's not—" Daria started. "I wouldn't . . . is that really what you think of me?"

"That is *exactly* what I think of you." Liz's hands were fists at her sides. She was ready to fight, ready to yell, ready to respond to whatever insults Daria threw at her.

But Daria didn't speak. For several long seconds, she didn't even move.

"Okay," she finally said.

She picked her briefcase up off the table and put her blazer over an arm.

"I'm sorry for wasting your time. Excuse me."

She walked around Liz to the door and let herself out. Liz watched her go, breathing hard. She had finally gotten to say everything she'd always wanted to say to Daria—but she didn't feel triumphant.

Liz took one last look around the conference room, then turned off the light. She shut the door gently behind her. And then she walked back to her desk, sat down, and started to cry.

18

The next day, Liz called in sick. She spent the day in bed, eating chips and rewatching *But I'm a Cheerleader* while she scrolled through Twitter. She couldn't pay attention to either, though, because she was having a continuous debate in her head: whether or not to tell Jane.

Normally, she would have told Jane everything, but she didn't know how Jane would react to hearing that Bailey had broken up with her based on a conversation that Daria had partially overheard. Plus, Liz couldn't think of a way to tell the story without admitting that she'd hooked up with Daria in Boston and never told Jane about it.

Liz channeled her rage into working on the article she'd started the night before, which she'd emailed to herself before going home. She got into a groove, describing what it had felt like to read the magazine in college and know she wasn't alone. She wrote about the people who worked there, how much they cared about the *Nether Fields* and how hard they had worked lately. And how they were being unfairly shut down before they had a chance to really turn things around.

After she finished the draft, Liz felt accomplished. But when she reread it, she realized it was over-the-top and clearly biased. Not trusting herself to edit it at the moment, she pushed her laptop to the side and stared at the ceiling instead.

Finally, sensing that if she didn't get out of bed now, she might never, Liz forced herself to get up and go for a walk. Her body felt heavy as she slogged her way past the Brooklyn Museum and into Prospect Park. The meadow was empty except for adults with little kids and the occasional person walking a dog. Liz took off down the path toward the other side of the park.

Moving made Liz feel better, but without anything to distract her, she found herself replaying last night's confrontation with Daria. And not just the yelling part. Also the kissing part. And the Daria-had-feelings-for-Liz-this-entire-time part.

Her phone vibrated once in her pocket, and Liz took it out, thinking it might be Jane checking in on her. But it was just an Instagram notification. She started to put it away when it buzzed again—another Instagram notification. Apparently she had a new follower and a message request. Probably spam. Liz opened the app to check and found herself staring at the longest Instagram DM she'd ever received in her life. From @DFitz.

For a second, Liz considered deleting it without reading. But she was deluding herself—she knew she didn't have that kind of self-control. Sitting down on a bench, she scrolled to the top and began to read.

> *Liz,*
> *I hope it's okay that I'm messaging you. It felt wrong to send this to your work email and I didn't have another way of contacting you.*

I'm sorry that I offended you last night. I genuinely thought that you knew how I felt. I had even convinced myself that you felt the same way. Clearly, I was wrong.

I also wanted to address two of the things you accused me of last night. Not to try to win you over—obviously, it's too late for that. But to clear my name, at least a little.

First: Weston. I don't know what she told you, but I doubt it was the whole story. We were roommates freshman year and we hated each other. I spent as much time as possible out of the room, with Bailey. I'd never had a friend like her, who allowed me to be myself and liked me anyway. Bailey was my only support when I came out—first to myself and then to my parents, who disowned me. Bailey helped me get through it. For that, I owe her everything.

Sophomore year, Weston started pursuing her. She acted like she was desperately in love and it worked—Bailey's always been a romantic. But Weston was terrible to her: making her feel special one week, then hooking up with other people and barely acknowledging Bailey the next. I tried to convince Bailey to stop seeing her, but Bailey was too in love to see how unhealthy it was. She spent all her time with Weston, smoking weed and drinking. She started skipping classes. Her behavior became erratic and she got so depressed, it terrified me. Eventually, I realized that she and Weston were doing a lot of other drugs, too. Weston was making a fortune dealing on campus and in town.

And then one of Weston's customers got caught with coke and Weston asked Bailey to take the fall for her.

*She made Bailey believe that if she did this one thing,
Weston would finally fully love her.*

*Bailey agreed. She was planning to confess, but I went
to the dean. I told her what had been going on and that
Bailey needed help more than punishment. They
searched Weston's room and found more than enough
evidence to have her arrested. She was expelled. The
school agreed to let Bailey come back if she took a year
off to get treatment, so Bailey went to an inpatient
program. She didn't speak to me for months.*

*Weston never visited her, even though Bailey begged her
to. It broke Bailey's heart. Eventually, she forgave me.
She realized how toxic Weston was, came back to
school, and graduated. I know she feels guilty about
Weston getting expelled. Weston has reached out to her
multiple times through the years, saying she loves her.
Bailey's managed to stay away, but she's also dated other
untrustworthy people who've used her and then abandoned her.*

*Maybe I'm a little overprotective of her now. But I was
worried when she started dating an employee. It seemed
like a disaster waiting to happen. Then I overheard
Lydia saying that had been the plan all along. And I
believed them.*

*I won't apologize for Bailey's decision to shut down the
magazine. I did advise her that was the prudent
course—she would have lost everything if she kept
going—but I'm only a minority investor, and it was
ultimately her decision. I did tell her what I overheard,
though. She trusts my judgment and it was easy to*

*convince her that she'd been wrong about Jane, the way
she was wrong about Weston and so many others. You
know Jane better than I do. If I was wrong about her,
I'm sorry. I'm still trying to learn how to have Bailey's
back the way she had mine in college, and I'm certainly
not doing it perfectly.*

*I'm sorry that I upset you last night. What I said,
though, about how I felt about you—I meant every
word.*
—DF

Liz read the message twice. Then she put her phone in
her pocket and started walking. She was determined not to
look at it again. A minute later, though, she'd stopped in the
middle of the path to read it again.

Daria Fitzgerald had slid into her DMs. Liz didn't know
how to feel or what to believe. She tapped on Daria's user-
name. Zero posts, zero followers, following one. She must
have created this account just to message Liz.

Liz put her phone back in her pocket and started following the footpath, thinking about what Daria had said about
Weston.

The way Weston had told the story, it had been Daria's
fault that she'd gotten kicked out of school. But the way that
Daria told the story, Weston had gotten caught on her own,
before Daria even got involved. And not only that, but
Weston had tried to get Bailey in trouble instead of her.

Surely Weston wouldn't do something like that. Liz *knew*
Weston. Surely Daria was just reinterpreting the story, spinning it to make herself feel better.

Except . . . the hot-and-cold, up-and-down thing. Liz had
to admit that dynamic *did* sound familiar. Because wasn't
that the way Weston had been acting with Liz? A hookup so

fantastic it made her feel giddy and then spotty contact for weeks? Weston was funny and sexy and good in bed. But Liz also felt like she never knew where they stood.

Liz turned off the footpath and went down a wooded trail toward the pond. Was it possible that Weston hadn't been fully honest?

Liz pulled her phone out again. There was at least one thing she could verify. After some quick googling, she found out what year Daria had graduated from Smith. Then she looked up Bailey and found it right there on an alumni website. Bailey Cox, graduation date one year later.

Liz walked down a set of wooden stairs and emerged on the edge of the pond. She sat down on a large boulder, next to a group of enormous geese pecking through the grass. It was a beautiful sight—the sun shining on the water, the trees still green, a few tourists in paddleboats on the far side. But none of it made Liz feel any cheerier.

It seemed like Daria could be telling the truth about Weston. Which would suggest she was telling the truth about Bailey and why Daria was so protective. It would explain why Daria had invested in the magazine, too—she was used to bailing Bailey out.

Then Bailey had fallen hard for Jane. Daria had been suspicious and unwelcoming from the start. But maybe she had reason to be suspicious of the people Bailey dated. And then . . . then she had overheard them talking in the kitchen. Liz's stomach twisted. She didn't remember exactly what they had said, but Lydia had been joking about how someone had needed to sleep with the new owner to keep her interested in the magazine.

And Daria, listening in, had believed every word.

Well, Bailey shouldn't have believed Daria. She had to know how much Jane cared about her. How could she have turned on Jane without even giving her a chance to defend herself?

With a guilty twinge, Liz wondered what would have happened if she'd overheard Bailey saying something horrible. Would Liz have been tempted to convince Jane to end things with Bailey?

She had to admit it was possible. But Liz knew Jane would never have broken it off like that. She would have listened to Liz, but she would also have given Bailey a chance to explain herself.

But for Bailey—with low self-esteem, a string of bad relationships, with a history of Daria being right about these things . . . would she have trusted Daria right away?

Liz kicked at a small rock half-buried in the dirt until it dislodged. She wished Bailey and Daria had never butted in to their lives, with their money and their feelings and their complicated baggage. Why couldn't they have just stayed on the Upper West Side and left the rest of them alone?

As she started trudging back up the wooden staircase toward home, Liz decided she would tell Jane everything. She couldn't keep something like this from her best friend. She put in her headphones. But even with "Huntin', Fishin' and Lovin' Every Day" blasting loud, she couldn't stop her mind from returning, over and over, to Daria's final, past-tense line.

What I said, though, about how I felt about you—I meant every word.

19

Before Liz told Jane, she had one thing left to do.

She texted Weston and asked if they could get a drink later that night. She had to ask Weston about what Daria had said. Otherwise, she'd be no better than Bailey, relying on Daria's word alone.

Or, a small voice in her head said, *no better than you were before, when you turned on Daria based on Weston's word alone.*

But she'd had no reason not to believe Weston. She had seemed so genuine. And it wasn't like she had gotten anything out of the lie . . . other than Liz sleeping with her and Liz spreading rumors around the magazine, damaging Daria's reputation.

Weston showed up twenty minutes late. By the time she got there, Liz had already drunk one whiskey sour and ordered another, the ice in the one she'd gotten for Weston slowly melting. Distantly, she knew that she shouldn't be ordering cocktails. She needed to start saving money if she was losing her job in three months. But there was a stronger voice in her head that told her it had been a shitty two days and she deserved this.

"Hey, babe." Weston kissed Liz quickly and sat down. "What's up?"

God, Weston really was hot. She was wearing a tight black T-shirt tonight, with a few long, layered necklaces over it. Liz wished she could pull off that kind of simple, boyish outfit. Why did skinny people look androgynous in everything?

"Daria and Bailey are shutting down the magazine." Liz hadn't intended to start there, but that's what came out.

"Ugh, I'm sorry." Weston squeezed Liz's hand. "That sucks. What are you going to do now?"

"I don't know." Liz dug her straw through her drink, trying to get the cherry out.

Now that Weston was here, Liz was tempted to just complain about the *Nether Fields*'s uncertain future; Weston was a good listener, and she would be sympathetic.

But no. Liz needed to know the truth—for Jane and for herself.

"So Daria told me something weird," Liz started casually. "I—well, I accused her of breaking up Bailey and Jane." She phrased her words carefully. She didn't want to mention that Daria had made a move on her. "And I called her an asshole."

"Good for you," Weston said. "She totally deserves it."

"Well, I mentioned you, too."

"Oh yeah?" Weston took a sip of her drink.

"Yeah," Liz said. "And she told me a story that was a little different from the one you told me."

Weston shrugged. "I'm sure she did. I'm sure she spun it to make herself seem like the hero."

"Kind of, actually." Liz traced her finger along the rim of

her glass. "She said you got caught selling coke, before Daria even got involved."

Weston snorted derisively, then leaned back, stretching an arm across the top of the booth. She looked entirely unconcerned.

"And then you asked Bailey to take the fall for you." Liz fought to keep her voice even.

"Of course she had some story ready." Weston rolled her eyes. "Bitch."

"But Daria went to the dean and told her the truth. And they searched your room and that's why you got expelled."

Weston shook her head. She was almost done with her drink, Liz noticed, even though she'd just sat down.

"Well?" Liz said. "Is that true?"

"Don't believe anything Daria says," Weston said. "She has major control issues and doesn't care about the collateral damage."

Liz succeeded in spearing her cherry with her straw. She chewed it, thinking. Yesterday, she might have agreed with Weston. But now that she thought about it, she had never seen Daria lie to anyone.

"I don't know," Liz said finally. "I've never seen her act like that."

"Are you seriously defending her?" Weston leaned over the table. "After she just fired you and all your friends? After what she did to me?"

"But—" Liz hesitated, then went on. "But if you were selling coke, then she didn't really get you expelled. You did that to yourself."

Weston waved a hand, as if the difference was just semantics. "She's the one who went to the dean." So that part, at least, was true. And Liz couldn't help noticing that Weston wasn't denying the dealing charge, either.

"To protect her friend," Liz said. Her voice was getting

JUST AS YOU ARE

louder. "Because you were going to make her take the fall for you."

"I didn't make her do anything." Weston tipped back her glass and finished the drink. "You're letting Daria manipulate you. Honestly, who do you trust more? Me or her?"

Liz looked into Weston's face—her sharp cheekbones, her handsome eyes. She thought about their first conversation in Scissors and that delicious kiss. Weston giving her the floral blazer on their third date. The on-and-off-again texting. Weston's annoyance when Liz left to take care of Jane. And she thought of Daria, renting a car to drive Liz to Boston so she could write her article. Who did she trust more?

She already had her answer.

"You are so full of shit," Liz said, and she stood up and walked out of the bar.

Weston didn't run after her or call her name. It wasn't until Liz was on the platform waiting for the subway that her phone buzzed with a texted *fuck you*.

Liz smiled—apparently Weston had just realized that Liz had stuck her with the tab.

20

Liz waited until Friday to talk to Jane. She ordered food from their favorite vegan Indian place and set up a blanket on the roof so Lydia wouldn't be able to eavesdrop. Then she told Jane everything: hooking up with Daria in Boston, Daria knowing they would never get that grant but adding it to the budget anyway, Daria confessing her feelings for Liz, and Daria convincing Bailey to break up with Jane after she heard Liz and Lydia joking around. She even handed over her phone so Jane could read Daria's message for herself.

When Liz finished, Jane tipped her head back to look at the sky and didn't speak. She stayed that way for a long time.

"I can't believe she would do that," Jane finally said. "Break up with me like that, based on something someone overheard? *Believe* that of me? What the fuck!"

"I'm sorry, Jane," Liz said. "And I'm *so* sorry that Lydia and I were talking about this in the first place. That really messed things up for you. I shouldn't have done that."

"Yeah, you shouldn't have been doing that in the office. But you were also *joking*," Jane said. "Anyone should have been able to see that."

"Are you . . . do you think you'll try to explain things to her?"

"Hell no." Jane crossed her arms. "If she really believed that I'd sleep with her to get ahead, then she doesn't know me at all. She doesn't *deserve* me." She was silent for a while longer, then added, in a smaller voice, "It is sad, though, what Weston did to her. I knew she'd been in some bad relationships, but I didn't know the details. I wish she'd told me."

"You're going to find someone else," Liz said. "Someone who actually deserves you. And you know why? Because you're absolutely gorgeous, you're ridiculously hilarious, and you're absurdly smart. You work so hard and you care so fucking much about your articles. You're always trying to make the world a better place. You're the whole package, Jane. Even if you can't keep track of your keys for shit."

Jane snorted. "Thanks," she said. "And I know. I'll find someone else eventually. But . . . I really thought that she and I might make it all the way."

Liz opened her mouth to continue the pep talk, but Jane suddenly shook her shoulders and sat up straight.

"Let's talk about *you* hooking up with *Daria*," she said, raising her eyebrows. "Why didn't you tell me?"

Liz covered her face with her hands. "I'm sorry! I was just so embarrassed. I couldn't believe I'd make a mistake like that. And you should have seen the way she treated me after. It was humiliating. Also, I warned you not to start dating Bailey and then *I* went and hooked up with our boss in the sloppiest, worst way possible. I couldn't believe how badly I'd fucked up."

"Yeah, you *really* fucked up," Jane said, laughing. "But now that we've established it, you *have* to tell me what Daria was like in bed."

Liz laughed. "Okay, well first of all, it wasn't so much 'in bed' as it was 'in kitchen.'"

"*What?*" Jane said. "Girl! Was it on a table?"

"I'll tell you the whole story." Liz shifted over so she could hold Jane's hand. "So it all started with the birthday dinner from hell . . ."

* * *

Liz and Jane stayed on the roof for hours that night, lying on the blanket, looking at the sky and talking until Jane seemed to be in a better mood. But after that conversation, she seemed sadder than before. Before, she had been industrious, trying to prove to everyone that she was "totally fine" by cooking complicated dinners or rearranging her entire room. Now she kept to herself, not baking on the weekends or hanging out in the living room after work. More than once, Liz leaned against their shared wall and heard crying on the other side. Liz tried to cheer her up by bringing her little treats from her favorite bakery or leaving sticky notes with encouraging messages on her door, but it seemed like what Jane mostly needed was time.

It certainly didn't help that all of their coworkers were in a slump, too. At first, the group chat had buzzed constantly with ideas for social media posts and suggestions of celebrities they could ask to speak up on the magazine's behalf. Lydia had set up the petition and the staff had all shared it on social media, but so far they had only gotten a couple hundred signatures. Liz felt guilty that she hadn't revised her article about the *Nether Fields*'s impact, but ever since receiving Daria's DM, she hadn't been able to figure out how to approach the subject of the sale. It had all been so much simpler when she'd assumed Daria was evil. Lydia kept asking Liz when the article would be done, but every time Liz blew them off with some vague excuse.

As hope began to fade, people started to panic about

their exit plans. All month, the *NF* staff checked various job boards and then huddled around the office, frantically whispering about who was applying for which job and what their chances were. *Autostraddle* was looking to hire a writer/editor, and almost everyone in the office had applied, even people who weren't in the writing department.

Liz, however, had not. She'd opened the listing and updated her résumé. But she just couldn't bring herself to apply. In part because she knew Jane had applied and was way more qualified. But also because the more she stared at the job posting, the more she realized she just really, really didn't want it.

But if she didn't want another journalism job, then what did she want?

When they'd thought the magazine was closing months ago, Liz had been so sure that she could make writing full-time work for her. But now she had actually tried writing a novel, and it had been painful. The few chapters she'd managed to eke out weren't even good. Whenever she read them over, they just sounded flat and lifeless.

Lately, Liz just couldn't seem to shake the little voice in her head that said she wasn't good enough. Not good enough to get people to care about Moira. Not good enough to write a book. Not good enough to land a decent girlfriend. Not even good enough at being herself—she went back and forth on everything: her future, her writing, her presentation. Liz was never enough for anyone.

Except, a little voice in her head said, *for Daria.*

It was silly to feel good about that, Liz knew. Especially because Liz would probably never see Daria again. There was no reason for her to come into the office anymore. And it wasn't like they'd run into each other somewhere. They led completely different lives.

That's a good thing, Liz told herself. It was a Friday night in late September and she was lying in bed, slowly descending into a spiral of anxiety about her future. Katie and Lydia had invited her to Scissors earlier, but Liz hadn't been able to summon the energy. Instead, she was staring at the ceiling, trying not to think about Daria.

It was *good* that she wouldn't see Daria again. Liz could leave this whole messy situation behind her.

Still, she couldn't help feeling a little guilty about how she'd acted that night in the conference room and all the horrible things she had said. Daria had definitely deserved some of them. But not all.

Liz closed her eyes, trying to remember what it had felt like when Daria kissed her that night. She could remember pieces, like how hard her heart had been beating and the sea breeze smell of Daria's cologne. But when she tried to visualize it, she could only seem to do it from the outside, like she was watching a movie.

It had been a spectacular kiss, though.

And then Liz had screamed at her. Daria had thought they were about to run off into the sunset, and instead Liz had called her an asshole. She had accused her of terrible things, but the biggest one hadn't been true. Even Bailey and Jane—Liz could sort of understand why Daria was so protective of her friend. The friend who had been there for her when Daria was a teenager and her parents disowned her. Liz tried to imagine how horrible it would have been if her parents had rejected her when she'd come out. What must that have been like for Daria?

Liz took out her phone and opened the message Daria had sent her. Should she respond? *No,* she told herself. *What would I even say?*

Still, she wanted to somehow signal to Daria that her message had been received and believed. That she knew the truth about Weston now.

Before Liz could talk herself out of it, she followed Daria's account back. It wasn't much, but Daria would get the notification and know, at the very least, that Liz didn't despise her as much as before.

It was something.

Liz threw off the blankets and headed toward the bathroom, wondering if taking a shot of whiskey to help her sleep would be an unhealthy coping mechanism. Halfway down the hall, she froze, her heart pounding. Two dark shapes were pressed against the living room wall. Robbers? Murderers? Ghosts?

Then Liz recognized the shine of Lydia's signature silver spandex shorts. They were locked in a tight embrace with someone they must have picked up at Scissors, one hand in their hair and the other already up their shirt.

"Ugh, Lydia, this is the living room," Liz said. She pointedly shielded her eyes as she walked past them. Lydia giggled.

"Come on," Lydia whispered to their date. "Let's go to my room."

"But I like it out here," a familiar voice said. Liz turned.

That was *Weston* pressing Lydia up against the wall. Weston with her hand on Lydia's spandexed ass. Weston smirked at Liz, looking completely unembarrassed to be caught.

Liz gaped at her, speechless.

"Oops," Lydia said, looking between them and giggling. "Sorry, Lizzie!" They took Weston's hand and tugged her down the hall toward their room. Weston let herself be pulled, but not before turning back to give Liz a wink.

"Good night, *Lizzie*," she said.

Liz watched them go, then ran to the bathroom and flicked on the light. She looked terrible. Her hair was sticking up, her One Direction T-shirt was baggy, and her boxers had holes in the sides.

She reminded herself that how she looked was not the priority right now. The priority was Weston in Lydia's bed. *Her* Weston in Lydia's bed.

Not hers anymore, she reminded herself.

How could Weston do this to her? But then Liz remembered the wink. They had been in the living room, not exactly being quiet. Was Weston doing this on purpose, to get back at Liz?

But what about *Lydia*? They were supposed to be friends.

Liz forced herself to go back to her room. Disturbing them would not give her the upper hand here. But she lay awake for hours, spite-listening to hear every creak of Lydia's bed, every moan that seemed a little too loud.

The next morning, Liz waited until she heard the front door close. Then she marched into the kitchen. Lydia was there, barefoot and making coffee. Katie was lying on the couch in the living room, staring at her phone. She looked like she hadn't slept much either.

Liz braced herself on the breakfast bar. "How could you?" she said. She was proud that it came out cold and angry, not shaky.

"What?" Lydia turned around. There was a hickey on the right side of their neck, just above the collarbone. They raised an eyebrow at Liz's expression and turned to scoop coffee into the machine, saying, "Weston? She said you ended things."

"We broke up three weeks ago," Liz said. "*Weeks.*"

"You didn't break up. You were never actually dating." Lydia set the machine to brew, then turned around. "What?" they said. "It's true."

"Do you seriously not see anything wrong with what you did?" Liz said. "We're supposed to be friends!"

"Oh, *are* we supposed to be friends?" Lydia said, leaning over the other side of the breakfast bar. "Because I think, if we were actually friends, you would care that we're all about to lose our jobs."

"What are you talking about?"

"I'm *talking* about the article," Lydia said, jabbing their finger at Liz. "The rest of us have been working our asses off trying to save the *NF,* but when we asked you to do one little thing to help us, you wouldn't do it! You've been making excuses for weeks."

"That's not—I was—" Liz sputtered shamefully, trying to think of a way to explain her situation. But before she could find the words, Lydia went on.

"And you're the one who actually *needs* this job, too. The rest of us will be fine."

"What do you mean?"

"I *mean,* no one else is going to pay you to write your dumb little quizzes! And it's not like you have any other skills. Charlotte *finally* let you write a real article and guess what?" Lydia slammed a hand down on the counter in emphasis. "No one read it. Because you can't handle writing real articles. Which is probably why you never wrote this one."

Liz gripped the breakfast bar so hard that she could feel the edges cutting into her hands. "You're just trying to distract from the fact that you're a bad fucking friend who slept with my ex."

"Just because *you're* jealous doesn't mean *I'm* a bad friend."

An image of Lydia and Weston pressed against each other last night flashed in Liz's mind, and she felt a rush of anger. Had they both had some sort of revenge sex against Liz? Why couldn't Lydia have just asked her about the article instead of bringing home the one person she knew would hurt Liz most? "Not a bad friend?" Liz shot back. "What about Katie?"

On the couch, Katie went very still.

"What *about* her?"

A small voice inside Liz's head was telling her to stop, but all the confusion and hurt and betrayal she'd felt in the past few weeks seemed to be exploding out of her all at once. "She's supposedly your best friend. But you treat her like your wingman, ditch her the second someone else looks your way, and then hook up with her as a last resort. Everyone knows she's in love with you. Even you're not stupid enough not to have noticed. But you just don't give a shit about anyone but yourself."

Lydia pushed past Liz and walked toward their bedroom. "At least I didn't get dumped and take out my insecurity on my friends!" they yelled.

"You're not my friend!" Liz screamed back.

"Good!" Lydia slammed their door so hard that a picture of the roommates at Coney Island fell off the living room wall and shattered.

Jane popped her head out of her bedroom, looking concerned. Katie got up from the couch, her eyes full of tears.

"Thanks a lot, Liz," she said.

"Katie, I'm sorry, I—" Liz started to say, but Katie went into her room and slammed her door, too.

"What happened?" Jane said, coming over.

Liz looked down at her feet. "Lydia slept with Weston," she said, and then she was crying, really crying, shoulders-heaving, lots-of-snot crying. Jane put her arms around Liz.

"Hey," Jane said tenderly. "Hey, it's okay."

21

I t was Jane's idea to go for a run. Liz had never once thought to herself that life might be improved by struggling to breathe while circling Prospect Park, but Jane insisted that it would make them both feel better.

So, the day after her fight with Lydia, Liz dug an ancient pair of sneakers out of her closet, last worn for her required college PE credit (a hula hoop dancing class, the least athletic of the available options), and out they went.

At this point, Liz was willing to try anything for a mood boost. She had no love life. She wasn't on speaking terms with at least one of her roommates and possibly two (she had left cupcakes and an apology note by Katie's door that morning, but Katie had yet to come out of her room). And pretty soon, she wouldn't have a job. If Jane said running would help, she would give it a try. Plus, Jane had promised to buy her a bagel after.

They went very slowly and were passed several times by ambitious walkers, but they ran a whole mile. When they finished, Liz could feel a small bit of hope breaking through the gloom she'd been feeling. Apparently out of her mind on this runner's high thing, she even agreed to run with Jane three times a week.

After two weeks, Liz casually suggested to Jane that they check out the Pride Runners. Jane was surprised that Liz even knew such a group existed but agreed that they should try a run. Liz wasn't sure why she didn't tell Jane that she only knew about the group because Daria had mentioned it. Probably because she didn't want Jane to think she wanted to see Daria. Because she didn't.

The group had casual runs on Wednesday evenings in Prospect Park and Saturday mornings in Central Park. Liz and Jane decided to give the Prospect Park meeting a try. Before they left, Liz spent thirty minutes digging through every piece of athletic wear that she and Jane owned, trying to pick an outfit. Why were sports clothes so gendered? She finally settled on a pair of athletic leggings and a slightly baggy T-shirt from high school.

When she and Jane showed up at the park, there was a large crowd clustered by the entrance, dressed in the kind of slick materials and bright colors that implied athleticism. It seemed to be mostly gay men. Liz and Jane hovered on the edge. Liz's hands were sweaty, but she felt very cold as she looked through the crowd. Was Daria here? She imagined how impressed Daria would be with Liz's newfound dedication to running. She imagined their eyes meeting. Imagined Daria sneering at her and pointedly turning away.

What was she doing here? She felt so nervous she was almost sick.

She looked around the entire group once, then again. Daria wasn't there. That was a good thing. So why was she disappointed?

Jane pulled Liz toward the person who seemed to be in charge. He introduced himself as Steve, said he used he/him pronouns, asked about their running experience, and explained that runs today would be between three and six miles. He must have seen Liz's face, because he assured her they had groups at every level.

"Everyone gets a buddy, okay?" he said. "Your buddy today will be someone who knows the route and is going your pace. Stick with them."

He paired up Jane first. Jane, being actually athletic, was going on one of the longer, faster runs.

"Now let's see." Steve peered at Liz, then frowned into the crowd. "How long did you say you've been running?"

"Um. Like, two weeks?" Liz was starting to wish she hadn't come.

"How fast do you normally run? Maybe an eleven-minute-mile pace?"

"Um," Liz said again. "*Maybe*." She tried to convey with her eyes that "maybe" actually meant much, much slower.

"Hey, J!" Steve beckoned someone over. "You said you wanted to take it slow this week, right? Liz, this is J. They/them pronouns."

"Hi, Liz," J said, smiling. "Guess I'm your buddy!"

Liz gave a small, awkward wave. J was bouncing on their feet as if they couldn't contain their excitement. They were Asian, somewhere in their late thirties, and had dark hair pulled back into a ponytail with purple streaks in the sides. Liz could see visible muscles in their arms and legs. She was pretty sure that she and this athletic-looking person were not on the same level of running ability.

Steve led the group through a warm-up that involved stretching while also running up and down a patch of grass. Liz was out of breath just from doing something called kara-oke. And then, all too soon, it was time to run.

They all started out together. In less than a minute, though, the other pairs of buddies had peeled away. Liz noticed J subtly slowing their pace to match hers. Liz's face turned red. Well, redder than it already was. She had visions of J abandoning her in derision halfway through the run.

"Sorry I'm so slow," Liz said.

"No problem!" J said, beaming as if they were having an incredible time. "This is great! I injured my IT band a few weeks ago and I'm just easing back. I need a reminder not to push myself."

Liz didn't bother to ask what an IT band was. She had a feeling it was painful.

"How'd you get into running?" J said.

"To be honest," Liz panted, "my friend made me. We're, um, about to be laid off. And kinda both just went through breakups. So she told me the exercise would be good for us."

"Oh, totally!" J said, enthusiastically. "Running is *great* for breakups. The first time I signed up for the New York City Marathon, I had just been dumped. I've never trained harder in my life. It's nice to not just sit around moping, you know?"

Liz nodded. She felt like her body might seize up if she had to answer any more questions. "So how'd you. Get into. Running?" she wheezed, hoping J would take over the conversation for a while.

Luckily, J turned out to be chatty. They loped along easily, telling Liz about how they'd run cross-country in high school. Eight years ago, they had met their wife in the Pride Runners, and now they trained for marathons together, when they weren't too busy with their kids, who were three and five, or with their two asthmatic pugs named Deadlift and Kettlebell.

Liz found herself charmed by J. Most of her friends were sarcastic and cynical and preferred smoking outside of bars until two A.M. to waking up early to walk wheezing pugs. J, in contrast, seemed genuine and cheerful and earnest. It was impossible not to like them. Plus, it was nice to meet a queer person who was happily married and had a family. It offered a little ray of hope for Liz's future.

"So why'd you decide to join the Pride Runners?" J asked.

Liz's lungs were feeling a little more functional now. "Actually," she hesitated, then went for it. "I heard about it from someone I used to work with. Daria Fitzgerald?"

"Daria!" J beamed in recognition. "She's the best, right?"

Liz was surprised by J's enthusiastic response. It was hard to imagine someone as upbeat as J getting along with Daria. "Does she come here a lot?"

"She only does the Manhattan runs, but I've seen her there every time I've gone. She's great with newbies, so Steve always pairs her up with first timers."

"She is?" Liz didn't manage to hide her disbelief. J laughed.

"When she first joined, she barely said a word to anybody. But you know Daria. She's just so shy. You get her one on one, though, and she really opens up."

Was Daria shy? The word felt like it didn't fit, somehow. It was too . . . too *feminine,* Liz found herself thinking, for such a masculine person—then she felt ashamed. Of course masc people could be shy. Liz had thought she was a little more open-minded than that.

"She comes through, too, you know?" J said.

"Daria?"

"Uh huh. There was this guy in the group, Marty, who broke his leg. He couldn't come to runs and was feeling super lonely, so Daria started going over to his place and cooking him dinner. Other people started going, too, and some nights we'd have ten or fifteen people in this guy's tiny apartment in Hell's Kitchen." J laughed. "We'd bring dessert and wine and stuff. It was a lot of fun."

"Oh, wow," Liz said. "That's—I worked with Daria for a bit. And she was always a little . . . closed off."

"I'm not surprised," J said. "It's tough for her, working in finance. It's such a boys' club. I think she kind of becomes someone else there, just to get by."

"That makes sense." Liz didn't correct J's assumption that she worked at Daria's investment banking firm.

"We've got, like, maybe four hundred meters to go," J said. "You want to sprint the hill?"

"Oh. I guess." Liz did *not* want to sprint the hill, but she also didn't want to wimp out.

"Three. Two. ONE."

J took off at an absurdly fast pace. Liz did her best to speed up, feeling like she might puke. The hill seemed to go on forever. How far was four hundred meters? A mile? Half a mile? She had no idea. Why had the metric system been involved at all? Her legs burned. She felt like she was running through sludge.

At long last, gasping and sweating, Liz reached the top of the hill where J was waiting for her, not even winded.

"Awesome job, Liz!" They held up their hand for a high five. "Welcome to the Pride Runners!"

"Thanks." Liz was wheezing harder than J's pugs, but she returned the high five and stumbled after them to join the group. Jane was already there, doing a butterfly stretch in the grass and chatting with her running buddy. She looked happier than Liz had seen her in weeks.

"This was such a great idea," she enthused as Liz flopped herself into the grass. "Apparently they all go to dinner afterward. Do you want to come?"

"I'm beat. But you should totally go," she said. "I can't believe I survived that."

"You're a real runner now," Jane said.

"I need proof or no one will ever believe I did this." Liz took out her phone and snapped a selfie of them in the grass, Jane laughing and Liz making a moaning, pained face. She added it to her Instagram story with the caption *People do this for fun??*

Liz did a few half-hearted stretches, said goodbye to J and Jane, then headed home. A heavy, melancholy feeling had settled in her stomach, and the walk felt longer than usual. She pulled up her Instagram story to distract herself and scrolled through the list of viewers. There, at the very bottom, was DFitz.

Daria had viewed her story.

Liz took another look at the photo, trying to see it from Daria's perspective. Liz was sweaty and making a face, but she looked okay. And Daria had seen it. Daria had, for however brief a moment, been thinking about Liz.

She put her phone back in her pocket and kept walking. It was a little brisk out, but warm for October. The sun was setting, turning the sky orange. A crowd was gathered around the Brooklyn Museum, sitting on the big wooden steps and queuing up at the Mister Softee truck parked in front. There were couples holding hands, kids running around, and someone selling enormous crystals and tiny succulents from a folding table.

It really was a beautiful day.

22

Liz didn't post on Instagram very often. She never seemed to have anything worth sharing. It was a lot of work, too—coming up with a caption, finding a photo that made you look good but not vain. But the next day Liz posted to her story again: a picture of her coffee mug in front of her bedroom window. She almost added "not a bad way to start the morning," but that felt so basic she deleted the caption and posted the photo without commentary.

After two minutes, there were five views. After five minutes, there were seven. After twenty minutes, when she was walking to the subway for her morning commute, there were twelve. And then, after thirty-eight minutes, when she had a brief spell of service between the Park Place and Chambers Street stops, Daria had viewed the story.

Liz's stomach lurched, and she dropped her phone into her bag as if she'd been burned. Then she immediately took it back out, because she was on the subway and what else was she going to do? She went to Daria's page.

Daria had added a profile picture—a small circular photo of her on a beach somewhere, squinting into the sun and laughing. She looked relaxed, with her hair blowing into her eyes and a dimple in one cheek. Liz kept trying to expand the photo, even though she knew that didn't work. She couldn't help herself; she wanted a closer look at this happy, carefree Daria.

Daria still had zero posts, but she was following a few more people now. Liz refreshed the page, hoping a post might magically appear. Then she went back and watched her own story again, trying to imagine what Daria had thought when she'd seen it.

Liz was distracted all day. Not that it mattered. They had six weeks left until the magazine closed, and everyone was doing the bare minimum. Charlotte had started asking for opinions on how they should say goodbye to their readers.

Thankfully the apartment was empty when Liz got home from work. After Katie had found the cupcakes outside of her door, Liz had apologized for what she'd said. Katie had accepted her apology, but an unfamiliar awkwardness still lingered between them. As for Lydia, Liz knew she should forgive them, if only for the sake of the atmosphere in the apartment. But every time she thought about what Lydia had said, she became filled with helpless rage.

It wasn't the most mature move, but Liz had been giving Lydia the silent treatment. Liz couldn't deny that she was feeling the effects of being on bad terms with half of her friend group. But, on the bright side, it meant she got plenty of alone time for once.

Liz sat down at her desk with the intention of looking for jobs, but instead she opened up her old blog, *Confessions of a New York Dyke*. She wanted to remember what it had felt like to actually enjoy writing. Back then, she'd had fun crafting Colby's adventures, and she hadn't bothered to care whether the posts were meaningful or even well written.

Liz scrolled to the first post and started reading, preparing to cringe. But, thirty entries later, Liz found that she was actually enjoying herself. The blog was *fun*. Colby's voice came through in every line, witty and sarcastic. Her adventures were over-the-top sometimes, like when she tried drag for the first time and immediately won King of the Year, but Colby was endearing. As Liz read through the entries, she could see Colby growing, too—becoming more confident in her identity, changing her style of dress, learning how to be a better friend and partner. Liz remembered what Daria had said on the beach months ago: There *was* something kind of powerful about watching a queer person just live everyday life.

Without really thinking about it, Liz clicked the new post button and started typing:

> *Hey queerdos! I know, I know—it's been FOREVER since I posted. Some of you have probably guessed why. After all, what's the most logical guess when a lesbian disappears for months?*

> *That's right. I'm ashamed to admit it but I, Colby Anderson, U-Hauled with a girl.*

The keys clacked under Liz's fingers as she kept going, having Colby explain all about this girl she'd met at a bar and immediately fallen in love with. Colby had always said that she wouldn't be the kind of queer who found a girlfriend and immediately ditched all of her friends, but she had done just that. She'd fallen hard and obsessively. But things had gotten codependent, then controlling, and finally Colby had realized it was time to divvy up the dildos and find her own place. Now, after a period of post-breakup bleakness, Colby was back, ready to make amends to her friends, update her blog, and dive back into the dating pool.

She was a little older, a little more cautious, but still optimistic that she'd eventually find The One.

When Liz finally checked her phone, it was almost two hours later. She couldn't believe it. She'd been having so much fun, she hadn't noticed the time passing. It was so easy to slip back into Colby's voice, so easy to think up hilarious misadventures for her to have. Normally Liz felt discouraged when she stopped writing, never sure if or when she'd start again, but today she felt energized. She wasn't sure if she was ready to rededicate herself to the blog, but she hit post anyway, sending the new entry out into the world.

Liz's stomach grumbled, and she sighed, trying to think what she could make for dinner out of the various scraps in her section of the fridge. Feeling uninspired, she lay down on her bed and opened Daria's Instagram page before she could stop herself. There was a colorful ring around her profile picture now: a new story. Liz opened it.

It was a photo of a sunset over the Hudson, taken fifteen minutes ago. The sky was pink and cloud-streaked over the water.

Liz watched the story three more times. Fifteen minutes ago, Daria had made the deliberate decision to take this photo and add it to her Instagram story. Liz checked—she was still Daria's only follower.

Which meant Daria had posted this story for Liz to see.

*   *   *

On Friday, Liz posted to her story twice. The first was a picture of two gourmet-looking breakfast sandwiches, made by Jane. Liz was glad Jane was cooking again. She seemed happier lately. It helped that she had an interview coming up for that position at *Autostraddle*.

The second photo Liz posted was a selfie. She took thirty different ones in the office bathroom during lunch, then went back to her desk, where she considered and reconsidered posting for twenty minutes. Finally, she picked the least embarrassing one. It was a mirror selfie. Liz had on her favorite denim jacket, and she gripped the collar with one hand, while giving what she hoped was a sexy smolder. She added the text *denim jacket season lfggg* in blue over the top.

She posted it before she could change her mind, then refreshed the list of viewers every few seconds. She got a pair of heart-eye emojis from Charlotte and a fire emoji from a girl Liz had made out with once in college. Weston viewed the story (ugh). Six others did.

And then, eight minutes after posting, Daria viewed it. Liz felt ridiculous for grinning at her phone. Was Daria checking Instagram obsessively, hoping Liz would post?

Of course, Liz was one to talk. Because when Daria posted a story that night, Liz noticed right away. She forced herself to get a drink of water and go to the bathroom before she checked it—for dignity's sake. As soon as she got back to her room, she snatched up her phone and opened the story.

There was Daria, sitting at an unfamiliar desk in a pool of lamplight, with the caption *Will I die in this office?* Daria was slumped over, her cheek propped on one hand, making a bored expression. It was casual, comedic—but surely it had to be intentional that the lamplight made Daria's cheekbones look even sharper than usual, that one piece of hair was flopped just so over her forehead.

Liz was sure that this photo was for her. A selfie to answer her selfie. A bat signal in the night. Had Daria seen Liz's photo and planned her response, maybe even posed and taken multiple outtakes like Liz had? It was like they were having a conversation without fully acknowledging it.

Liz's stomach felt like she'd just taken a shot of whiskey. This photo seemed to indicate that Daria still cared.

But how did *Liz* feel? She sat down on the edge of her bed, trying to organize her emotions. She was posting photos with Daria in mind. Was she interested in Daria, or was she just desperate for attention?

She didn't know. She had no idea what she was doing or what she was feeling or what she wanted. But she watched Daria's story again and again, studying her face, and she couldn't stop smiling.

23

The next day, Liz went to meet the Pride Runners in Central Park. At nine in the morning. On a Saturday. In Manhattan, which was an hour subway ride away. Truly, Liz was out of her mind.

She felt guilty about it, but she hadn't told Jane she was going. She knew that Jane would be suspicious. She also thought Jane might offer to go with her, which Liz didn't want. She was half-convinced that she would chicken out, and she didn't need an audience for that.

It took Liz almost twenty minutes to find the John Lennon memorial where the group met. By the time she showed up, she was eight minutes late and already sweating. Luckily, the group hadn't left yet.

A truly obnoxious amount of people were gathered there, all wearing brightly colored windbreakers and spandex and running leggings. Some of them even had water bottles on straps around their waists. Liz had on a pair of baggy lime-green shorts and one of Katie's long-sleeved T-shirts that clung a little too tightly.

Clearly, she didn't belong.

If Liz was going to turn around, this was her moment. She could pretend she was just walking through the park, headed somewhere else.

But then she saw J chatting with someone at the edge of the group. Liz took a deep breath and went over, keeping her eyes down. She couldn't tell if she was more afraid of seeing Daria or not seeing her. Her heart was hammering a little harder than it should have been, considering they hadn't started running yet.

"You're back!" J said, giving Liz a hug.

"I—yeah." Liz's voice came out a little squeaky. "Thought I'd just keep showing up."

"I'm glad! We can be running buddies again."

Steve shouted that everyone should finish warming up. Liz did a few hasty stretches.

"Liz?"

Liz was standing on one leg to stretch her thigh and almost toppled as she whirled around, narrowly avoiding crashing into Daria.

"Daria!" Liz's voice sounded several octaves higher than normal. "Hi! Wow! What a— Hi!"

Daria was wearing one of those shiny, expensive wicking T-shirts and a pair of shorts that showed off some seriously toned thighs. Her hair was messier than usual, as if she hadn't showered this morning. She looked a little confused, but not in a bad way.

"Hi," Daria said. "Are you here for the run?"

"I—yup. Here to run." Liz pointed at J. "With my running buddy."

"I didn't know you'd joined Pride Runners," Daria said.

"I just started," Liz said. Then, because she couldn't seem to shut up, she added, "I'm really slow."

"You're not that slow," J said kindly. "You'll be kicking our butts in no time."

Liz let out a hyena-like cackle and then quickly shut her mouth.

"Welllll," Daria said. She drew out the word, and Liz thought she was going to say goodbye, but instead she turned to J. "J, you were saying you wanted to go a little faster today, right?"

"Yeah, but I don't mind," J said, elbowing Liz in a jovial way.

"I was actually thinking I want to take it easy today," Daria said. "So I can take over as Liz's running buddy." She glanced at Liz and then away. "If you don't mind, I mean."

Liz shook her head.

"Are you sure?" J seemed a little dubious, but then their eyes flicked between Liz, who was very red in the face, and Daria, who was intently focused on tightening the strap of her watch. They started to smile. "You know what? Great idea!" They backed up into the crowd, still grinning. "Have fun out there, kids!"

"There's a good route through the trees," Daria said, ignoring J. "It's six miles, but we could take a shortcut to get it down to four. Is that too far?"

"Not at all," Liz said, even though the farthest she'd ever run was those three miles with J on Wednesday. Anything sounded better than staring at her shoes awkwardly because she couldn't make eye contact with Daria.

"All right," Daria said. She jerked a thumb over her shoulder. "Shall we?"

"Yu-up," Liz said in a strangled, faux-casual tone she'd never heard herself use before.

Daria checked for bikers before stepping into the road that looped around the park and crossing over into the pedestrian lane. Liz followed, and they started jogging, Daria keeping pace beside her. Liz felt fidgety and tense, but at least her anxiety was giving her some much-needed energy. After about a minute, the proximity became unbearable, and she started to pull ahead.

"Maybe we should start slower," Daria called from behind her.

Liz shook her head. "I'm good."

Daria picked up her pace, pulling up beside Liz. They ran like that for a few seconds before Daria said, "I was surprised to see you."

It had to be obvious that Liz had come here on purpose to see Daria. Right?

"I just . . . wanted to give running a try. It seemed like a good idea."

It was a terrible idea. What if Daria still hated her for what she had said? What if Daria was mad that she was here, encroaching on her turf? What if she thought Liz was ridiculous for showing up?

But if she was mad at Liz, she wouldn't have volunteered to be her running buddy. Right?

As they ran, Liz kept sneaking glances at Daria, acutely aware that there were only a few inches between them. Daria was wearing some seriously short shorts. Liz found herself wanting to stop and study her. But she also found she couldn't keep her eyes on Daria for longer than a few seconds at a time. Every time Daria's head turned and it seemed like their eyes might connect, a jolt ripped through Liz as if someone had tied her stomach to a doorknob, the way you would with a loose tooth, and then slammed the door.

After another minute or two, Daria pointed at a smaller path branching off the main road. "Through here."

They crossed the road, dodging cyclists, and Daria led the way up a small hill that left Liz's calves burning. The path was too narrow for them to run side by side, and Daria took the lead. Liz couldn't stop staring at Daria's straight posture, her shoulders moving under the fabric of her shirt, the sharp edges of her recently cut hair. Liz was so mesmerized, she almost forgot how much she hated running.

Minutes passed in silence. Liz was just starting to panic, wondering if she should start a conversation, when Daria glanced over her shoulder and said, "I've been thinking a lot about your article."

"My . . . article?" Liz tried to disguise how hard she was breathing so Daria wouldn't think she was out of shape.

"The one about the photographer," Daria said. "It was really good."

"Oh," Liz said. "Thank you."

"There was a quote in there that you mentioned in Boston." Daria paused, and Liz saw her shoulders tense, as if she was psyching herself up to keep speaking. "The one where she talks about how sometimes people will do or say terrible things to you. But as awful as those moments are, that's not the worst part. It's when you let those moments get to you. When you start to let the fear of those moments run your life."

The path widened and they fell into step next to each other, but Daria didn't take her eyes off the trail ahead. She could almost have been speaking to herself.

"I think I've been letting that fear run my life," Daria went on. "I love the way I look. It's who I am. But I also hate feeling hyper-visible. I hate when someone's rude to me in a store, and I don't know if it's because they're having a bad day or because they hate me for who I am. Every time I walk into a room I'm on edge, worried someone will say something. I'm always having fights with people in my head, planning out how I'd respond if they *did* say something. Even though, nine times out of ten, no one does. So then I'm just walking around scared and mad for no reason."

Daria took a shuddering breath. Liz wanted to say something reassuring, but she also didn't want to interrupt. She felt like if she did, Daria might not get started again.

"You know about what happened with my parents." Daria gave Liz a nervous half glance over her shoulder. "I guess I never got over the feeling that people were going to hate me for who I am."

The path narrowed again, forcing them closer together, so close that their elbows brushed a few times. "I know it's not an excuse," Daria said quietly. "I'm white and cis and well-off and live in a liberal city. I have so much privilege. But still, most of the time, it's just easier to default to—to being cold. To not caring. To being an asshole sometimes. So, I'm sorry."

They held each other's gaze for one second, two, three. Liz's face flushed. Then they reached an uneven part of the path and Daria looked away to get her footing.

Liz knew she should say something, but she needed a minute to process. Cold and aloof Daria Fitzgerald had been desperately scared of rejection all along. And Liz had rejected her in the most dramatic way possible. Had called her every name Daria had just called herself.

So why was Daria there, running next to her, telling her all this?

"My family, they—" Liz said between gasps of air. Then she stopped and bent over to grab her knees. "Oh my God, can we walk for a minute?"

"Of course." Daria halted, seeming startled. "Are you okay?"

Liz waved away her concern, breathing hard. Then she straightened up. She couldn't see anyone else on the trail;

they were surrounded only by trees, their leaves rustling in the wind. It felt unexpectedly intimate. Liz suddenly wished they hadn't stopped.

"Um," she said, her voice still breathless. "Should we— walk?"

"Sure." Daria turned, and they started down the path again. If Liz had lifted her hand, she could have wiped the sweat from the back of Daria's neck. She could have run her fingers down the muscles in Daria's arm.

Daria glanced at Liz, and Liz quickly looked away.

"So," Daria said. "Your family?"

"Oh. Right. My parents." Liz tried to remember what she had been about to say, feeling a little self-conscious. "They always used to say that when they had a kid, they knew they were signing on the dotted line. They didn't know who I'd be, but they were signing up to love me, no matter what."

Daria kept quiet, listening.

"And they stuck by that, even when things were tough," Liz continued. "When I wasn't sure who I was or what I wanted, whether I was straight, bi, gay, nonbinary, who knows, I always knew that I could count on that one thing. That they would love me no matter what." Liz hesitated, searching for the right words. "I can't imagine how hard it's been to go through life without that. But I can understand why you might . . . need to protect yourself like that. I'm sure I would do the same thing in your shoes. So, I'm sorry, too. For being so judgmental. For not giving you the benefit of the doubt."

Liz reached out and placed her fingers lightly against Daria's shoulder. Daria looked up, startled, and there was something undeniably endearing about her wide-eyed, deer-in-the-headlights expression.

"It's your parents' loss," Liz said. "They're missing out, not knowing you."

Liz's heart was beating so hard it almost hurt. Her stomach lining seemed to have turned into an electric fence. Daria's eyes—a soft, warm hazel with green flecks—were close, so close, and Liz's hand was still on Daria's shoulder, meaning they would only have to lean in slightly and there would suddenly be no distance between them or their lips.

Liz hadn't thought this through. She hadn't thought enough about what showing up at this run would mean, let alone putting her hand on Daria's shoulder like this. Did she want to be this close? Did she want to close the distance between them?

"Do you want to try running again?" she said abruptly, pulling her hand back.

Daria let out a soft breath, as if she'd been holding it. "Good idea. We're almost at the shortcut."

They didn't speak again as they finished the run, but every so often they'd catch each other's eyes and smile shyly. When they reached the memorial, a group of runners was already gathered, stretching and chatting. J waved them over.

"How was it?" they asked.

"Hard." Liz was bent over again, trying to catch her breath. "I can't believe this is your idea of fun."

"Hey, you're one of us now," J said. "So this is your idea of fun, too."

Liz groaned, but she liked the way J said that. It felt nice to be part of this group.

"Are you coming to breakfast, Daria?" J asked.

"I can't." Daria grimaced as she sat down to do a butterfly stretch. "I have a work call in half an hour."

"Come on! We miss you," J said.

"I'll come to the next one." Daria's eyes were on Liz as she spoke. "Next Saturday?"

"Next Saturday," Liz said back quietly, and Daria grinned.

24

On Monday, Daria responded to Liz's Instagram story.

It was a photo of a whole-wheat cinnamon loaf, made by Jane, next to a jar of apple butter from the farmers market. Liz was halfway through her second slice when the notification came through. Apparently, they were moving past the point of plausible deniability.

Obviously, she couldn't open it right away. She tried to figure out what the appropriate amount of time to wait was. Five minutes? Ten? Daria had taken a chance and messaged her—Liz didn't want to make her wait *too* long.

She finished her toast, washed her plate, wiped crumbs off the counter, and then couldn't wait anymore.

Did you make that?? Daria's message read.

Liz grinned as she typed. *If you think I made this you know nothing about me.*

She put her phone down and went to take a shower before work. Halfway through, she started worrying that Daria might read her message as dismissive, rather than self-deprecating. Why hadn't she added an emoji? She cut her shower short and ran back to her phone. Daria hadn't seen

JUST AS YOU ARE

the message yet. Liz didn't think there was a way she could salvage it now, though—an *lol jk!* sent five minutes later didn't exactly scream nonchalant. She left it as it was.

Daria responded while Liz was walking to the subway. She didn't even try to make herself wait to open it this time.

So Jane made it?

Yup she's trying to find the perfect bread recipe. AKA very extra. Who actually makes their own bread?

She went into the subway and endured an agonizing twenty minutes of spotty service before she finally got Daria's reply.

I made my own bread this weekend. The message included a photo of a truly impressive round ciabatta. *Extra?*

VERY extra, Liz wrote as she walked into work. *So much work for something you can buy at the store.*

Daria sent back a passionate defense of the higher quality of homemade bread as Liz was settling in at her desk. To which Liz responded that she didn't doubt the higher quality, but nothing could ever induce her to spend *several hours* making something that cost less than five dollars.

It was impossible to get any work done that day. When she wasn't responding to a message, Liz was waiting for one. Or planning her next reply. Or overthinking whatever she'd just said. Or, if it had been longer than ten seconds, double-checking to make sure she still had cell service.

Liz tried putting her phone on silent. She tried putting it in her backpack. She tried putting it in her desk drawer. But each time, she'd fish it back out again after only a few minutes.

All day, two questions pulsed through Liz's mind. Could Daria still be into her after all the terrible things Liz had said in the conference room? And, somehow scarier to consider . . . was Liz into Daria?

Maybe, Liz thought, smiling to herself as her phone

buzzed again. Or maybe they were both figuring this out as they went along.

Either way, Liz didn't want it to stop. Maybe she was just addicted to terrible decisions, but this felt . . . good. A bright spot in an otherwise gloomy time.

Their messaging spilled over into the next day, then the one after that. It started out light—Daria talking about her love of cooking, Liz making her promise to go out and buy *Paul Takes the Form of a Mortal Girl,* which Daria had never read—but by Wednesday, Liz found herself confiding in Daria about her desire to write an important queer novel and how poorly it had been going now that she'd actually tried to write.

In turn, Daria told Liz about her breakup with Caroline. Growing up, Caroline had been Daria's best friend. They'd lived in the same neighborhood, and when Caroline switched to Daria's school in third grade, Daria had thought she would end their friendship once she realized how unpopular Daria was. But instead of ditching her, Caroline had spent the next few years fighting off Daria's bullies, both verbally and physically. By the time they made it to middle school, everyone knew not to mess with Daria.

But, when they began dating a few years after college, Caroline started to urge Daria to act more masculine, rolling her eyes when Daria ordered a girly drink or cried at a movie. It started to feel like Caroline was more worried about how their relationship looked from the outside than what it was like on the inside. As if she wanted to prove to everyone that they weren't any different from a straight couple. So Daria had broken things off, but everyone (Caroline, Daria's aunt, their friends, even Bailey) seemed to expect that Daria would eventually come to her senses and they would get together again.

Over a screen, conversation flowed easily. Liz worried,

though, that when they saw each other in person on Saturday, all of these confessions would weigh too heavily on them. Real life wouldn't be able to live up to this private, online space they'd built.

On Friday night, Liz was sitting in her room, staring at her DMs, when Jane came in and sat on her bed, leaning against the wall with her knees tucked up to her chin.

"What's up?" Liz said, locking her phone and turning it facedown on her desk. She longed to pick Jane's brain about Daria, but it felt wrong to analyze a potential flirtation when Jane was still recovering from her breakup.

"Bailey texted me," Jane said without preamble.

"What?" Liz said. "When? What did she say?"

"She wants to talk. She apologized for ending things so abruptly and says she understands if I don't want to see her, but she really wants a chance to explain herself." She held out her phone and Liz scrambled over to her side to read the text.

It was a pretty good message—remorseful without being simpering.

"She misses you," Liz said, handing the phone back to Jane. "What are you going to say?"

"Ugh! I don't know." Jane buried her face in her knees. "I was just starting to get over her, too."

"Were you?" Liz said, in what she hoped was a kind tone. "I mean . . . you've been pretty sad lately."

"That's because of the magazine," Jane protested.

Liz gave her a look.

"Okay, and the breakup, too," she admitted. "But I don't know if I can trust her. After she broke things off so abruptly without trying to fix things? Who's to say she won't do that again?"

"I guess you can't know," Liz conceded. "But you could hear what she has to say and then go from there."

Jane grunted noncommittally, examining her toenail polish.

"Do you miss her?"

Jane sighed. "I'm upset at the way she handled things," she said. "But yeah. I do. A lot."

"Maybe it's worth just listening to what she has to say, then," Liz said. "But don't forgive her too easily. You have to make her work for it, okay?"

"Oh, that's a given," Jane said.

They debated how long Jane should wait before responding to the text and settled on ninety minutes. It took nearly that whole time for them to compose a text that was the appropriate mixture of aloof and open. Bailey responded right away and agreed to a Saturday afternoon coffee in their neighborhood—because if Bailey wanted Jane back, she was going to have to leave Manhattan, dammit.

Once it was settled, Jane and Liz decided to reward themselves with drinks at a nearby Western-themed gay bar. Liz had a feeling you weren't supposed to go out for drinks the night before a morning run, but she couldn't pass up the chance to spend some quality time alone with Jane. Lately, they'd been either busy or sad or both.

They settled onto tall stools at the bar, reminiscing about nights they'd spent at Switch 'n Play, the amazing queer burlesque show held in the back room. When Liz had first moved to New York, they had gone with Katie and Lydia almost every month. Each time was a little explosion of joy—especially when the drag kings performed. Liz had a thing for drag kings (although honestly, who didn't?). Now she couldn't remember the last time they'd gone.

"Well, we're going to have more time in a month, when the magazine closes," Jane said.

"Yeah, more time to hide inside the apartment, trying not

to spend any money," Liz said. "Have you heard back about that *Autostraddle* job yet?"

Jane swirled her straw through her dark and stormy. "I have a second interview on Tuesday."

"Jane! That's amazing!"

"I mean, I don't have the job yet," Jane said. "But if I did get it, they'd want me to start right away. Which would mean leaving the magazine before it's officially shut down."

"That's okay," Liz said. "You don't have to go down with the ship, Captain."

"What are you going to do once this is all over?" Jane asked.

Liz thought about what she'd said to Jane earlier. If Jane could take a chance on trusting Bailey, Liz could take a chance on trusting her dearest friend.

"Okay, remember when we thought the magazine was closing back in April?" Liz said. "Well, I had this idea that I could use the severance payment to try writing full-time for a few months. Because, well, I've always really wanted to write a novel." Liz studied Jane's face, searching for hints that she thought this was a terrible idea.

But Jane beamed at her. "That sounds so cool. Is that still your plan?"

"Welllll . . ." Liz hesitated, drawing out the word. And then it all started to rush out of her: how she'd finally dedicated herself to trying to write; how everything she'd written had been absolute crap; how, ever since her article on Moira Campbell had flopped, Liz had felt completely stuck; how she had no idea what to do with her life because all she'd ever wanted was to be a real writer, but that didn't seem like an option for her anymore since all she was capable of writing was fluff.

Jane listened thoughtfully as Liz poured out all her worries, nodding along sympathetically. When Liz finally finished, Jane sipped her drink for a second before speaking.

"Don't take this the wrong way," she finally said. "But what if you *are* a fluff writer?"

"Ouch."

"No, no. What I mean is—you are really good at writing fun, lighthearted things," Jane said. "Your quizzes are always *so* creative. Your advice columns are hilarious. Your listicles get great click-through rates. And think of all the people who have written in over the years to tell you that your advice column has helped them, or who've left comments on your blog telling you how meaningful it is to see a character struggling with her identity."

Jane put her hand on Liz's arm. "Your writing means a lot to people. Art doesn't have to be super literary to help people. And honestly, I can't really imagine you writing something super literary and serious, because that's just not who you are." Jane took her hand back and raised her glass. "Like it or not, Liz Baker, you're fun."

Liz frowned down at the bar, processing. What Jane was saying made a lot of sense. But she couldn't help feeling . . . embarrassed at the idea of admitting that maybe she wasn't the award-winning author she'd always wanted to be.

"I've been updating my blog again," she said, running her finger around the rim of her glass. "It's been nice, actually. To remember that writing can be fun."

"That's amazing!" Jane said. "I bet if you really focused on it, you could build an incredible following."

Maybe Jane was right. Maybe Liz could focus on her blog and try to turn it into something. Maybe Daria had actually been right all those months ago, when she'd said that Liz was just a silly fluff writer.

But maybe that wasn't such a bad thing.

25

On the subway to Central Park the next morning, Liz wasn't sure if she was more likely to fall asleep or puke. On the bright side, though, focusing on not dying left very little room for Liz to worry about if it would be awkward when she saw Daria.

"Liz, hey!" J called as Liz approached the group, enthusiastic as always. "How are you doing? Missed you at the Prospect Park run this week."

They'd been chatting with Daria, who smiled at Liz and said hello. She was wearing a black running tank top that showed off the sharp lines of her collarbones and the soft curve of muscle in her upper arm. Liz realized too late that she was staring.

"Hi," Liz said, suddenly shy. "I, um, had to work late." She figured that sounded better than the truth, which was that she'd stayed home to rewatch *Saving Face*.

They made small talk for a while. When the run started, J left to run at an athletic-person speed, while Daria and Liz set out on the same route they'd run the week before. Liz lasted less than three minutes before she had to admit that she was hungover. Daria laughed but slowed the pace. Liz stumbled along as best she could, cursing herself.

"Oh my God, this is terrible," Liz gasped. "Can you, like, distract me?"

Daria laughed. "Well, that's my apartment building," she said, gesturing to a building near the park with the words THE PEMBERLEY BUILDING in cursive over the golden revolving doors. "And let's see. We have a new client at work." She started telling Liz about an entitled brat of a man who always referred to Daria as "sweetie," while Liz worked out the geography in her head, realizing that Daria had gone completely out of her way to pick up Liz in Brooklyn for the drive to Boston.

As she loosened up, the run started to feel, if not good, at least marginally less terrible. Liz found, to her delight, that it was as easy to talk to Daria in person as it was over DMs. They went back and forth: childhood birthday party mishaps, broken bones, the time that Charlotte had gotten arrested at a protest the night before an important meeting with Heather Media and Liz had tried to bail her out in time. Before Liz knew it, they were almost back to where they'd started.

After stretching, they joined the group for breakfast at a nearby diner. Liz was much more into this aspect of the running club, getting a double order of pancakes and drowning herself in water and coffee. People kept coming over to their table to say hi, and Daria introduced Liz to all of them. After breakfast, Daria offered to walk Liz to the subway.

"How's Jane doing?" Daria asked as they started down the sidewalk.

"She's okay," Liz said. "She's actually— Have you talked to Bailey lately?" She had been about to tell Daria that Jane was preparing to meet Bailey in Crown Heights later that day, but stopped herself just in time, not wanting to spill the beans in case Daria wasn't aware.

Daria chuckled. "Don't worry. I know she's seeing Jane today."

"Gotcha," Liz said. "And did you have anything to do with that?"

Daria turned toward Liz—not just a glance, but an extended look. Meeting her eyes felt like trying to force two magnets together. Liz had to look away, focusing on the sidewalk in front of them.

"Bailey missed her," Daria said. "A lot. She's been moping since they broke up. I shouldn't have interfered in the first place. I know that now. So I told Bailey that and apologized for getting in her way."

They had reached the entrance to the F train, pausing just outside the stairs. Liz forced herself to look at Daria. Her chest felt like a hot tub—warm and roiling.

"Thank you," Liz said. "For doing that."

"You're welcome."

They were standing less than a foot apart, a little to the side of the subway entrance. People hurried by, not paying them any attention. The day was bright and sunny and crisp. Autumn air blew leaves down the sidewalk around them.

Daria took a small step closer. Liz stopped breathing.

"It was really nice to see you today," Daria said, her voice very soft.

"It was—yeah. Also nice today. To see you, I mean." Liz's brain wasn't working. Her tongue wasn't cooperating. If they kissed, would she do a terrible job because her tongue was on strike? Were they going to kiss? Did she *want* them to kiss?

She'd been thinking of nothing but Daria all week, but she still hadn't made up her mind. They made no sense together. It was a terrible idea. Daria was the reason all her friends were losing their jobs. Liz had hated her for so long. And yet . . .

And yet, and yet, and yet.

Daria leaned forward, just a little. They were only inches apart. Their hands brushed.

Liz half closed her eyes in anticipation. But Daria stayed where she was. The message was clear—if Liz wanted to kiss her, she would have to cross that line herself.

"I'll see you next week, right?" Liz said instead. "For the run?"

Daria took a small step back. If she was disappointed, she didn't show it.

"I'll be there." Her warm hazel eyes lingered on Liz's. "Every Saturday, every week."

The words were casual, but they felt like an oath.

"I'll see you there, then," Liz said, suddenly desperate to get on the subway. "Have a good rest of your weekend."

"You too."

Liz looked back once from halfway down the subway stairs, just a quick glance. Daria was still there, watching her walk away.

Liz's hands shook as she swiped her MetroCard.

She had almost kissed Daria Fitzgerald. Again. But those times in Boston and in the conference room didn't really count. Those kisses had been impulsive mistakes. If they kissed now . . . this time, it would mean something.

The F came, and Liz wedged her way on. It was crowded for a Saturday. She pushed her way toward the middle of the car and held on to a pole.

Liz caught her reflection in the darkened windows of the train car. She looked like someone else—wearing athletic clothes, up and productive before noon, smiling to herself on the subway.

She grinned even wider at her reflection. Maybe, just maybe, this thing with Daria could actually work.

26

On Sunday evening, Lydia called a house meeting via group text. Liz planned to skip it, but Jane insisted that she couldn't shun her roommate forever and they still had to find a way to live together, even if they weren't friends.

So Liz begrudgingly attended, on the condition that Jane recount every single detail of her coffee date with Bailey. Which she did, gladly: When Jane showed up, Bailey had been waiting with her favorite tea and a fresh scone. Bailey had thanked her for agreeing to meet, then started to apologize profusely. She said that she was completely and utterly in love with Jane and had been miserable ever since they broke up. She had messed up, badly, and should never have broken things off like that without talking to her first. She would do anything to win back Jane's trust, if Jane would just give her another chance.

To Jane's credit, she had played it very cool. She told Bailey how much the breakup had hurt her and that she wasn't sure she could trust her anymore. They would have to take things slowly this time, not rush in and spend every second together like before. It would take time. But Jane still had strong feelings for Bailey and was willing to give it a shot.

Of course, Jane had shown no such restraint when retelling the story. On the contrary, she had pounced on Liz, and squealed repeatedly. It was hard not to be excited when someone confessed that they loved you and hadn't stopped thinking about you for weeks. Just like Liz couldn't stop replaying what Daria had said in the conference room: *Don't you know how into you I am?*

Liz was delighted for Jane. She was less delighted about the house meeting, however. She tried to express her mood by slouching as low as possible on the couch with her arms crossed, glaring at the wall and refusing to look at Lydia.

Lydia, as usual, was uncowed. They stood in front of the dark living room windows, facing their roommates. Only Jane looked back. Next to her, Katie picked at her chipped black nail polish, avoiding eye contact.

"What's this about, Lydia?" Jane asked from the couch.

"Two things." Lydia crossed their arms. "First, Liz, I don't think it's fair that you're still mad at me. It's been, like, a month. And you were already broken up."

Liz looked away pointedly.

"I shouldn't have slept with her," Lydia said when it was clear Liz wasn't going to respond. "But that doesn't mean you get to be mad at me forever!"

"Wanna bet?" Liz muttered. She knew she was being overdramatic, but still. It was infuriating how Lydia acted like *Liz* was the irrational one here.

"Whatever," Lydia said. "That's not even the point. I called this meeting to discuss saving the magazine. We have four weeks left to find a buyer. I set up the social accounts, I set up the petition, and I've been promoting it every day. We have five hundred signatures, which is great, but it's not enough." She turned and pointed at Liz.

"Liz, you said you were going to write that article on the *NF*. Have you even started it?"

Liz's thoughts flashed guiltily to the draft she'd written in a haze of anger weeks ago and hadn't looked at since. She could barely remember what she'd written, but she knew it had been more of a rant than an ode to the *NF*. "I wrote, like, half of it."

"Well?" Lydia threw up their hands. "Are you going to finish it?"

"No, I don't think so," Liz said carelessly, just to annoy Lydia a little more. Lydia let out an exasperated breath.

"Jane, you were going to reach out to your connections and try to get them to promote the petition," they said. "Have you done that?"

"A little," Jane said, wincing. "But, Lydia, a petition, no matter how many people sign it, isn't going to save the magazine."

"But it will show that people actually care about what happens to us!"

"Show who?" Liz sneered. "Random people on the internet? They're not paying our bills."

"Show Bailey and Daria!" Lydia said. "If we make this into a bad enough PR disaster, they won't be able to shut us down. Those assholes will have to give us a real chance."

"Oh, grow up, Lydia," Liz said, standing. "Throwing a temper tantrum online will make *us* look bad, not them."

Jane stood up too. "I'm sorry, Lydia," she said. "But I don't think there's anything we can do. The magazine is closing and I'm heartbroken, but I think we need to accept that and start figuring out what comes next."

"Oh, fuck you." Lydia looked at Katie, who shrank into the couch. "Thanks for the backup, bitch." They stomped down the hall to their bedroom and slammed the door behind them.

"I'm going out," Liz said. Her dramatic exit was hindered somewhat by having to spend five minutes tugging on her Doc Martens. But once they were laced, she huffed her way out of the apartment. It felt good to clomp around in her boots, acting moody and gay.

She strode through Crown Heights with purpose, even though she had no destination—she was just fueled by anger. She knew that she had held on to this grudge against Lydia for too long. Yes, Lydia had said some terrible things, but it wasn't like they'd never fought and made up before. But every time Liz thought about smoothing things over, Lydia's words would swim into her head: *You can't handle writing real articles.*

Lydia had said that only because they *knew* how much it would hurt Liz. Right?

Or maybe they meant it. Maybe everyone secretly thought the same thing.

And could Liz really say they were wrong? Maybe she *couldn't* handle real articles, just like she couldn't handle writing a novel. Maybe Liz just didn't have enough substance to her. She'd never write a real book, never have a real career, never find real love, never even find a real label that fit her.

Liz walked for more than an hour, hoping the movement would burn off some of her anger and help her pull her thoughts together. But by the time she headed home, long after the streetlights had started to glow, Liz felt just as insignificant and stuck as before.

27

Monday was particularly brutal. Liz was still in a bad mood from the house meeting, and work only made things worse. The Page Printer was jammed. The Carlile Copier (named, of course, after Brandi Carlile) was broken. Liz decided to treat herself to a hot sandwich for lunch, but it ended up being dry and lukewarm. At that point, she wrote the day off completely. Liz spent the next half an hour reading *BuzzFeed* articles, then got up to get some tea, hoping for a reset.

"Hey," Finn said when Liz walked into the kitchen. They were washing out a Tupperware bowl at the sink. "I saw your article."

"Which one?" Liz scrounged through a couple boxes and found a green tea bag.

Finn looked surprised. "The one that went up today," they said. "It was . . . intense." Finn handed her a mug.

"I didn't have an article go up today," Liz said, taking the mug.

"The one about the magazine shutting down?" Finn prompted. "It went up, like, half an hour ago?"

Liz froze, one finger on the hot-water button, dread flooding her body. Then she fast-walked back to her computer, leaving the tea behind. She clicked desperately, cursing as she mistyped her own password, then opened the *Nether Fields* home page.

It was there, right at the top. "Dear Readers, We're Shutting Down—But We Shouldn't Have To." By Liz Baker.

"Shit," Liz muttered. "Shit, shit, shit." An email popped up in the corner of her screen, with the subject line *Saw your article*. Liz ignored it and started skimming. It was the rant she'd written weeks ago, right after she'd found out they were closing.

The article started with a paragraph on the *Nether Fields*'s history. Then it announced that, in a few short weeks, all of that history would be lost when the magazine closed down. How had it gotten to this point? The article explained, in detail, the saga of the last year. Heather Media's lack of support. The hurried sale to unqualified private individuals. How, just when their numbers had started to improve, Bailey and Daria had decided to put the magazine up for sale, knowing there were no interested buyers.

From there, it only got worse. Liz forced herself to keep reading. *You have to ask yourself: Why did they even buy the magazine in the first place? Did our running joke have more truth to it than we realized—that maybe they just wanted to find people to sleep with, the way Bailey eventually started sleeping with one of her employees? Or was it more sinister than that? Did they have some creepy need to exert control in one small corner of the universe? A need that came at the expense of twenty hardworking, earnest queer individuals who were just trying to make a living while also making a difference in the world?*

Because let me be clear: From day one, the owners—or at least Daria—made it clear that she was too good for a maga-

zine trashy enough to include quizzes and clickbait. The only time she opened her mouth was to criticize us or mock our content. No one could figure out why she'd invested in the magazine in the first place. The only reasonable explanation seems to be that she enjoys controlling everyone around her. If only she'd read the sex toy reviews and dating advice columns she hated so much, she might have loosened up enough not to eliminate twenty jobs.

Someone had gone through and edited the article a little, correcting grammar and shortening some sentences. But otherwise, the words were Liz's until the very end, when someone had added two new paragraphs, calling on readers to protest the closing of another queer institution and sign the petition to keep the magazine going.

Otherwise, every single word belonged to Liz. It was her voice, her writing style, her damning opinion. It was not objective journalism—it was melodramatic, full of cruel comparisons and mean names. It was an article that Liz would never have handed in, not in a million years, no matter how upset she was.

How had this article gotten onto the website? She hadn't shared it with anyone. It was saved to her personal computer.

Lydia had to be behind this. But how could they have gotten on her computer? They didn't know Liz's password.

But Katie did.

Liz closed her eyes as the horrible realization sank in. Katie knew all of their passwords. Katie always laughed at them for not taking their digital security seriously. Katie, who was hopelessly in love with Lydia.

Liz stood up and hurried over to Lydia's cubicle. It was empty. So was Katie's. Cursing, she scanned the office and spotted Lydia huddled in the corner, chatting with Daniela.

"Take it down," Liz said, rushing over.

Lydia smirked at her. "What do you mean?"

"Take it down right now." Liz wanted to grab Lydia by the shirt and shake them. "What the fuck do you think you're doing? You had no right to post that."

Lydia's mouth twitched, as if they were barely holding back a laugh. "I don't know what you're talking about."

Liz didn't think she had ever been so angry in her life. She needed to get that article down now, before anyone else read it. Before Jane read it. Before Daria read it.

"Can you not be a completely terrible person for once and just take this down?" She was shouting now, making a scene, but she didn't care.

"Liz," someone said sharply. Liz whirled around. Charlotte was standing in the doorway of her office. The rest of the office had stood up from their desks, staring. "Conference room. Now."

"It wasn't me! They posted it," Liz said, gesturing wildly at Lydia. "They took it off my computer and posted it without asking me."

"Lydia. You too. Conference room." Charlotte looked imposing in a way that Liz had never seen, her arms crossed and her eyes blazing. "Finn, get that article off our front page. Erase any trace of it if you can."

Finn nodded, their eyes wide.

"Jane! You too!" Charlotte called, and Jane scrambled over. Charlotte marched down the hallway toward the conference room. The other three followed in silence. Liz dug her nails into her palm. How many people could have read the article in forty-five minutes? How many could have shared it? They were closing because they didn't have that many readers, right?

Charlotte threw open the door of the conference room and held it as they shuffled inside. Jane gave Liz a questioning look; Liz grimaced back at her, realizing with an awful pang that she must not have seen it yet. How could she have written those things about Jane's relationship?

"Sit," Charlotte ordered, shutting the door behind them. They obeyed.

"What's going on?" Jane said, looking between the three of them.

Charlotte's jaw was clenched. Liz had never seen her look so angry.

"I was in my office, working, when I got a phone call from the head of Heather Media," Charlotte said, sitting down at the head of the table. "Asking what the hell I was thinking. When I didn't know what he was talking about, he explained that there was an article on our front page, written by one of my reporters, shitting all over his company. Apparently, it's being promoted very heavily on Twitter, where it's going viral in, as he put it, *our community*. I took a look at our front page and sure enough, there was an article announcing our closing and complaining that we were mistreated."

Jane's eyes got very wide. She darted a look at Liz, who looked away.

"Liz," Charlotte said. "Did you write this article?"

"Lydia posted it! Without asking me. They took it from my computer."

"But did you write it?" Charlotte said.

"I— Yes." Liz felt almost physically sick with shame.

"Why?" Charlotte said.

Liz wanted nothing more than to run from the room, but she gripped the bottom of her chair and forced herself to answer, knowing she owed Charlotte an explanation. "After we found out the magazine was closing, we wanted to save it somehow. That's when Lydia started the petition. And I said I'd write an article, to get people invested. I wrote a draft when I was upset, then . . . stopped. I never meant for anyone to read it. Ever. I had no idea it was even up until

Finn told me." Liz paused briefly. She didn't want to bring Katie into this—the last thing she wanted to do was cause even more damage. "But Lydia took it off my computer without my permission."

"You can't prove that," Lydia snapped.

"We can track who logged in to post and from what computer," Charlotte said, her tone icy. "A system we have in place for exactly this reason. So, Lydia, I'm going to ask you a few questions, and I want you to think very carefully before you answer. Did you post that article?"

"Yes," Lydia said defiantly, crossing their arms.

"Did you have Liz's permission?" Charlotte asked.

"No," Lydia said. "She was never going to get her act together to—"

Charlotte held up a hand, cutting them off. "Do you have any idea what you've done?" she said. "Not only have you damaged Daria's and Bailey's reputations, Liz's reputation, my reputation, and the reputation of this entire magazine, but you've also opened all of us up to lawsuits."

Jane turned to Liz, horror dawning on her face as she tried to puzzle together just how bad this article was. Liz tried to silently convey how sorry she was, but Jane seemed to see only confirmation in her face. She looked away.

"We just wanted to save the magazine," Lydia protested.

Charlotte took a deep breath before answering, as if she was doing her best not to yell. "And you thought going behind my back was the best way to do that?" she finally said. "Do you think I haven't tried everything I can to save this magazine? Do you think if there was a magic way to keep us afloat, I wouldn't have already done it? This magazine is closing, okay? And that's not Daria's or Bailey's fault, just like it's not mine."

Liz sank deeper into her chair.

"This article is whiny and unprofessional and beneath us," Charlotte continued, looking at Liz now. Liz's cheeks burned with shame and the effort of holding back tears. "This publication is my *legacy*," Charlotte said. "How many magazines founded by queer people of color can you name? I'll be damned if this article becomes what people remember about us instead of two decades of good work.

"And on top of all that," Charlotte said as she turned back to Lydia, "you've robbed us of the chance to say a respectful, caring goodbye to our readers. There are people who have read this magazine for almost twenty years, who love it, and because of you, we didn't get to thank them for their support or tell them how much we've loved writing for them. Instead, they found out that we're closing through inappropriate, mean-spirited clickbait."

Even Lydia looked troubled. Liz hadn't had a chance to comprehend the full implications until Charlotte laid them all out, and it seemed that maybe Lydia hadn't fully thought them through, either. Liz couldn't hold back her tears any longer. How could she have written that article?

Charlotte's mouth was set in a grim line.

"Lydia," she said. "You're fired. Effective immediately."

"What!" Lydia shouted, but Charlotte ignored them, picking up the conference room phone and calling someone. A moment later, Finn opened the door, looking apprehensive.

"Finn, please escort Lydia to their cubicle so they can retrieve their personal items. They are not to touch their computer or any other *Nether Fields* property."

"You can't do that!" Lydia stood up. "I'm the only one trying to *help* this place."

"Do I need to call security?" Charlotte's voice was hard. She waited until Lydia shook their head. "Building pass," Charlotte said, holding out her hand.

Lydia glared. "Fuck you," they said, raising their middle finger at Liz, then slammed their building pass onto the table and left, Finn following close behind.

Charlotte stood. "We're going to make a statement, retracting that article," she said. "Jane, meet me in my office when Lydia's gone so we can draft something. Then, Liz, you're going to write a formal apology."

Liz opened her mouth to protest, but Charlotte shook her head.

"I don't care that you didn't post it. Those were your words, published under your name. You have to take responsibility. Not only for the *NF*, but if you ever want to be employable again. I don't want you to write it right away—it needs to be levelheaded. Take the rest of the day off and get me a draft tomorrow."

Charlotte made to leave but paused in the doorway. "I'm disappointed in you," she said to Liz, then shut the door softly behind her.

Liz dropped her head to the conference table. How had everything become such a mess so quickly?

"Liz," Jane said. "How bad is it?"

Liz squeezed her eyes shut. She knew how hard Jane worked, and she hated the idea that this article might have repercussions for her friend. "It's bad," she said. "I—I didn't say anything about you specifically, but I . . . the article does say something about the owners sleeping with the employees. Not a direct accusation but—I'm so sorry. I didn't think anyone would read it."

Jane let out an exasperated breath. "You never think, do you? You never fucking think, and then the rest of us have to deal with the consequences."

Liz looked up, shocked. "Jane, I—"

"Not now." Jane held out a hand to stop her. "I need to

read this before I talk to you." And with that, she turned and walked out of the room.

Liz wanted to run after her and beg for forgiveness. She wanted to find a way to make things right between them. But she knew she had to respect Jane's desire for space.

So instead, Liz stood up and went for the door. Jane didn't want to talk right now, but there was one person who hopefully would. Another person who Liz needed to explain herself to and find a way to make things right with.

Liz needed to go find Daria.

28

Everyone stared at Liz when she came out of the conference room. There was no sign of Lydia. She headed straight for the elevators, but Finn caught up to her as she was pressing the call button.

"I took the article down," Finn said. "But—it was posted on a blog, too. A personal blog that Lydia seems to have set up in case we took the article down."

"What does that— Is there anything we can do?"

"I'm sorry," Finn said. "We don't have access. I reported the blog to try to get it taken down. But without the password, our options are limited."

"*Shit!*" Liz said, stabbing at the elevator call button. "I'm sorry, Finn. Thank you. But—*shit.*"

Finn nodded sympathetically before heading back to their desk.

As the elevator descended, Liz pulled out her phone. Had Daria seen the article? It's not like she was one to sit around refreshing the *NF* home page or Twitter. But Bailey was, and if Bailey knew . . . no, there was zero chance Daria hadn't read it by now.

Liz went to call Daria, then remembered she didn't have Daria's number. Instead, she DMed her, asking if they could meet somewhere today to talk. It felt inadequate, but what else could she do? Send her an email?

Hating herself, Liz started walking uptown, hoping vaguely that she'd be able to recognize the apartment building Daria had pointed out on their run just a few days ago. It was almost the end of the workday. Or it would be in a couple hours. Maybe Liz could just . . . hang around outside Daria's building and hope Daria didn't call the police when she saw her.

With nearly every step she took, her phone buzzed with a new text, mostly from her coworkers, asking if she was okay and what had happened. None of them were from Jane. Liz ignored them all. She would have put her phone on silent, but she didn't want to miss a notification from Daria. She walked on autopilot through Midtown, holding her phone open to Instagram, waiting and trying not to walk into anyone. It was almost Halloween, and all the cheerful pumpkins and wide-mouthed ghosts in the store windows seemed mocking, like they were laughing at Liz's distress.

Somewhere between a Duane Reade and a coffee shop, Daria's status changed to "Active now," and the message was marked as seen. Liz's heart leapt into her throat. She waited one block, then two, then three, but Daria didn't respond.

Liz kept walking, willing Daria to write back. Liz didn't realize she was crying until a few tears landed on her screen. She was desperate to tell Daria that she didn't mean what she had written. How sorry she was. That she knew now that Daria wasn't condescending and controlling. That Daria was kind and funny and thoughtful and sensitive and . . . someone Liz had completely, hopelessly, fallen for.

It was true, Liz realized. She was fast-walking half of Manhattan because she had feelings for Daria.

Liz wiped at her eyes, but she couldn't stop the tears from coming. She was falling in love with Daria, possibly already had, but she'd been so stubborn that she hadn't been able to see it until now.

By the time Liz saw the golden doors of Daria's apartment building up ahead, she'd stopped crying, but her cheeks were sticky with dried tears. She checked the time—it was only four thirty. She walked into Central Park and sat down on a bench that allowed her to see Daria's apartment doors, then sent another message: *please just let me explain.*

A minute passed. Two minutes. Then the bubbles that indicated Daria was typing popped up. Liz breathed out in relief—but a moment later, the bubbles vanished. A few seconds later, they came back, then disappeared again. Finally, finally, Daria seemed to come up with a message she was happy with.

Fine. When?

Liz messaged back at once. *I'm in Central Park, near—* she looked around for a landmark, realizing how weird it would be to say she was in front of Daria's building. Not too far away, she could see the memorial where the Pride Runners always met. *Near the John Lennon memorial,* she wrote. *Come whenever you can.*

As soon as she hit send, she started sprinting toward the memorial, as if Daria might materialize within seconds and she'd miss her chance. She paced around the mosaic, craning her neck in every direction, her pulse taking off every time she saw someone with short brown hair or a well-tailored suit.

When forty-five minutes had passed with no word from Daria, Liz sat down on a bench, hugging her knees to her chest against the crisp fall wind. She wasn't sure how far away Daria's office was. Or if she was even coming. How long should she sit here, waiting?

And then, as the evening sun started to shroud the trees with an orange glow, Liz saw her. Daria was approaching from the south side of the park, walking like someone used to New York: shoulders a little hunched, hands in her pockets, eyes straight ahead, moving fast. A wave of tenderness rose in Liz that was so strong it almost hurt. She stood up, smoothed her clothes, and steeled herself for whatever was coming her way.

"Hi," she said when Daria was within earshot, her voice cracking a little around the word.

"Hi," Daria said. Her voice was flat, her hazel eyes hard.

"Can we walk?" Liz asked. She was hoping that some movement might help her gather her thoughts, or at least calm the shaking of her hands.

"Okay." Daria took off toward a nearby footpath. Liz hurried after her, trying to figure out where to begin. Everything felt too open and exposed for this kind of conversation. This was not a New York City, surrounded-by-people kind of talk. This was a tucked-away kind of conversation. They needed a scenic barn, maybe, or a quiet mountain near a pond. Liz imagined her and Daria on vacation, somewhere in New England, not too far from where she'd grown up. Hiking together and then stopping by an old cabin, Daria pressing her up against the side of the building to kiss her, no one around . . .

She shook her head, pulling herself together. She needed to get this moment right or there would be no others.

"Daria," Liz said. She was slightly out of breath from how quickly Daria was walking. "I'm so sorry."

"For what?" Daria said, her voice cold.

"For the— Did you see the article?"

"Let's think," Daria said. "Did I see the article that mentions me by first and last name, that ran in the magazine that I own? I did, actually. Thank God no one in my office reads anything queer, or I would have had some seriously uncomfortable conversations with my boss today."

Liz hadn't thought it was possible to feel more horrified, but she did. "Daria." Liz reached up to put a hand on Daria's back, then thought better of it. "I am so, so sorry. I didn't—I never meant for that article to be published. I wrote it before we—right after you and Bailey said you were putting the magazine up for sale again. I haven't looked at it since then. Lydia took it off my computer and published it without telling me. I had no idea. It was never supposed to—I never thought anyone else would read it, let alone . . ." she trailed off.

"But you wrote it, right?"

"I—not all of it. But. Yes."

Daria ran a hand over her face, into her hair.

"I knew you didn't like me," she said. "But I had no idea how much you hated me."

"I don't hate you," Liz said desperately. "Daria, please listen to me. I was wrong. That's not how I feel. Not anymore. I didn't know you then. Now, I—"

"You wrote it that night, didn't you?" Daria said. Her hands were fists at her sides. "The night I told you I had feelings for you, that I'd been thinking about you for months. You went home and wrote this."

"Not that night," Liz said miserably. "The next day."

Daria shook her head. "I am so fucking stupid."

"No! You're not!" Liz reached for Daria's arm, hoping to stop her so Liz could look her in the face and say—say *something* to make her understand. But Daria shrugged her off.

"And this whole time, I've been thinking that *maybe*—" She gestured toward Liz. "So fucking stupid," she said again.

"No," Liz said miserably. "I'm the stupid one. The things I wrote were horrible. Mean. Wrong. I was angry and rant-ing. I know Bailey didn't buy the magazine to"—she cringed, remembering her own words—"sleep with people. I know you're not . . . that you're nothing like how I described you. Getting to know you has been the best part of my life these past few weeks. I joined Pride Runners so I could have an excuse to see you. I spend all day hoping you'll message me. I—" Liz stopped walking. "I go to sleep thinking about you," she said, echoing Daria's words from weeks ago. "I wake up thinking about you. I—" She broke off, her voice threatening to turn into sobs.

Daria was only a few feet from Liz now, hair shining in the sunset, face unreadable. Tentatively, Liz reached out and took one of Daria's clenched fists in her hands. Daria didn't pull back, and Liz pressed her lips against Daria's knuckles.

For a long moment, Daria didn't speak or move. Her hand was warm. Slowly, it relaxed out of its fist. She intertwined her fingers with Liz's. But then she let go.

"That article," Daria started, then paused to wait for a pair of runners to pass them on the footpath. "Makes me look like a heartless monster bent on controlling everyone around me. Strangers are tweeting about me. It's the first thing that will show up when a client googles my name. You know how hard I try to just—just fly under the radar. And now." She shook her head. "You've made my life seriously complicated."

Liz started to say how sorry she was again, but Daria cut her off.

"However this article got written or posted, I—things just got a lot harder for me. And I can't do"—she gestured between her and Liz—"this right now. Whatever this is."

"Oh," Liz said. "Okay." She bit down hard on the inside of her cheek, but it wasn't enough to stop the tears from coming. Daria looked just as sad as Liz felt. Liz wanted to comfort her, to wrap her arms around her. For a second, she thought Daria would let her. But then Daria stepped back, clearing her throat.

"I have to go," she said.

Liz nodded, unable to speak. Daria gave her one last, long look. Then she turned around and walked back toward the park exit. Liz stayed where she was, hugging her elbows, watching her go. Now, more than ever, Liz felt sure that together, she and Daria would have just *fit*. Now, when it was too late.

Liz watched until Daria was out of sight. But Daria never looked back.

29

On the subway home, Liz finally read her texts. There were more than a hundred of them, mostly from her coworkers. Apparently everyone had tried reaching out to Lydia, but they had refused to take down the blog and weren't answering their phone.

Liz opened Twitter. The gay internet was an echo chamber and her article seemed to be the controversy of the day. The original link no longer worked, but enough people had linked to the blog where it still lived. Liz tried to compute the scope of the damage. It hadn't gone as viral as Lydia had hoped. A couple thousand people had liked or shared or commented. A couple thousand was better than twenty thousand or a hundred thousand. But it was still too many.

Most of the comments were calling Bailey and Daria jerks, saying they should be ashamed of themselves for treating their employees so badly. But there were also people saying the article was unprofessional and questioning who Liz Baker was to make all these judgments. And a few who said no one had even heard of this magazine anyway, so no wonder it was closing.

Liz set her account to private and forced herself to delete the app. There would be more backlash soon, she was sure, and she wouldn't want to read it. Then she texted Lydia. Her first draft was full of f-bombs, but by the time she got off the train, she'd landed on: *Lydia, you were right to be upset with me for not writing the article like I promised to. I'm sorry. That was unfair to you and to the entire staff. But please, take that article down if the magazine, Charlotte, or our friendship has ever meant anything to you. I'm begging you.*

She stared at the text for the rest of the subway ride, but it didn't go from delivered to read (Lydia was, of course, the kind of person who had read receipts on, so you knew if they were ignoring you). Then Liz stumbled home. Her back ached, her feet hurt, and her face was still swollen from crying. She felt thoroughly pummeled by this day.

When she opened the door to the apartment, she found Katie lying in the armchair by the living room window, her feet dangling over the side, staring at her phone. The lights were off, and the room was dim.

Liz shut the door and flicked on the overhead light. Katie sat up, startled.

"I didn't know what the article said," Katie said before Liz could speak. "I'm so sorry, Liz. Lydia said it would save the magazine. I wanted to help. I wish I'd never given them your password. I can't tell you how much I regret it."

Liz opened her mouth to yell but found she didn't have it in her. Katie had started to cry. Liz wanted nothing more than to have this all be someone else's fault. But how could she fault Katie for doing something desperate for a crush when Liz had overlooked so many red flags for Weston? When she would do anything to go back in time and treat Daria differently from the very beginning?

"Come here," Liz finally said, holding out her arms, and they collapsed into each other.

■   ■   ■

Jane came home at seven. Liz waited in her room for ten minutes before going over to her door, telling herself she was giving Jane a moment but really taking the time to muster up her courage. When she finally knocked, Jane hesitated before telling her she could come in.

Liz closed the door behind her. Jane was sitting at her desk chair, looking drained and listless. Liz wanted to hug her, but wasn't sure if Jane would want that, so she settled uneasily on the edge of Jane's bed instead.

"Did you talk to Bailey?" Liz asked.

Jane shook her head. "She didn't want to talk."

Liz squeezed part of Jane's quilt between her fingers. "Jane," she said. "I am so sorry."

"I know Lydia posted it without your permission," Jane said. "But how could you write those things? About Bailey? About *me*? I know you didn't mention me by name, but everyone will be speculating about who it is."

Liz opened her mouth to try to explain, but Jane cut her off. "I'm a Black trans woman writing in the public eye, Liz. I can't just be good at what I do—I need to be better. I can't give anyone any reason to doubt me or my credentials."

"I'm sorry," Liz said miserably.

Jane shook her head. "I know you would never have published this article as is," she said. "But sometimes it feels like you get so focused on your own feelings that you don't think or care who might become collateral damage. Including me."

It was worse, somehow, that Jane didn't sound angry as she said it. Instead, she sounded tired and resigned. How long had she felt this way? Jane's quilt blurred as tears filled Liz's eyes.

"You're right," Liz said quietly. "You're right and I'm sorry."

"You're like a sister to me, Liz. You've been there for me so many times and you've welcomed me into your family in a way I didn't know I needed," Jane said. "But I just potentially lost Bailey. My entire career is up in the air. That article tarnished our magazine's reputation, and I'm the head writer, so I might not get that *Autostraddle* job now. Because of something *you* wrote. We've been friends for a long time, and we'll still be friends after this. But not tonight. Not for a while. And I'm going to need you to work really hard to earn back my trust."

"Okay," Liz said. She would have thought she'd cried as much as she could that day, but apparently not. She stood up. "You're right. I understand. I love you."

Jane didn't respond.

Liz closed the door softly behind her and went back to her room. But it turned out she actually could feel a little worse, because when she checked her phone, Lydia had written back: a photo of them and Weston at a bar, cheeks pressed together, flipping off the camera. The text read: *fuck u bitch thx for getting me fired.*

Liz wanted to throw her phone, but she knew she couldn't afford it. She put it in her desk drawer and threw her pillows instead. Then she sat down on her bed and buried her head in her palms. This was the worst day of her life. And she had absolutely no idea how to fix it.

30

It took Liz a second to remember why, exactly, she felt so terrible when she woke up the next morning. Then the previous day came rushing back to her, and she covered her head with her pillow, hoping the world would just go away.

It did not go away. In fact, the world knocked at her door two minutes later, in the form of Jane.

"Oh. Good morning," Liz said, sitting up in bed as Jane pushed the door open, hovering on the threshold.

"Morning." Jane looked like she hadn't slept much. Her face was drawn, and her eyes were puffy. "I just wanted to let you know—the article is off the blog."

Liz closed her eyes in relief. "Thank God. What made Lydia decide to take it down?"

"They didn't, actually," Jane said. "Katie guessed their password and deleted the site."

"Oh." Liz slumped back against her pillows.

"Yeah," Jane said. "Anyway, I'm heading out." She shut the door, and Liz slowly slid down until she was lying on her back again. She had never wanted to go to work less. But she had an apology letter to write.

When Liz sat down at her work computer, she had more than a hundred emails. Most of them were from queers offering their support. Saying they were so sorry to hear the magazine was closing and that they were furious at how the *NF* staff had been mistreated.

Liz closed her eyes. She didn't know what she had expected. A million emails calling her a bitch for hurting her best friend? A restraining order from Daria? An email from some president of the Associated Press, telling her she was barred from ever working in journalism again? But no. People believed her article. They agreed with her. Which was infinitely worse, because it meant there were hundreds of people out in the world right now, believing every careless, cruel thing Liz had said.

Liz opened a blank Word document, staring at the blinking cursor. She thought about Jane, squealing after her coffee date with Bailey. About Daria, stretching in the grass after their run, her cheeks flushed.

An hour later, Liz emailed a draft of her apology to Charlotte, who gave her approval to pass it along to their lawyer for review. Liz sent it off, then went to Charlotte's office and knocked tentatively on the door. When she opened it, Charlotte had her head flat on her desk. She moaned to acknowledge Liz's presence.

"What an absolute shithouse of a day," Charlotte said, raising her head and rubbing at her eyes.

"Seriously." Liz slumped into a seat across from her. "I'm so sorry, Charlotte. I never meant for that article to be shared. But we also shouldn't have planned it behind your back."

"No, you shouldn't have," Charlotte said. "But I also know you didn't mean for anyone to see it." She sighed. "I know you, Liz, and I know your heart is in the right place. So I forgive you."

Liz felt almost light-headed with relief. She gave Charlotte a tremulous smile.

Charlotte waved her hand in the direction of the office. "I mean, this is all ending soon anyway. What does it even matter?"

"You don't mean that," Liz said.

"No, I don't," Charlotte admitted. "I've spent nineteen years of my life loving this magazine. But, honestly, as long as I get the chance to say goodbye to our readers properly and put a good last issue to bed, I actually feel ready to let it go."

"Really?" Liz said, surprised.

"Really." Charlotte leaned back in her chair. "I mean, I started this magazine when I was younger than you are. I got a couple of my friends to write articles, I laid it out in Microsoft Word, and I passed it out to people in gay bars. It felt exciting back then, to create a platform for myself when no one else would publish my work, to put myself out there in a way I'd never seen a Chinese lesbian do. And as it got more successful and official, it took on new meaning. I was able to publish articles about important issues, able to hire a lot of queers of color, able to support our community." She shrugged. "But somewhere along the way, it became something that I was doing for other people, not something that I was doing because I loved it."

Liz stared. She had always assumed that Charlotte would want to hang on to the magazine as long as possible. She'd never considered that Charlotte might feel just as burnt-out as Liz.

"I mean, don't get me wrong," Charlotte said, leaning forward. "I love all of you, and I'm proud of the work we've done. But I'm ready to move on."

"What are you going to do?" Liz asked.

"Long term, I'm not sure," Charlotte said, sounding unconcerned. "But for now, I'm going to take that severance money, fix up my motorcycle, and ride across the country with a couple of friends from Dykes on Bikes. See some things, have some fun, and not have to be in charge for once."

"You're going to ride across the country on a *motorcycle*?" Liz said. "That is ridiculously cool."

Charlotte winked at her. "What about you?"

Liz didn't know what to say. After a moment, Charlotte reached across her desk and patted her on the elbow.

"You'll be okay," she said. "You're smart and hardworking and talented. I know you'll figure this out. And I'll be around to help."

Liz opened her mouth to try to put into words how much that meant, but Charlotte spoke again.

"I mean, as long as Heather Media doesn't sue us. 'Cause if they sue us, we're *all* screwed."

"Great," Liz said, laughing. "Thanks for that."

Charlotte turned to her computer. "Are you sure this is the apology you want to post? It could just be two paragraphs saying you never meant for that article to go public and you're sorry for any harm you caused."

"Yes," Liz said. "Definitely."

Charlotte looked back at Liz. "But I thought you hated Daria."

"I did," Liz said in a small voice.

"You don't need to make her seem like a saint just because you feel guilty," Charlotte said.

"I meant what I wrote," Liz said. "I want to make this right. I did once think Daria was . . . all the things I wrote in the article Lydia posted. But I just didn't know her well enough. She's actually really great."

"Really?" Charlotte raised an eyebrow.

"Yeah," Liz said. "Really. I've—gotten to know her more."

"Oh, *have* you?" Charlotte said insinuatingly, but when Liz didn't respond she didn't ask any more questions.

"Okay. Well, in that case, legal just wrote back. You have our approval."

■   ■   ■

Half an hour later, Liz's apology went live:

Dear Readers,

Yesterday afternoon, an article was published on the Nether Fields site with my name on the byline. It was posted by a now-terminated employee, disgruntled over the closing of the magazine, who took the article off my computer without permission. It was never my intention for those words to be read by anyone but myself.

I'm upset about the violation of my privacy. Still, those were my words. I wrote them in a moment of anger, right after we found out the magazine was being put up for sale again, knowing we were unlikely to find a buyer. My words were more diary entry than clearheaded reporting, and it's my responsibility to explain that the article didn't paint an accurate picture.

I've worked at the Nether Fields for four years. I love this magazine, its readers, and its staff. When Heather Media planned to shut us down in May, we were all devastated. But then Bailey Cox and Daria Fitzgerald bought the magazine, giving us a second chance. They worked hard and cared deeply. They made changes that helped keep our doors open for the past six months. Ultimately, though, they couldn't afford to keep trying. Running a magazine, let alone a queer magazine, is a brutal business. It is no one's fault that we couldn't make this work. Everyone is heartbroken to see the magazine go— including Bailey and Daria.

The article I wrote was cruel and careless. I have a bad

habit of being judgmental, especially when I'm angry, and I leapt to judge two individuals who were just trying their best to save the Nether Fields. Bailey Cox, from the beginning, was warm, friendly, and passionate about creating community for queer women. She's a generous and caring person. I owe her an apology.

I also owe an apology to Daria Fitzgerald. I called her many unflattering names in that article, none of which she deserves. Daria is thoughtful and quiet, which I originally misread as being cold and conceited. I've since come to realize how wrong I was. Daria is smart and kind. She's funny. She stands by her friends and commitments. Ask anyone who knows Daria and they have a story: a time she helped them, a time she was there for them, a time she went out of her way to make them feel supported and loved. She never compromises her values. She apologizes when she's wrong and looks for opportunities to grow. She's the kind of person I hope to someday be more like.

I want to apologize to Charlotte Liu and the entire Nether Fields staff. You've all worked so hard to keep this magazine going, and this controversy was not the way we should have ended our time here.

Lastly, I want to apologize to you, readers. This was never how you should have found out our magazine was closing. Please know that we love you and it has been a privilege to write for you. We're working on our final issue now, which will be devoted to celebrating you and this entire magazine.

I hope you'll find a way to forgive me and give everyone mentioned in that article the privacy and grace they deserve—even me.

Sincerely,
Liz Baker

■ ■ ■

By the time Jane got home that evening, Liz was putting the finishing touches on dinner. Jane tugged her shoes off and put them on the mat by the door, eyeing Liz suspiciously. "You never cook," she said.

"I know," Liz said. "But I wanted to make you dinner."

"One dinner isn't going to make everything right between us again," said Jane. "I wasn't kidding when I said I need to see some changes in the way you act."

"I know," Liz said. "I know I need to stop being so impulsive. And I know that I need to work on being a better friend than I was before."

"Yeah," Jane said, crossing her arms. "You always say things without thinking. And that can create a lot of issues. Especially for someone like me, who can't get away with saying random shit like you can. So I need you to start thinking *before* you act, not just apologizing after."

"You're right," Liz said. "And I hope you'll let me prove to you over time that I'm going to be different. I actually booked a therapist appointment today so I can start figuring out how to be better about that."

"Good." Jane side-eyed Liz for a moment, then drifted over to inspect what she was stirring.

"It's vegetarian chili," Liz said. "And there's cornbread in the oven."

Jane leaned over the pot to sniff it.

"Go ahead," Liz said, stepping back.

"What?"

"You can taste it and add whatever spices you think I'm missing."

Jane smiled, just a little, then took out a spoon, tasted it, and headed over to the spice cabinet. Liz leaned back against the breakfast bar while Jane stirred and tried to choose her next words carefully. "I'm really sorry, Jane," she said. "I should never have written those things. Even for myself. And I know I'm not always the easiest to be friends with. I really am going to work at being better from now on. Because you're my favorite person in the whole world and knowing that I've hurt you, or put you at risk, or made you uncomfortable—that's just not okay."

Jane turned around and faced Liz. "It helps to hear you say that. And don't get me wrong, I'm furious at Lydia," she said. "But it's hard not to be mad when your best friend is the reason your girlfriend breaks up with you."

"Bailey broke up with you again?"

"Not yet." Jane hugged her arms across her chest. "But I haven't heard from her. We only just got back together. I just—I don't think we're going to make it."

Liz studied the floor, noticing a few shriveled peas that had found their way into a corner. "I'm so, so sorry, Jane."

"Me too," Jane said softly. "But," she added tentatively, "if she breaks up with me over something that wasn't my fault, then fuck her, right?"

"Yeah," Liz said. "That's true."

There was a pause while Jane tasted the chili one last time, then turned off the burner. "That was quite the apology letter," she said eventually.

"I hope it was enough," Liz said.

"It was pretty good," Jane said. "But—since when are you in love with Daria?"

"I— What?"

"I mean. That apology was basically a love letter."

"It was not a—" Liz cut off. "It's kind of a long story."

Jane took two bowls out of the cabinet. "Tell me over dinner?"

Liz grinned, trying not to cry. She knew she still had a

long way to go to earn back Jane's trust and friendship again, but she was willing to go all that way and more. Jane deserved that. And Liz wanted that for herself, too. She wanted to grow, to become the kind of person who really thought things through, who was considerate, who didn't rush to judge people. The kind of person who deserved Jane's friendship.

"Absolutely."

31

Liz briefly considered going to the Central Park run on Saturday morning, but she couldn't stomach it. Daria hadn't reached out after the apology—not via Instagram, email, or even LinkedIn, all of which Liz checked obsessively, just in case. Plus, the queer world was small, and she was sure many of the runners would have heard about the article. She had just started becoming friends with J, too, and now she felt sick imagining their reaction. Would they even let her run with them, after what she'd done? Liz didn't want to find out.

Which was why Liz was still in bed on Saturday at eleven when someone knocked on her door. She called for them to come in, thinking it was Jane, but it was Katie. They hadn't spoken much since the night they'd hugged in the living room, and Liz sat up, feeling nervous.

"Can we talk?" Katie asked, shutting the door behind her.

"Of course," Liz said.

"I wanted to tell you I'm sorry," Katie said, sitting down on the edge of Liz's bed. "I read a pretty great apology letter recently and it made me realize how powerful saying sorry can be." She gave Liz a small smile. "So—I'm sorry. For invading your privacy. For giving Lydia the password to your computer when I knew what they were planning to do."

Liz reached out and squeezed Katie's hand. "I'm sorry too," she said. "I never should have brought you into my fight with Lydia. That wasn't fair. You deserve better friendship than that."

"I do," Katie said, nodding. "Which is why I told Lydia we're done. I told them I don't want to be around them anymore."

"Whoa," Liz said. "That's a big change."

"I should have done it a long time ago," Katie said, rubbing her wrist with one hand. "I guess I just never realized how bad it had gotten. It always felt like my fault. The way they treated me."

"You thought they cared about you," Liz said, feeling a rush of sympathy for her friend. "There's nothing wrong with that. How Lydia treated you was *their* fault."

"Yeah, but," Katie shrugged. "I let them do it to me."

"It's hard not to," Liz said. "When you really like someone. I've done the same thing."

"Thanks," Katie said, giving her a faltering smile. "I love you."

"I love you too," Liz said. "There's no one I'd rather be huntin', fishin', and lovin' every day with."

Katie laughed and half hugged, half tackled Liz into the mattress. Liz hugged her back, only letting go long enough to open her phone and play their song before she wrapped her arms back around her friend.

■ ■ ■

The next morning, Liz was woken up by the apartment buzzer. She kept her eyes closed, hoping Jane or Katie would answer it. No luck—it rang again. Liz groaned and shuffled down the hall to the buzzer intercom, asking who was there.

"Delivery," a voice said. Liz pushed the button to let them in, then leaned against the wall with her eyes closed while she waited for them to climb the stairs. Maybe someone had ordered her a breakfast sandwich. A girl could dream.

When the doorbell finally rang, Liz opened the door to find an entire meadow's worth of spring flowers in front of her. She couldn't even see the delivery person behind two gigantic vases full of bright pink, purple, yellow, and blue blossoms.

Hope kick-started her heartbeat. Were these from Daria?

"Delivery for Jane Wilson," said the person who presumably existed behind the wall of flowers.

"Oh." Liz felt ridiculous for being disappointed. "You can put those down wherever there's space. Here." She swept a pile of magazines and junk mail off the coffee table. "Thank you."

Liz stared at the floral explosion for a minute, then went to find Jane, who was at her desk, wearing headphones and scrolling through a job board. She jumped when Liz tapped her on the shoulder.

"You got a delivery," Liz said, feeling oddly shy. She and Jane had eaten dinner together again last night, but things definitely weren't back to normal between them.

"What?" Jane pulled off her headphones.

"Just come see."

Jane followed her down the hall. She gasped when she saw the flowers.

"They're beautiful! Who are they from?"

"I mean, I have a guess," Liz said. "But go find out."

Jane bent over to smell the flowers with a dreamy expression. She read the tiny card that was poking out between a lily and a tulip, then wordlessly handed it to Liz. All it said was Jane's name.

"They have to be from Bailey, right?" Liz inspected the arrangement. "I mean, they look pretty fancy."

"I don't know," Jane said. "But how embarrassing would it be if I texted her after she told me she needed space to ask if she sent me flowers and she didn't?"

"Well, who else could have sent them?" a voice said from the other end of the living room. Katie had come out, looking like she'd just woken up.

"Charlotte?" Jane asked doubtfully. "Or maybe this is Lydia's way of saying sorry?"

Liz grunted. "Yeah, right. Also, why would Charlotte send you *two* flower arrangements?"

"Why would *anyone* send you two floral arrangements unless they're trying to sleep with you?" Katie said.

"But then why not include a note?" Jane bent over to smell them again.

They had started debating whether Jane should text Bailey when they were interrupted by the buzzer.

"The delivery person must have forgotten to include the card and come back," Katie said, pressing the button to let them in. But when she opened the door, a different delivery person was waiting with an enormous wicker basket.

"Jane Wilson?" they said, holding out a clipboard. Jane, bewildered, signed for the package. Liz took the basket and placed it on the coffee table. Nestled inside, surrounded by paper packing shavings, were a baguette in a white sleeve, a long thin box of macarons, a bottle of red wine, and various jars and boxes.

"No note," Katie said, inspecting it.

Jane started rummaging through the basket, passing each item to Liz and Katie for inspection. It was like a mini

Christmas. There was some Dijon mustard, a jar of tiny
pickles, pink salt, a pastry box with two croissants, and a
package of smoked ham.

"I don't get it," Jane said. "Why send me flowers *and* food?
With no note?"

"Maybe she came to her senses and realized she can't let
you go," Katie said.

"She hasn't said a word to me all week," Jane said. "Why
do that and then suddenly hit me with gifts?"

"You have to text her!" Liz said. "Or else she'll think you
don't like her weird pickles."

"Okay, okay. I'll get my phone." Jane stood up but had
barely made it down the hall when the buzzer rang again.
She whirled back around to gape at Liz and Katie.

"No way," Liz said, laughing for what felt like the first
time in days. "This is getting out of control."

A few seconds later, a delivery person was standing on
their doorstep with a large wrapped package in their hands.
Jane brought it over to the couch and tore into the wrapping
paper. She pulled out a black-and-white striped long-sleeved
shirt.

"Ew," Katie said, making a face. "That is seriously not
cute."

"She should have stuck to tiny pickles," Liz added.

But Jane didn't respond. She was staring at whatever else
was in the box. When she looked up, her eyes were full of
tears.

"It's Paris," she whispered.

"What?"

"The trip we were planning to take," Jane said, starting to
actually cry. "We were going to go to Paris together, but then
we broke up."

Liz grabbed the edge of the box and tipped it toward her.
Inside, nestled in tissue paper, was a black beret.

"Oh my God." Liz grabbed Katie's and Jane's hands. She looked at the baguette and the croissants and the lilies. "It's Paris."

Jane was bawling now. Katie handed her the beret, and they all laughed as Jane tried to balance it on top of her braids.

"You look ridiculous," Liz choked out, starting to cry too.

And then the doorbell rang. They all looked at each other.

"That had better be an enormous cake shaped like the Eiffel Tower," Liz said, wiping her eyes.

But when Liz opened the door, Bailey was standing on the other side.

Liz stepped back to give her a view of Jane, sitting on the couch surrounded by jars and flowers. Jane jolted to her feet and the beret fell onto the couch behind her.

"Jane," Bailey said, stepping inside. She took a deep breath. "I'm so in love with you. I love how smart you are. I love that you care so much about making the world a better place. I love your scary obsession with Harry Styles. I love your fashion sense and your quest to bake the world's best cinnamon rolls and how much fun I have with you every day. There are a million amazing things about you. And I love every single one. So unbelievably much."

Katie sniffed loudly. Jane started crying again, apparently unable to respond.

"I never should have broken up with you," Bailey went on. "And I never should have let a ridiculous article get in our way. I've never felt like this about anyone before, and I really, really don't want to lose you. So if you give me a third chance, I promise I won't let you down again."

She crossed over to Jane. "So, will you go to Paris with me? And—will you date me again?"

Jane nodded, still sobbing, and threw her arms around Bailey.

Behind them, Liz closed the apartment door as quietly as possible. She and Katie made excited eye contact, then started tiptoeing away toward their respective bedrooms. By the time Liz reached hers, Bailey was reaching up to cup Jane's cheeks in her hands as they kissed.

32

Liz didn't hear from Daria the next week, either.

On Saturday, she was desperate enough to go to the morning run in Central Park even though it was freezing outside, hoping an in-person apology might change Daria's mind. But Daria wasn't there. The other runners whispered and stared as Liz desperately scanned the group, trying to find her. J pointedly turned around without saying hello, and Liz's face burned. She was paired with a new running buddy, a short white man who was so focused on trying to breathe during the run that they didn't talk. Afterward, Liz didn't even stick around to stretch before slinking away from the group in shame.

At this point, Liz supposed she should just try to move on. The end of November was approaching, and the magazine was officially closing on December 1. Liz had been presented with her severance package and, other than finishing up the final issue, there was nothing left to do. The shutdown felt a little bit like a breakup that had gone on for months. She just wanted to be done.

Liz was starting to panic a little every time she thought

about What Comes Next. She had applied for a few jobs at different magazines and newspapers but hadn't gotten any interviews. Some small part of her was relieved—she didn't want to work for those places anyway. She was half-convinced that she should just get a part-time job some-where and try to make her blog work, like Jane had suggested. But she worried that a gap in her résumé would make it much harder to find journalism jobs in the future. Was her blog really worth taking that risk for?

Liz was sitting in her room one night, writing another blog post, when Katie knocked on her door.

"Hey," she said, sticking her head in. "I thought you'd want to know that Lydia's moving out. They're coming to get their stuff on Thursday while we're all at the office."

"Okay," Liz said carefully. "How do you feel about that?"

"Relieved," Katie said. "Do you want to get takeout? I'm thinking of ordering from the vegan Indian place."

"Yeah, I'd love to," Liz said. "Let me just finish up here, and then I'll come hang out."

Katie crouched to peer at Liz's screen. "What are you working on?"

"It might be a waste of time," Liz said. "But I'm thinking about rebooting *Confessions of a New York Dyke* and trying to make it a little more official."

"No way!" Katie shoved Liz's shoulder with her own. "That's a great idea! You were getting pretty good views on that back in the day, right?" Her eyes took on a faraway qual-ity, the way they always did when she started to plan some-thing. "And that was completely organic, with no advertising or anything. Imagine if you did a little promotion, built your social media platform, maybe placed a couple of ads on Instagram and Goodreads—oh! You should set up a Patreon! I bet a ton of people would pay for early access and bonus content and stuff." Her mouth fell open. "We could do cross-promotion with my meme account!"

Liz swallowed, feeling overwhelmed. "I don't know," she said. "That sounds like it would take a lot of time. Shouldn't I be focusing on something I can do for a living?"

"Why not do *this* for a living?"

"I just—" Liz took a deep breath. "I don't know if I'm a good enough writer to actually make money. I mean, you heard Lydia. No one cared about my article about the photographer."

"Liz, that wasn't about your *article*," Katie said, rolling her eyes. "Our magazine is literally being shut down for not having a big enough audience. That's why it didn't get more attention."

"Maybe."

"It's normal to be insecure about your writing," Katie said. "I worry I'm a terrible writer all the time, and journalism is way less subjective than creative writing. But don't let that fear hold you back, okay?"

Katie's words reminded Liz of what Moira Campbell had said during their interview. How people focused so much on what they could lose by living as their authentic selves that they forgot to focus on what they could *gain*.

Maybe Katie and Moira had a point.

"Thanks, Katie," Liz said. "What about you? Have you been applying to jobs?"

"Yeah!" Katie grinned. "I've got a couple of second-round interviews coming up. Mostly at online publications, but a few at newspapers. And ¡*Pussy Putas!* has started to get attention—I got invited to guest host a couple episodes of this podcast about young Latine people interviewing their parents and grandparents about their experiences immigrating to the United States. Which is going to be amazing exposure for me." She smiled again. "I actually think this could end up being good for me. I'm going to miss the *NF,* but I think I'm ready for the next step."

"You definitely are," Liz said. "I mean, you're an incredible reporter. Once you're at a bigger company, you're going to take off."

"Thanks, bud." Katie squeezed Liz's shoulder. "Love you."

Liz spun around in her chair and hugged Katie around the middle. "Love you too."

"I'm really glad." Katie kissed the top of Liz's head. "Also I'm ordering garlic naan, whether you want to be around my breath or not."

"Get two orders," Liz said. "I'm not a monster."

■ ■ ■

The next day, Liz was sitting in her cubicle, putting the finishing touches on her final article (an advice column on how to deal with your favorite magazine shutting down) when her desk phone rang. Liz answered it, a little hesitantly—no one ever called her work number.

To her surprise, it was Jane.

"Why are you calling me? Where are you?" Liz said, double-checking the caller ID.

"Lena Lounge," Jane said in an ominous voice. "Get over here. Right now."

"Why? Is everything okay?"

"Just get over here!" Jane hissed and hung up.

Liz put the phone back, bewildered, and headed over to the lounge. When she opened the door, Jane tackled her.

"Holy shit!" Liz yelled, losing her balance. Jane wrapped her arms around her and started jumping up and down.

"I got the job I got the job I got the job!" she screamed.

"What?"

"The *Autostraddle* job! I just got the *Autostraddle* job!"

Liz screamed and started jumping too.

"Oh my God!" she said. "You got the job?"

"I got the job!"

"You got the job!" Liz stopped jumping because she was out of breath. "When did you hear?"

"Thirty seconds ago!" Jane said. "They just called! It pays way more and it's *Autostraddle* and everyone there is so nice and oh my God I have a job and I have a career and I'm going to be okay!"

"You're going to be okay!" Liz said. "You're going to be more than okay! You're going to be their top reporter in, like, two months!" She shrieked again. It felt amazing to be happy with Jane like this. Things had been improving between them lately, but this was the first time it had felt like they were getting close to being unreserved with each other again.

"I was sure I wouldn't get it after the article," Jane said. "I didn't hear from them for, like, three weeks after my final interview. So I said that on the phone, that I hadn't expected to hear from them at this point."

She grabbed Liz's arm and looked intently into her eyes. "And do you know what they said?"

"What?" Liz said.

"They admitted they were a little on the fence after the article came out. But then they got a *call*." She waggled her eyebrows at Liz, who furrowed hers dramatically.

"Okay . . . ?"

"A call from *Daria Fitzgerald*."

"What?" Liz dropped her exaggerated confusion face and grabbed Jane's elbow right back.

"Yeah! Apparently, Daria called and gave me a glowing recommendation. She explained that I had been unfairly caught in the crosshairs of an irate employee's poor decision-making and they should disregard the article completely. She said that, as the owner of the magazine, she was consistently impressed with my professionalism and performance, and that I was an incredible journalist."

"Oh my God," Liz whispered. She sat down on the couch.

"I know," Jane said, bouncing in place. "I didn't think she liked me, let alone thought I was a good journalist."

"She would have to be completely oblivious to not know that," Liz said.

"But she went super out of her way to do this," Jane said. "Which seems kind of weird. *Unless* . . ." she trailed off meaningfully.

Liz shook her head. "This isn't about me. She's not even speaking to me right now. And I can't blame her, really."

"Or maybe—" Jane started to say in an insinuating tone.

"No," Liz interrupted. "She's just that kind of person. It was the right thing to do—you deserve this job. Plus, she kind of owes you for breaking you and Bailey up."

"Are you sure?" Jane said, sitting down next to her. "'Cause she's literally never seemed to care about me before now."

"I'm sure," Liz said heavily. "You got your girl, but I don't think I'm going to get mine."

Jane put her hand over Liz's and squeezed. Liz smiled at her, then shook off her gloom.

"Enough about me," she said. "More about your glamorous new future! Have you told Bailey yet?"

"Not yet!" Jane said. "I wanted to tell you first."

"Call her, call her!" Liz said. "And tonight we're celebrating, okay?"

Jane beamed at her. "Deal."

33

———

Jane was moving out. She told Liz on Saturday, over tea at their favorite café on Franklin Avenue.

"At the end of the year," she said apologetically. "I just think it's time."

Liz tried not to let her face fall, but she knew she didn't fully succeed. "You're not . . . moving in with Bailey, are you?" she said, trying not to sound too horrified.

"No. We're not *that* gay," Jane said. "We're taking it slow. I just need space of my own, you know? And now I can afford it."

But what about me? Liz wanted to say. What if she barely saw Jane anymore? Was Jane still mad at her? Was that why she was leaving Liz behind?

No, Liz reminded herself. This was a good thing for Jane. It was understandable that she would want her own space, especially after everything that had happened, and Liz was going to be a good friend. This was a chance for her to actually practice thinking before she spoke.

"I'm really happy for you," Liz said. "This sounds super exciting."

Jane beamed. "I found a studio in this neighborhood, so I won't be very far. We'll still hang out all the time."

"We'd better."

Jane smiled at Liz over the rim of her teacup.

"You seem really happy," Liz said, smiling back.

"I am," Jane said. "I almost feel bad being this happy, since the magazine is closing. But . . . maybe it was time, you know?"

"Yeah. Maybe." Liz broke off a large chunk of croissant and put it in her mouth.

"I haven't wanted to stress you out by asking," Jane said cautiously. "But are you still thinking about focusing on your own writing for a while?"

Liz shrugged, all her fears racing through her mind like ticker tape.

What if writing didn't work out?

What if no one wanted to read a silly lesbian blog?

What if she wasn't a good enough writer to pull this off?

"I know you're afraid of all the what-ifs," Jane said, as if reading Liz's mind. "But I have a few to add to the list that you might not have considered."

Liz frowned at her.

"What if you never give yourself a shot?" Jane began. "What if you regret not trying for the rest of your life? What if you *are* good enough?"

Liz swallowed. Those were definitely what-ifs she'd never allowed herself to consider. But she shook her head, not wanting to think about it right now. "Maybe Katie and I should move too," she said, to change the subject. "Living there without you sounds too sad."

Jane hesitated, but then seemed to accept Liz's dismissal. "Maybe you could find a two-bedroom somewhere."

They fell into reminiscing about the apartment. The time

Jane had caught the ceiling on fire trying to make crème brûlée. The time Katie had locked herself in the bathroom after a bad breakup and Liz had to pee in the kitchen sink. Even the time Lydia organized a seven-deadly-sins party so rowdy the landlord threatened to evict them.

When Jane got up to go to the bathroom, Liz took out her phone to stop herself from wallowing. The only notifications she had were three work emails: two from Charlotte and one with the subject line *Congratulations!* Probably spam. Liz opened it anyway.

Congratulations! the email read. *We're thrilled to let you know that you've made it to the final round of selections for our Emerging Writers Fellowship.*

Liz froze in her seat and double-checked the sender— some place called the Literary Arts Council. They had a fancy, legit-looking logo. The email address wasn't a random string of numbers. And it was addressed to her by full name.

She scanned the email, her heart racing. It said that she should be proud, because making it to the final round was a great achievement when they had so many applicants. Their final decision would be announced on December 15, and the fellowship would begin January 1.

Hands shaking, she googled the organization. A reputable-looking website popped up, along with several articles from different news outlets about their work. She even recog nized the names of some of the writers who'd previously been fellows. Jane came back and sat down, but Liz asked her to wait one minute while she checked something.

She navigated to the website's fellowship page. There it was. The Emerging Writers Fellowship. Every year, they of-fered ten fellowships to writers who had never published a book. Fellows would receive a monthly stipend, be paired with an experienced mentor, and share work with one another in monthly virtual workshops. Over the summer, they would attend a weeklong writing workshop in Vermont, all expenses paid.

Liz's breath caught in her throat. It was everything she hadn't known she wanted. But the application deadline had been three months ago.

Surely there must have been some mistake. Liz had never even heard of a writing fellowship. Writing residencies, sure. MFA programs, yes. But nothing like this, where you could stay in your city and not move to Iowa or Minnesota.

She should have done more research. She should have scoured the internet for every opportunity that would allow her to write for a living. Because now it was too late, and she would have to wait until next year.

Except.

Liz went back to the email. She realized there was an attachment, and she opened the document. It was a letter from someone on the selection committee, telling her how much he had loved *Confessions of a New York Dyke*. He was a gay man in his fifties, and it would have meant the world to him to have this kind of story when he was young, about someone just figuring out life while being queer. A fun, engaging story like this would have gone a long way toward helping him realize that being gay was not only okay, it was something that could bring a lot of joy to his life. He was sure that her writing could make a big difference to a lot of queer people.

Liz stared at the document, reading it over again. Then she stood up and grabbed her jacket.

"I have to go."

"What?" Jane said, bewildered. "Where?"

"I have to get Daria back!"

Liz didn't wait to see Jane's reaction. She took off at a half jog toward the subway, then ran down the stairs a few at a time and caught a train into the city just as it was pulling in. Luck was with her today.

Of course, once she was on the train, she had forty minutes to start doubting her plan. After Liz got to Daria's apartment, what then? What if the doorman wouldn't let her up? What if Daria wasn't home?

What if Daria still didn't want to see her?

Daria had said she couldn't "do this." And Liz was pretty sure "not doing this" didn't involve Liz showing up at her apartment unannounced.

But even though she didn't have proof, she just *knew* that Daria had submitted her for this writing fellowship. Daria had also called *Autostraddle* and given Jane a recommendation. Surely that was all a good sign. Surely Daria still cared.

And if Daria still cared, even a little bit, then Liz needed to try. She needed to stop focusing on what could go wrong if she went after what she wanted and start focusing on what could go right instead. Jane's words rang in her head: *What if you regret not trying for the rest of your life? What if you are good enough?*

Because Liz *was* good enough, dammit! She was always doubting herself: her writing, her looks, her gender presentation. But Daria liked Liz anyway. And, more important, Liz liked *herself* this way. Maybe someday she'd drift more toward one end of the gender spectrum, but for now Liz liked ping-ponging back and forth between them.

It was time to be brave. To focus on what could go right. To focus on possibility, instead of fear.

When she finally reached Daria's apartment building, Liz threw her shoulders back and walked directly over to the doorman, full of purpose. She had a feeling that if she looked at all skeptical, the doorman wouldn't let her upstairs.

"I'm here to see Daria Fitzgerald. She's expecting me," she said, trying to sound rich and bored. She prayed the doorman wouldn't call Daria to check.

The man looked her over and hesitated, but then said 12C.

Liz spent the whole elevator ride fixing her hair in the mirrored ceiling. She found 12C a little too quickly. She paused in front of the door. Her mouth was very dry. She was sweating.

Possibility, not fear, she reminded herself. *Possibility, not fear.*

She knocked.

Silence. She knocked again. Maybe Daria wasn't home. In which case, Liz's only option was to lurk outside the building like a creep and hope that she came back soon.

Then she heard footsteps on the other side of the door. She smoothed down her hair one last time and tried to put on a normal facial expression. The footsteps got closer. It was too late to go back now. She was here, and she was going to tell Daria just how much she had fallen for her. How desperate she was not to lose her. And then she would kiss her, like Daria had kissed her in that conference room.

The door opened.

"Well. Isn't this a pleasant surprise," Caroline Hillier said.

34

Liz tried her hardest to project nonchalance, as if showing up unannounced at her former employer's apartment were an extremely casual thing to do. Unfortunately, her bright red face and inability to form a coherent sentence were possibly giving her away.

After several seconds of stuttering, Liz finally came up with: "What are you doing here?"

Caroline raised one very thin eyebrow. "I think a better question is what are *you* doing here?"

"I'm . . . here to see Daria."

"Does Daria know that?" Caroline said.

"No. I—I just thought I'd drop by."

"How charmingly old-fashioned," Caroline said, shifting to block the entrance. "It does seem a little odd for you to 'just drop by' after that article, though, doesn't it?"

Liz debated making a break for the elevators. She craned her neck, trying to see behind Caroline, hoping Daria would come to check who was at the door.

"That article was never supposed to be published," she began.

"Oh, yes. I read your apology. It was"—Caroline paused, seeming to search for a word that was appropriately cutting—"touching."

"Can I just talk to Daria?" Liz said.

"About what?"

"Just . . . something," Liz said. She tried not to cringe. Was that really the best she could come up with?

"Personally, I think it's very inappropriate that you're here," Caroline said, leaning against the doorframe. "I mean. You get Daria to open up to you, you get her to chauffeur you around, introduce you to her family and friends. Then you ruin her reputation and call her every terrible name you can think of. And yet, here you are. Showing up at my girlfriend's apartment even though she clearly doesn't want to see you."

Girlfriend? Liz's stomach twisted. "I'd rather hear it from Daria if she doesn't want to see me."

"She's not here," Caroline said, then smirked. "But I'm glad I can take this chance to thank you. Your horrible article brought us back together. Because when she needed support, I was there. And your little love-note apology doesn't change that."

Liz stared at Caroline, too dismayed not to show it. Daria and Caroline were back together?

"She's not here?" was all Liz managed to say.

"No," Caroline said. "And I don't think you should be, either. So I'm going to call down to the doorman and ask him not to let you up next time."

Liz didn't bother coming up with a snarky response. It didn't matter anymore.

She turned and got back into the elevator. Her reflection looked lonely and pathetic. In the lobby, she hurried past the doorman without glancing at him. Then she hustled toward the park, trying to get as far away as possible from the building. The only thing that would make this situation

JUST AS YOU ARE   279

worse would be Daria coming home to find Liz sobbing outside of her apartment.

When Liz found a hidden bench, she sat down and gave
in to tears. What had she been thinking? That Daria had
done all those things because she still wanted to be with
Liz? The writing fellowship, maybe. But the deadline had
been before the article. The rest was just her being nice. Liz
had stomped all over her heart. Of course Daria didn't want
to be with her.

And now Daria was back with Caroline. Liz had driven
Daria right back into her arms. She didn't think Daria would
be happy with Caroline, but what did she know?

Liz covered her face with her hands and let herself sob.
For the magazine shutting down, for Jane moving out, for
her uncertain future. And, most of all, for Daria.

Daria, who Liz had unfairly judged. Daria, who she'd realized too late she was in love with. Daria, who had decided it
was time to move on.

Liz cried until her face felt raw, then dragged herself to
the subway for the most depressing trip of her life. When
she finally got back to the apartment, no one was home. She
took a long, hot shower and got into bed. She was going to
deal with this the only way she knew how: ordering an ob-
scene amount of Thai food and watching *Portrait of a Lady
on Fire* on repeat until work on Monday.

It was time to let Daria go, Liz told herself as the opening
credits rolled. Their timing had been off since they'd met,
and clearly, at this point, it wasn't going to happen. The best
thing to do would be to try to stop thinking about her at all.

Thirty minutes later, Liz was deep into reading through
every DM she and Daria had ever sent to each other, starting from the beginning. The early ones were tentative and
cautious. Later, they got longer and more frequent. Every
message felt like a piano falling on Liz's head—look how

caring and articulate Daria was. How smart and interesting. And Liz had blown it all.

It took her a few minutes to see that there was a new story ring around Daria's profile picture. When she finally did notice, she dropped her phone on her face in surprise.

Rubbing her potentially broken nose, she scrambled to grab her phone again. Daria had posted a snapshot of the entrance to Prospect Park, bustling with bikers and runners, with the words *Beautiful day for a walk*. There was a second photo, too, this time with no caption, of the big meadow near the entrance.

Liz sat upright. Daria was in Brooklyn. Daria was at Prospect Park, only a mile away from Liz's apartment. And Daria had posted it to her Instagram story.

It was a message for Liz. She was sure of it.

She checked the story again. It was time-stamped fifteen minutes ago. Prospect Park was a twenty-minute walk away, and it would take even longer to figure out where Daria was. She could try to take a cab, but with traffic that would be even slower. How long would Daria wait?

She would just have to run for it.

Liz wriggled into a T-shirt and leggings, then stuffed her feet into sneakers as she stumbled down the hall. She took the stairs as fast as she could, and then she started sprinting.

At first, she felt great, striding along with purpose and adrenaline. Three blocks later, though, she started to feel sick. Sprinting a mile was not going to work. She slowed down a little. Her body begged her to walk, but she thought of Daria and kept pushing.

She chugged down the sidewalk, wheezing. Her lungs burned. It would be just her luck if Liz managed to find Daria and then immediately threw up on her.

Finally, at long last, she made it to Grand Army Plaza. She jaywalked across the street to the Brooklyn Public Library but then got stuck waiting for the light. She took advantage of the moment to bend over her knees and gasp for air. When the light changed, she sprinted across and into the park, then down the path until she could see the meadow.

She stopped, uncertain what to do next. The park was crowded with people sitting on picnic blankets, throwing footballs, and walking dogs. She took out her phone. Daria had added another photo of the park to her story. It was from five minutes ago. She was still here.

Liz turned in circles, holding up her phone, trying to figure out which way Daria was facing. She spotted the library poking out from behind some trees—Daria must be on the other side of the meadow, looking back toward where Liz was standing.

Liz groaned. Of course she was on the wrong side. She started running again, dodging kids and dogs, trying to ignore the sharp stitch in her ribs. Her left shoelace was coming undone, but she didn't stop to tie it. She was pretty sure that if she did, she wouldn't be able to start running again. She couldn't believe she had ever signed up to do this voluntarily. Running was terrible and anyone who did this for fun was delusional.

When she reached the other side of the field, she pulled out her phone to see if her view matched Daria's picture. Close, but not quite—she was too far off to one side.

She headed east, checking her phone until she was pretty sure she was in the right spot. She scanned every picnic blanket and bench. If Daria hadn't moved on already, she had to be nearby.

Liz turned in circles, squinting around. There was a person with long hair lying on a picnic blanket, someone with a golden retriever, two kids tossing a Frisbee—and there was Daria, leaning against a tree with her arms crossed, watching Liz.

Liz had been breathing hard before, but now she couldn't breathe at all. She thought about trying to wipe some of the sweat off her face, but there was so much that she didn't think it would make a difference. She walked over.

"Oh, hi!" Liz called when she was in earshot. Her voice had never reached such a high pitch before in her life. "I was just—out for a run. What are you doing here?"

Daria gave her a look that plainly stated she had just watched Liz run across the entire meadow, holding up her phone. Liz stopped just outside the shade of the tree, leaving a few feet between them. She pressed one hand against the stabbing stitch in her side, trying to look like she wasn't about to die.

"I heard you came by my apartment," Daria said. Liz couldn't read her tone. Had she come all this way to tell Liz to leave her and Caroline alone?

"I—um—yes. I sure did," Liz said. "You know. I thought I'd just—pop by! Say hi to my good pal Caroline."

Daria's lips pursed to one side. Liz was acting absurd. She knew this.

"Actually," she said, taking a deep breath. "I came by to ask—did you submit me for a writing fellowship?"

"I did, actually," Daria said. Liz still couldn't read her tone. "A while ago. I hope that's okay."

"Why?"

Daria shrugged and turned to watch two kids riding their bikes across the grass. "I know you want to write, but it's hard when you're working. And I also felt like you needed some external validation that your writing could be fun and still be meaningful. So, when I saw the fellowship while researching grants for the magazine, I went ahead and submitted your blog. Because I thought if I suggested it, you might not apply out of spite."

"I wouldn't have ⎯" Liz stopped herself. "Okay, fair. But thank you."

"How did you find out?" Daria was still focused on the kids, who were now being chased by their parents.

"They sent me an email. I'm a finalist. I'll find out if I got it next month."

"Really?" Daria looked back at Liz. "That's incredible. Congratulations."

"I haven't won yet," Liz said. "But if I did—it would be life changing. So thank you."

"It was your work that got you there." Daria looked away again.

"But it was you who made it happen."

"Well. You're welcome, then."

They stood in silence for a moment. Then Daria said, "What will you do if you get it?"

"I mean, take it, obviously," Liz said. She took a deep breath. "And even if I don't get it, at least now I have some validation, like you said. Which I really needed. So I think, either way, I'm just going to go for it. Stick to a regular posting schedule, set up a Patreon, try to build a platform. Really try to make this work. And if it doesn't, at least I'll always know that I tried, right?"

"Right." Daria nodded. There was another beat of silence and then, "Was that the only reason you wanted to see me?"

"I wanted to say thank you," Liz said. This was not how she had imagined this moment going when she had sprinted the mile from her apartment. She had imagined running into Daria's arms, not this awkward stiffness. "For that and for everything else. For calling *Autostraddle* and helping Bailey and Jane get back together. For everything. You've done so much recently, for—" She paused. "For people I care about."

Liz took a step closer, but Daria didn't look up. She had her hands in her coat pockets, and her shoulders were hunched.

What was Liz doing here? What had she expected, when Daria had a girlfriend and had explicitly told Liz to leave her alone less than three weeks ago? Why did Liz think she would be able to change her mind?

Maybe it was hopeless. But if Liz was going to have her heart broken, she might as well do it thoroughly.

"I'm in love with you," Liz said, in a rush. "I know you're still mad at me about the article, and I know you're with Caroline now. But I am completely, hopelessly, in love with you. I was so wrong about you. From the beginning, I was offended that you thought my articles were beneath you, so I believed the worst about you whenever I could. But now that I'm actually paying attention, I realize how kind you are. How caring. And I know maybe we don't really make sense. And you're still totally stuck up, sometimes, and rude and *scared*. You're so damn scared of everything. Of rejection, of other people, of being yourself. But I'm scared, too. Scared that I'll spend the rest of my life regretting that I almost had you, but then I blew it. Because I'm pretty sure"—Liz took a deep breath—"that I could never forgive myself for that."

Daria studied a tree root at her feet, not saying anything.

Oh God. Liz needed to get out of here now, before she had a crying breakdown in her second city park of the day. At least she'd gotten a chance to say it all, she thought bitterly. At least Daria would know absolutely everything when she rejected her.

Daria glanced up, but then quickly looked back down. "I'm not with Caroline," she said. "Did she say that?"

"Uh, yeah," Liz said. "She did. She was in your apartment."

"I just— She offered to come to New York, after the arti-

cle came out, and cheer me up. And I was feeling lonely, so
I said yes. But we haven't—we're not. That's it."

"Oh. Okay."

Daria poked the tree root with one of her loafers. Liz's
heart, which had finally calmed down from her run, picked
up speed again. Daria wasn't with Caroline. Maybe there
was hope after all.

"Look," Daria said, and then she paused. "I really appreciate all that." She paused again.

It was like a glass of ice water had shattered in Liz's throat.
She could feel cold dread dripping down her chest into her
stomach. A wash of heaviness, a wave of *Of course*, a pain
that she could tell would only build with time.

"I get it," Liz said. "I really do. And—I just can't listen to
you say it again. So. Okay. Sorry. Bye."

She turned and took off running across the meadow, fast.
Daria shouted her name, sounding startled, but Liz didn't
turn. She would spare them both from the awkward rejection speech. She would rip off the Band-Aid.

It would have been a lot easier to run if her throat hadn't
felt like it was closing up. She just had to make it to the trees
and then she could cry. Liz tried to pick up the pace. Her
vision was blurry with tears now, and she hoped there
weren't any large rocks or holes in her path.

"Liz!" Daria called from behind her, her voice closer than
it had been before—she was following her. "Stop!"

Liz kept running. Why was Daria drawing this out? Didn't
she realize this way would be easier on both of them?

"Jesus fucking Christ, Liz," Daria shouted. "I'm wearing
loafers!"

"Just leave me alone!" Liz shouted. She bent her arms
into ninety-degree angles like an Olympic runner and tried
to power through. After today, she was never going to run
again.

"Liz, please!"

A sob finally escaped Liz's throat, slowing her down. Daria caught up. She was missing one loafer and running with a limp to keep the other one on her foot. Her face was red and her hair was a mess and she looked extremely annoyed.

"When did you get so fucking fast?" she gasped.

"Just—I don't want to hear it," Liz said, stumbling forward.

"Liz, can you *please* just stop?"

"Why?" Liz sobbed.

"So I can kiss you, dammit!"

Liz stopped. Daria almost slammed into her but caught herself at the last second. She bent over, grabbing her knees, and groaned. Her sock and her remaining loafer were covered in mud.

"You," she said, looking up at Liz, who was wiping tears and sweat off her face, "are a piece of fucking work." And then she grabbed the front of Liz's shirt, pulled her in, and kissed her.

They were both out of breath. They were both sweaty and disheveled and panting. Liz was still crying. But when they kissed, Liz felt like her fingers were sparklers, like her stomach had filled with confetti, like her blood had been replaced with champagne. Her whole body felt *awake*, and Liz pressed herself against Daria, not caring about how sweaty she was, only caring about the feel of her hands running through Daria's hair, the solid warmth of Daria's hand pressing against her lower back. Their mouths opened, and Daria's palm cupped Liz's cheek, bringing them closer together. Their tongues touched, then touched again. Liz bit Daria's lower lip just a little, and Daria groaned into her mouth.

They kissed until Liz remembered that they were in a public park, surrounded by families. Even when they broke

apart, she kept her arms around Daria's waist. If this was a
hallucination, or a mistake, or a onetime experiment, she
wasn't going to be the one who let go.

"Elizabeth Baker," Daria said, pressing her forehead
against Liz's. "You are absolutely out of your mind. And I am
so in love with you."

"You are?" Liz said.

Daria nodded.

"Do you . . . will you forgive me? For that article?"

"I will," Daria said. "If you'll forgive me for being a judgmental jerk when we met."

Liz laughed. "Deal."

She leaned in and kissed Daria again. It was just a short
kiss, but the ground still seemed to tilt beneath her—
although that might have been Daria shifting her weight to
balance on one shoe. Then Liz wrapped her arms around
Daria more tightly, burrowing her head in Daria's neck.
Daria squeezed her back. They looked at each other and
both laughed in amazement.

"What now?" Liz said.

"Welllll . . ." Daria said, drawing out the word seductively.
"You live around here, don't you?"

"I do," Liz said, taking Daria's hand and kissing her knuckles lightly. Then she twined her fingers into Daria's and
started pulling her in the direction of the fallen shoe.

"Let me show you," she said.

Acknowledgments

This book never would have seen the outside of my computer screen if it weren't for the help and support of many, many people.

First of all, thank you to Katy Nishimoto. You are my dream editor! Thank you for all the love, care, and dedication you poured into this manuscript. This book is infinitely stronger (and has infinitely fewer glances and sighs!) because of your editorial notes.

Thank you to my incredible agent, Jessica Alvarez, for believing in this story and helping me make this dream come true. Thank you to the whole BookEnds team for your kindness and support. A huge thank-you to Phoebe Schmidt for your enthusiastic love of Liz and Daria. And thank you to Veronica Vega for your excitement and guidance.

Thank you to the entire Dial Press team, particularly Whitney Frick—from the very beginning, your enthusiasm made me feel like I'd found the perfect home for Liz. Thank you to Emma Caruso for your brilliant editorial insights. A giant thank-you to Sandra Chiu for this absolutely gorgeous cover! And thank you to Cara DuBois, Avideh Bashirrad, Debbie Aroff, Jordan Forney, Melissa Folds, Maria Braeckel,

Rebecca Berlant, Kevin Garcia, Jo Anne Metsch, Leah Sims, Donna Cheng, Jordan Pace, and Michelle Jasmine for all the work you've put into helping this book find its way onto shelves.

An extra-special thanks to Hannah Koerner, who read a version of this manuscript that was fifty thousand words longer and still managed to find encouraging things to say about it. Another extra-special thanks to Stuart Yandell, who gave me editorial notes and encouragement via long-distance video game chats.

Maybe the biggest thank-you of all to my family: Mom, Dad, Baird, Cole, and Asher. I love you all so much. I'm so lucky to have a family like you. Thank you for all your support. I'm sorry about the sex scene.

A million thanks to Maia Sacca-Schaeffer and (again!) Hannah Koerner. Our friendship brings so much love, support, and joy to my life. A million thanks to Rachael Morris: You're a soul mate of a friend, and meeting you has made my entire life better. A million thanks to Elizabeth Keto for helping me develop my never-ending *Pride and Prejudice* obsession and for being my constant partner in crime. Thank you to Alyssa Miele, Carolina Ortiz, Laura Harshberger, Rose Pleuler, Shannon Cox, and Stephanie Guerdan for all the Cubbyhole nights—you're the queer friend group I always dreamed of. Thank you to Emily Hewitt for teaching me to love New York. Thank you to Brenna Christensen for all the adventures. Thank you to Maria Messick, Sarah Manhardt, and Kinza Baad for being lifelong friends. And a shout-out to Crescendo—I love being on your team.

A special thank-you to every author who has written a book about being queer: Your stories made me feel less alone when I had no idea what my future might look like or if I even had one. And, finally, a huge thank-you to everyone who reads this book—I love you all, just as you are.

JUST AS YOU ARE

Camille Kellogg

Dial Delights

*Love Stories
for the
Open-Hearted*

Susie Dumond, Author of *Queerly Beloved,* Interviews Camille Kellogg

Susie Dumond: To start from the beginning, what inspired you to write *Just as You Are*?

Camille Kellogg: Mostly, I wrote *Just as You Are* because this is the book that I needed to read. When I was in my early twenties and just coming out, I felt so lost. I didn't know any older queer people, I didn't know any queer people in long-term relationships, and I didn't know where to find any sort of community. I had lived my whole life imagining one future, and suddenly I had a very different one ahead of me. I wanted someone to, like, grab me by my shoulders and give me advice. But I didn't have that person. So I was very desperate for books, movies, media that talked about what being queer was like. The hard parts, the good parts, but also the everyday parts. The day-to-day experience of being queer. I really just wanted to see queer people living their lives and get that reassurance that queer people *could* have full lives and get happy endings. So that's where the idea to write this book really came from.

SD: That's wonderful. And I think it really comes across. In reading it, for me, I saw so many of my queer experiences reflected in it. It's so rare to see something that looks so much like my life on the page. So I definitely would have been really moved to read this in my early twenties, just as I was now, in my early thirties.

This novel is a retelling of *Pride and Prejudice* by Jane Austen. Can you talk about why you chose to do that and how you approached retelling such a beloved classic?

CK: *Pride and Prejudice* is probably my favorite book of all time. I reread it every year. I just think it's the perfect love story. And I'm a huge romcom fan in general. I really love all of the classic romcom books and movies, but over time I started to think, "Why am I spending so much time consuming media that I can't see myself in?" I wanted something that would give me the same fluttery, longing feelings and also reflect my experiences as a queer person. And because *Pride and Prejudice* has so many satisfying twists and so much satisfying sexual tension, it seemed like a good place to start. I had a lot of fun working in little references. When I figured out the name of the magazine being the *Nether Fields,* that's when I was like, "Okay, I think this could actually work."

SD: It was really fun to find the Easter eggs, even as someone who hasn't read *Pride and Prejudice* as many times as you have. I really love that instead of the family, it's more of a queer found family. And I also really love that in the place of these high-society parties they have, like, a Pride pool party.

CK: Yes! It's pretty much a ball.

SD: How about the title? Where did *Just as You Are* come from?

CK: I spent a long time trying to find a title for this book. Somewhere on my computer is an embarrassing document with a hundred horrendous title options, most of which are queer puns. And where this title came from is actually another adaptation—*Bridget Jones's Diary.* Colin Firth tells Bridget he likes her "just as you are." And I like nodding to that classic romcom in addition to *Pride and Prejudice.* But

I also think there's a really nice queer theme to this title. Which is that you're allowed to be just the way you are. I think a lot of queer people, when they're growing up, don't have that acceptance, and they feel the pressure to pretend or hide parts of themselves. I like that this is a relationship where both Liz and Daria can be honest about who they are and can be their authentic selves.

SD: You're a book editor in addition to being an author. How has your experience as an editor impacted your author life?

CK: I actually think I learned more about being an editor by being an author than the other way around. And what I learned is that it is *so* scary to be an author! I work with authors every day and I didn't realize just how nerve-racking it is to send your work out to someone and say, "Give me feedback!" It's really vulnerable. So this experience gave me a lot of respect for the authors I work with.

I also gained a new appreciation for the editorial process, because at the end of every round of edits, I thought, "This book is so much better than it was before." That was a really nice feeling, to see firsthand how big of a difference an editor can make to a book.

SD: Gender presentation is really important in the book, and we see a lot of characters have different experiences with gender. Can you talk about why it was important for you to depict that?

CK: Gender expression has played a big role in my experience of coming out—that's not true for everyone, but for me, in discovering my sexuality, I had to think a lot about how I wanted to dress and act and who I really was. Figuring out your sexuality, your presentation, what labels fit, your gender—it's so hard! You really have to look into yourself in a way that most people aren't taught to do growing up. And the public narrative about queerness is almost always one of certainty. The whole idea of coming out is that you say, "I am XYZ label." And it's often coupled with sentiments like "I was born this way" or "I've always known." But I think so many people *haven't* always known. A lot of people figure it out later in life or it takes them a long time or they're just not sure. And it's really easy to feel insecure about that. So I wanted to show that uncertainty is normal. I also wanted to show someone who's uncertain but doesn't necessarily find one set answer. Identity changes a lot over your lifetime, and I wanted to show someone who learns to be okay with that, instead of learning to hide that uncertainty and go for an easy answer.

SD: That's powerful. And it feels very realistic, too. I really love the specific parts where you're pointing out that not only does your gender matter in terms of how you feel but in terms of how people treat you. Can you talk about that?

CK: It's easy to say "be yourself," but how do you know who your self is? How do you figure that out? And also, you're not yourself in a bubble. You're yourself in a world. You talked about this in your book, *Queerly Beloved,* how you might choose to compromise or hold back on parts of yourself for safety or for comfort. And when is that a good idea and when does that end up hurting you? It's really hard to tell.

SD: Do you have any advice for people who are still figuring out their own identities?

CK: I think the best advice I can give is: Experiment. Start small. Pick a shirt or a hairstyle or a lipstick and try it out. If it feels good, keep going in that direction, and if it doesn't, try something new. I think letting yourself take the time to try things and not putting pressure on yourself to know immediately is so valuable. My other piece of advice is to try to have fun! It can be so exciting to put on a piece of clothing that feels good. Let yourself find those moments of joy and celebrate them.

SD: That's great advice. You're not committing to something forever if you decide that you like it once. I feel like that's really part of it, too. It can change day to day, year to year, and over the course of your whole life.

CK: Yes, exactly! When I was experimenting, I wanted to know the answers and I wanted to know now. I didn't realize that those things could and would shift over time, because no one had told me.

SD: Absolutely. I'd also love to talk about Liz's love interest, Daria, being a masc of center person. That's something that's obviously also important to me because the love interest in *Queerly Beloved* is as well. Can you talk a little about butch representation and showing desire for masculine of center people and what that means?

CK: Yes! I mean, the main reason that Daria is butch is because butch people are hot. And I thought it was important that everyone knows that (*laughing*). Also, Mr. Darcy to me is very much someone who's tall, dark, and handsome. So Daria was always going to be tall, dark, and handsome. So those are the surface level reasons why Daria is butch.

More seriously, masc queer people don't get a lot of media representation. The majority of mainstream sapphic rep is feminine women. And when I was growing up, I didn't even really know that butchness was an option. I thought the options were "feminine woman" or "masculine man," and you had to pick one. And now, most of my friends are somewhere in the middle, figuring out their own labels and identities. So a lot of the people in this book are somewhere in that in-between area. As someone who myself identifies as part of that in-between, masc of center area, it was really important for me to show that. Because I think people really need those examples, to realize just how many possibilities there are for how you can identify and present.

SD: I love it. And yes, shout-out to the hot butches.

CK: Yes! They're in your book, they're in my book, they're hot.

SD: Put them in more books! I'm into it.
   I love the group of friends in this book. Can you talk about chosen family?

CK: Yes! The scenes with the roommates were some of my favorites to write because they just love each other so much and they know each other so well. They have so much fun and banter together. I also really love how different all four roommates are—they have totally different personalities and backgrounds, which sometimes makes things fun and sometimes creates tension. I felt like the fact that they all met through work allowed for them to have a friend group that might not exist in any other scenario, because they're all so different that they might not normally be hanging out in the same spaces. But I think those kinds of friend groups actually happen a lot in the queer world. When you meet people who recognize and celebrate you for who you are, you want to hold on to them. Because you know firsthand just how valuable that can be.

SD: I also love in the book how you talk about the power of what you call fluff writing. It felt very meta, because this is a feel-good love story, but it also is so powerful. Can you talk a little about what that meant to you and what it meant to your characters?

CK: I was worried it was a little too on the nose! But so much of queer media is depressing. The first couple of books and movies that I saw with queer representation were all horrifyingly sad. I think it's so powerful to see a story about someone with your identity who's happy. It helps you realize that you can have a happy life, too.

Also, I know Liz is a bit harsh about her advice articles sometimes, but sites like *Autostraddle* have all of this amazing advice: how to flirt, how to go on a date, how to figure out your style, all from a queer lens. And I read those articles *religiously* when I came out. Because I didn't have *any* advice. When you're straight, you're inundated with advice and relationship models. They're everywhere. And so having articles like that was so important and valuable to me. Even just to see that other people were out there with the same questions, with similar experiences, it made me feel so much less alone.

SD: Yeah! And I actually think one of the most fun parts of being queer is inside jokes. Because we have so few pieces of queer media to reference. I feel like there are a lot of references for queer readers in this book that I loved seeing. And you don't always see those in books, especially when you know that a lot of the audience will be straight readers who just won't get it. So I really appreciated the inside jokes for the queers.

CK: I love that point! That having so little media is why we all know the same references. I've never fully thought of it like that. But yes, I wanted to write a book that was really *for* queer people. And the language in this book really reflects the way I talk to my queer friends. I know that including a lot of pop culture references runs the risk of dating the book but, like you said, we have so few that our references tend to last a long time. So I had a lot of fun working in as many as I could.

SD: What do you hope readers will learn and take away from the novel?

CK: I actually have three things that I hope readers will take away from this. I think the first one is this sense of queer joy, how being queer can bring so much to your life and you can be really happy not in spite of being queer but *because* you're queer.

I also would love for readers to take away that there's no wrong way to be queer. That you don't have to act a certain way or dress a certain way or be X adjective enough or Y adjective enough. There are no rules. You can be queer in whatever way you want and still be part of this community.

The final thing I want readers to take away is that everyone belongs. Right now, in this country, queer and trans rights are under attack, and what we really need to be doing is banding together and saying, "Everyone has a place here." And saying that we're going to fight for the most vulnerable members of our community, especially trans people and people of color. It's all of our responsibilities to make sure that those members of our community feel supported, protected, loved, and fought for by our community. So I would really love readers to take that away as well.

SD: I think they will. Those messages are so strong, and the book is such a warm embrace of those messages. It feels very natural in the story.

So, final question, what are some LGBTQ+ books that you've read recently and loved?

CK: Oh my God. I'm going to have to hold myself back here. This is a really hard one. I'll start with romcoms. Obviously, *Queerly Beloved*. I read it last month and I loved it so much. I just loved the bar setting, all of the friendships and the community, and I loved that theme we talked about: How much of your identity do you share with the world and how much do you hold back and what cost does that have for you? Sticking to romcoms, I also really loved *Something to Talk About* and *Honey Girl*, those are two of my favorites. Recently I read *Love and Other Disasters*, which was so cute and I loved all the cooking descriptions, and *For the Love of April French*, which was SO sexy and just melted my heart.

Outside of romcoms, *In the Dream House* is one of my favorites. *Stone Butch Blues* and *Fun Home* were really iconic for me and my gender expression. Others are *Paul Takes the Form of a Mortal Girl* and *Detransition, Baby*, and I have to shout out *We Are Okay* by Nina LaCour, since I am a YA editor.

SD: That is a really great list. I hope everyone who reads this runs out and goes to the bookstore and buys them right now.

CK: Yes! Every single book I just mentioned, read them *right now.*

SD: Well, thank you so much for chatting with me and for writing this really wonderful book. I cannot wait for readers to get their hands on this amazing story.

CK: Thank you so much!

Questions and Topics for Discussion

1. Liz feels a lot of insecurity about not being settled in her gender presentation. Where do you think that insecurity comes from? Have you ever felt pressure to figure out a label for your identity?

2. How do you think Liz grows and evolves throughout the novel? What encourages her to change? What makes that growth difficult?

3. Liz and Jane have an extremely close friendship, but in the second half of the book, Jane expresses that Liz needs to start being a more thoughtful friend. Do you think Liz will learn to be a better friend to Jane? Have you ever been in a similar scenario—either as the friend who needs to grow or the friend who had to ask someone to change?

4. In Liz's interview with Moira Campbell, Moira says that queer people should focus more on the possibilities that open up when you come out, rather than the fear of what could go wrong. Do you agree with Moira's opinion? Why or why not?

5. As readers, we get to see firsthand why Liz feels attracted to Daria. What do you think draws Daria to Liz? Do you identify more with one of them?

6. For most of the book, Katie is deeply in love with Lydia even though Lydia doesn't return her feelings. Have you ever been in a similar situation? How did it feel?

7. Why do you think Liz struggles so much to find the right approach to her writing? Have you ever gone through a similar struggle?

8. Liz often feels insecure about her articles for the *Nether Fields* because they're considered "fluff pieces." Do you

think lighthearted articles like those are important? Why or why not?

9. Liz spends a lot of time thinking about what her ideal style would be and how she would dress if she could afford to buy new clothes. How do you define your personal style? Has it evolved over time? Is the way you dress or wear your hair important to your identity?

10. Liz sometimes feels like it's hard to consistently be herself when she's around other people, because she's tempted to change in order to fit their expectations of her. Do you ever feel that way? If so, how do you counteract that pressure?

11. Liz finds interviewing Moira Campbell, and seeing her with her wife, very affirming. Why do you think it's important to record stories from queer elders? Have you ever had the experience of being inspired by elders or ancestors?

12. Art plays a big role in this novel, from Moira's photographs to Liz's writing. What is the importance of art? How would you define "success" when it comes to making art?

13. In the second half of the novel, much of Liz and Daria's romance takes place over social media. How do you think social media and technology have changed dating?

14. Discuss Lydia's decision to post Liz's draft article and the apology Liz writes afterward. Have you ever had your privacy violated in a similar way? What did you think about Liz's apology?

15. Betrayal plays a big role in this novel, from Lydia and Weston's hookup and Lydia's decision to post Liz's article to Katie giving Lydia Liz's password and Liz writing the article in the first place. Have you ever betrayed a

friend, or been betrayed by a friend? How did that impact the relationship?

16. At the end of the novel, Liz decides to pursue her dream
of writing full-time. Do you have a dream you wish you
could pursue more decisively, or spend more time focusing on? What stands in the way of your ability to
follow that dream? What kinds of things would you
need in order to feel like you could take more action
around your dream?

17. Despite the characters' efforts, the *Nether Fields* eventually shuts down. Do you think the characters should
have been successful in their effort to save it? Why do
you think the author made that decision?

Camille Kellogg is a queer writer based in New York City, where she works as an editor for children's and young adult books. She studied English and creative writing at Middlebury College and attended the Bread Loaf Writers' Conference on a fiction scholarship. She's passionate about queer stories, cute dogs, and bad puns.

camillekellogg.com
Twitter: @kellogg_camille
Instagram: @kellogg_camille

ABOUT THE TYPE

This book was set in Fairfield, the first typeface from the hand of the distinguished American artist and engraver Rudolph Ruzicka (1883–1978). Ruzicka was born in Bohemia (in the present-day Czech Republic) and came to America in 1894. He set up his own shop, devoted to wood engraving and printing, in New York in 1913 after a varied career working as a wood engraver, in photoengraving and banknote printing plants, and as an art director and freelance artist. He designed and illustrated many books, and was the creator of a considerable list of individual prints—wood engravings, line engravings on copper, and aquatints.

*The Dial Press, an imprint of Random House,
publishes books driven by the heart.*

Follow us on Instagram:
@THEDIALPRESS

Discover other Dial Press books and
sign up for our e-newsletter:

thedialpress.com